TENTH
AVATAR

TENTH
AVATAR
A QUEST FOR ANSWERS

KANCHAN A. JOSHI, PH.D.

Braveship
BOOKS
Aura Libertatis Spirat

Tenth Avatar: A Quest for Answers

Braveship Books

www.braveshipbooks.com

Aura Libertatis Spirat

Print Edition:
ISBN 13: 978-1-64062-017-9
ISBN-10: 1-64062-017-6

Kindle Edition:
ISBN 13: 978-1-64062-018-6
ISBN-10: 1-64062-018-4

ePub Version:
ISBN 13: 978-1-64062-019-3
ISBN-10: 1-64062-019-2

Printed in the United States of America

Dedication:

Dedicated to my parents, all the brilliant and dedicated scientists, Sadhguru, Shree Swami Samarth, and Lord Hanuman.

INTRODUCTION

By the time, I finished my Bachelor's degree in Engineering, I thought I knew everything about science. When I finished my Doctorate, I realized I knew nothing.

Once I completed college, I thought I knew everything about human history and the journey humans have undertaken so far. When I saw research on the amazing things our ancestors have done, which is not taught in the textbooks, I realized I knew nothing about history.

I thought people worked to take care of themselves and their families. But then, I saw people give their lives for others' well-being, I realized there was more to life than what met the eye.

Eye opening experiences such as these inspired me to write this book. The book explores various questions about the true nature of life and the universe from both eastern-spiritual, intuitive and western-logical, scientific perspectives—all wrapped in the package of a fast-paced, fictional adventure. It explores the quintessential human quest for uncovering the true nature of our experiences and aspirations, the mysteries of our history, and the application of the scientific method for answering these questions in the form of a gripping thriller.

I hope you have as much fun reading as I had writing the book!

CHARACTERS AND PLACES

Hanuman	A warrior, yogi, immortal being
Anjani	Hanuman's human mother
Kesari	Hanuman's biological father, army General, simian
Vali	Brutal, powerful king of Kishkindha
Sugriv	Vali's younger brother
Ravan	Powerful demon king of the southern island of Lanka
Kishkindha	Region in ancient southern India
Vanara	Forest dweller
Mahadev	The Great God
Angad	Vali's son
Rishi	Ascetic, scientist, learned, wise man
Muni	Philosopher, sage
Jai Vanara, Jai Lanka, Jai Mahadev	Battle cries

Ashtavakra	Bent man, great philosopher, visionary scientist
Agastya	Visionary scientist, philosopher, innovative Teacher
Ram	Fearless warrior, noble human and yogic master
Lakshman	Ram's volatile and brave brother
Sita	Accomplished yogi, Ram's wife
Indrajit	Ravan's powerful son
~~	~~~~
Krish	Brilliant physicist, mathematician
Dave	Krish's advisor, professor at Cal Tech
Kathy	Krish's lab mate, extraordinary scientist from MIT
Mark	Experimentalist, a scientist and a macho man
Prisha	Krish's love interest
Brooke	Brave federal agent
Ramanujan	Genius, self-taught mathematician, single handedly developed mathematics with applications in number theory, mock theta functions used to understand black holes. Fellow of Royal Society, Fellow of Trinity College

TABLE OF CONTENTS

CHAPTER I

THE BATTLE

~~~~~~~

Ancient India

~~~~~~~

Freedom does not come without a fight, for an individual or a society.

F ATHER, PLEASE TELL ME THE STORY OF THAT FAMOUS BATTLE you talk about," Hanuman said pleadingly, pulling his father's hand to make him sit for story time.

"I would love to, son," his father said. He set aside his heavy mace and sat down.

Hanuman's father, General Kesari, had fought in the battle of Kishkindha. It was an incredible honor. As he described it, his enormously strong chest swelled with pride and his eyes sparked with a special jyoti, light. Kesari took a deep breath and arranged the different pieces of the battle in his mind before describing them to Hanuman in vivid detail.

Hanuman felt as if he had been there by his father's side.

Kesari relished the opportunity to remind his son of the great history and the beautiful geography of their homeland.

Hanuman's mother looked at her husband adoringly as he told the story. She was proud to be the wife of the great General Kesari. She enjoyed watching the father-son interaction. Listening intently, she thanked the Great God Mahadev, in her heart, for her beautiful family.

Hanuman belonged to the Vanara community—the forest dwellers. They had long body hair, some had tails, and some suffered swollen jaws. This was the price they paid for their superior physical build and strength. They were bred this way by the use of special technology by the Rishis, the scientists. Most Vanara, who were not of nobility, lived in the forests. Vanara made political and military alliances with human kings during times of war.

The bloodbath had taken place in the Kishkindha Mountains in the southwest part of Ancient India.

Hanuman sat captivated as Kesari narrated the story:

"The brave King Vali paced rapidly through his battle formation. His golden pendant shone in the sun. The pendant was a gift from his father, Indra—the king of the gods. It increased his strength two times over. The pendant boosted the king's already sky-high confidence and made him feel invincible.

'It is a yantra, a machine,' whispered some of the soldiers.

'He grunts like an elephant in musth, clinching his teeth,' another general said to his captain.

Vali uprooted small Sal trees and tossed them casually at the enemy to strike fear into their demonic hearts.

'Victory to the king of the Vanara,' shouted Vali's army, raising their maces. The army arranged themselves in the eagle formation. The beak of the eagle formation was a wedge-shaped pack of the most elite fighters, led by Vali himself. Vali gave them enormous strength and belief—belief that they would survive and return home, belief that they could win this brutal fight against a great invader. The beak was followed by the head—made up of heavily armed fighters. The beak and the head were designed to crush the five-headed serpent formation of the enemy. The wings of the eagle formation had five columns of soldiers, each with the fastest and most skilled warriors on the outside. The body of the eagle was created by the rest of the army.

The warriors wore no armor because of the hot weather. Sugriv, who was Vali's brother, and I were at the head of the eagle formation.

'You strike hard after I hit these Asuras,' Vali commanded. Sugriv made eye contact with him and nodded obediently.

Vali's enemy was Ravan, the king of demons, the Asuras, who had come from across the ocean to the south. He planned to steal the superior human breeding technology of the Vanara and combine it with his own weapons technology to form a super army that would have no equal. He was a great visionary with tremendous power. Some claimed he obtained his powers from the Great God Mahadev in the Himalayas.

The strong and confident Vali appeared not to be worried about Ravan, especially on his familiar home turf. After all, it was well known that the invading army would lose half of its strength just getting to the battlefield through the difficult Kishkindha Mountains.

Everyone knew Vali was interested in his brother's beautiful wife. He had scant respect for his brother. Vali thought Sugriv was timid and soft and did not deserve to have such a beautiful lady as his wife. He didn't believe that Sugriv deserved to have any power either. Vali believed power, just like the 30kg mace he carried with great skill, should only rest with people like himself, who had the brawn to handle it. And because of their superior strength and fighting power, only a few special people deserved to rule and enjoy the most beautiful things in life.

Vali glanced contemptuously toward Sugriv. He had just turned his gaze away from his brother when a flying machine was seen rising above the plateau. It started raining mukta—hand launched—and mantramukta—sound launched—weapons at the Vanara army. The

Vanara, without helmets or armor, were easy targets. The brave soldiers took the heat without breaking rank.

'I will break their amateur eagle formation with a few strikes of astra- my weapons. And when they literally run with their tails between their legs, my brave Asuras will swallow this little eagle without even a burp,' Ravan was overheard boasting to his general.

The general let out the battle cry, 'Victory to Lanka! By this time tomorrow, we will be on our way home with their beautiful women, wealth, slaves, and secrets of breeding!' he exclaimed with lustful eyes.

However, Vali had other plans.

'I will teach this egomaniac such a lesson that his seven generations will not dare even look at Kishkindha with evil intentions,' Vali said to his captain. Vali decided to take the battle to the enemy.

'No point in waiting! Let us send these barbarians back to the ocean!' Vali shouted to his men.

'Jai Vanara-raj! Asuras die in the ocean!' the soldiers roared back. Vali charged forward. He was furious about the sudden attack from the flying machine.

'I cannot wait to crush the skulls of these Asuras,' Vali said to his captain.

The Vanara slammed into the Asuras. They used powerful blows from their maces to break helmets, skulls, and rib cages into pieces. In addition to their regular army, as soon as the battle cry was heard, hordes of Vanara appeared from the forest line with uprooted trees and boulders. Ravan's army was encircled.

Ravan knew he had to do something. He was playing into the hands of Vali. By attacking Ravan's army in such a short time, and with everything he had, Vali had negated his opponent's advantage of superior weaponry. Ravan could not use the weapons when there was no way to selectively target the enemy.

'This disgusting monkey is too smart,' Ravan roared with contempt toward Vali. 'Do you not know you are fighting the Great Ravan? You scum of the forest who calls himself a king,' he said, trying to get under Vali's skin. Ravan knew he had to act quickly. He attempted to target the Vanara generals, and Vali, by flying low and slow, merely a few feet from the ground.

Vali noticed his tactic immediately. He asked the bodyguard fighting next to him to fetch Sugriv.

After only a few moments the bodyguard returned with Sugriv. 'Put this on,' Vali said as he handed over his shiny golden pendant to Sugriv. The two brothers looked identical. The Vanara army would not notice the absence of their king. Vali ran toward the forest and quickly climbed a Sal tree. He patiently waited for the right moment, as a skilled hunter would. In a few moments, he heard the flying machine just behind his position, and rapidly approaching. He took a monumental leap from the tree. For a moment, he himself appeared to be flying. He hit the door of the machine and slammed it open as he landed with his mace at the ready.

Ravan was stunned by this raw display of valor by the king. Before Ravan could adjust to the fact that his enemy was standing right next to him, Vali landed a mighty blow to his face.

Due to the commotion, the pilot of the aircraft lost control and crash-landed.

Ravan did not even get a chance to retrieve his mace; Vali caught his neck in a vice grip under his armpit and chocked it with his enormous biceps, cutting off his airway and rendering him defenseless.

Vali came out onto the battlefield holding the still struggling, great King Ravan in this humiliating position before his men. Ravan's army was utterly astonished. The flying ape had ended the battle in one daring leap.

Vali imposed a demeaning treaty on Ravan. As further reminder not to cross his path again, Vali personally cracked open the skulls of five of Ravan's captains—after challenging them to a duel they knew they could not refuse per the warrior's code of conduct, the kshatriya dharma."

Kesari paused to be sure that he still had his son's attention. "After the battle, Vali asked a few Rishis to be brought to his palace.

'Write down the full description of the night sky. Note the location of the five visible planets—Mercury, Mars, Venus, Saturn, Jupiter, the sun and the moon. Spread the folklore to all Vanara in a way that is easy to remember. The great Vali, and this day, should be remembered for eons. Exaggerate if you have to, understood?' Vali said condescendingly to the scientists.

Yes, he was the king, but the Rishis were higher in the social hierarchy and had to be shown respect... at least outwardly.

Vali's female servants helped him put on his short dhoti, gold bracelets, thick anklets, intricately carved arm ornaments, and heavy gold chains with rare jewels.

Vali celebrated his victory with a big feast."

Kesari's description of the battle filled Hanuman's heart with excitement. He too dreamed of becoming a great warrior. He urged his father to tell him more stories.

Kesari looked at his beautiful, ideal, pativrata wife. She smiled approvingly and nodded her head gently. She had finished her chores while listening to the story. It was a starry night with the crescent moon adoring the sky. The family sat around the fire pit outside their home.

"Why was Sugriv banished from the kingdom? Why does he live in the Rishyamukha hills?" Hanuman asked.

Hanuman hung on Kesari's every word as he began a new tale:

"A demon challenged Vali to a duel. Per our kshatriya dharma, as you know, Vali could not refuse when challenged."

"I think the clever Rishis came up with all these rules to protect the weaker sections of society, and more importantly themselves, from the anger, pride, and jealousy of the powerful warrior class," Hanuman's mother theorized.

"Never challenge a warrior to a duel unless you really want to fight, and don't challenge a lady to a debate unless you really want to argue," Kesari chuckled.

"All right, continue your story," Hanuman's mother said firmly. "I am sleepy." She thought she was just stating facts.

Kesari continued.

"In the middle of the night, Vali came out of his palace to accept the challenge posed by the demon.

Sugriv ran after him to prevent him from fighting in the dark with this other worldly creature who possessed strange powers—such as levitating, changing forms, becoming invisible, and other such black magic tricks.

Vali did not care about all the trickery, especially while wearing Indra's golden pendant; it had metal arms attached to it, specifically designed for duels.

At the sight of Vali, the demon started running.

Sugriv thought it was a trap but Vali did not give two hoots. He was eager to smash the demon's skull into a thousand pieces. He had not killed an Asura in some time, and his hands were thirsty for blood. Vali charged ahead. Thankfully, there was some moonlight present.

The demon ran for a while in the darkness. He suddenly disappeared into a hole near what appeared to be a cave.

Hanuman, I must add here that these Rishis talk some nonsense about different worlds being connected through such holes. Maybe the demon came from another world. I have no idea. As such, a particular sect of these Rishis consumed peculiar drinks; maybe that is why they came up with such strange ideas," Kesari said. Not knowing if this was truth or fantasy, he felt compelled to mention it because of the strange powers and appearance of the Asuras.

Kesari continued, "Vali followed the demon into the hole. He instructed Sugriv to stand guard outside, to avoid any possibility of being trapped. Sugriv guarded the entrance of the hole for an entire year. Then, he heard the demon make an awful sound and saw blood gushing out of the hole. He assumed the worst, that Vali had been killed in the battle. He plugged the hole with a huge boulder to seal it, then returned to Kishkindha.

Now, there is another incredible idea by the Rishis. When the Rishis travel to God Brahma's world, time passes slowly. They think they have only spent but a few moments, however, here in Kishkindha, one hundred years may have passed. It is strange, but some Rishis say that is exactly what happened to Vali. He thought he was gone only a few moments, but in Sugriv's time, it had been over a year," Kesari paused. "I have no idea how all this works. I am a warrior. I kill the enemy in front of me. I heard all these things when the Rishis described them to Vali. Honestly, the king does not believe or understand these talks either. He just humors the Rishis. But hey, it makes for a good story!" Kesari chuckled.

Hanuman smiled at him, pleading, "Please continue with the story, honorable father."

"Vali had been gone for a year. Ravan and other enemies were looking for an opportunity to avenge their humiliation at the hands of Vali and destroy Kishkindha. The ministers decided to crown Sugriv as king for clarity of command. But, Vali returned after pushing away the boulder that Sugriv had placed over the hole. Vali was furious that his weak brother had tried to kill him and take over his kingdom by deceit. He tried to kill Sugriv, but somehow Sugriv escaped to the Rishyamukha hills.

Vali dared not go to those hills. A Rishi, who had developed incredible weapons in his ashram—a hermitage that also served as a laboratory—lived there. He did not like Vali's arrogance, and because of that, there was bad blood between them. The Rishi warned Vali to stay away or be killed.

Sugriv would be safe there. Vali had often mistreated him, had taken away his wealth, and even his wife. These actions were not befitting of a king and a brother," Kesari said, concluding his story.

Hanuman agreed with his father. Sugriv was a brave and fair person. Vali was immoral and unjust to his brother. Justice had to be delivered to him. Hanuman touched his father's scars from the battle. He had goose bumps. He was fascinated by the Rishis—their technology, knowledge of astronomy, intellect, mantra-hymns, and their fantastic talk of other worlds. He wanted to learn everything, but first, he wanted to be a great warrior like his father.

Kesari's scars and stories were shaping the world views and ambitions of the chiranjiv, the immortal one.

CHAPTER 2
THE FOG

~~~~~~~

Modern Day California

~~~~~~~

Battles are fought both inside and outside.

I**T WAS PAST 2 AM. O**NE OF THE RISING STARS OF THEORETICAL physics and mathematics, Krishnanujam, was getting some sleep after another long day at the lab. Krish was a good-looking young man. He liked to work out in the gym as much as he could. At six feet tall, clean-shaven, with black hair, thin rimless glasses, and a serious looking face, he appeared every bit a scientist. His lively eyes reflected an energetic and active mind. He was a gold medalist at the International Mathematical Olympiad and a chess champion.

Krish woke up violently from a deep sleep. "What the hell?" he yelled. He was in a cold sweat—his heart trying to pound its way out of his chest. He kept his eyes shut tightly and covered his ears with moist palms. "What's going on?" he wondered.

After what seemed like an eternity—but was only a few seconds in Earth time—Krish opened his eyes and squinted around the room cautiously. His lamp came into focus, as if it was in the process of being created. He glanced at his analog watch, noticing the jerky movement of the second hand. In reality, it was moving smoothly.

"This never ceases to surprise me," he muttered. He reached for his glasses. He could have sworn that he'd left them on the nightstand before he fell asleep. His hands fumbled blindly in the dimly lit room, but they were not within reach.

Ugh, my brain hurts, he thought rubbing his temples. *Maybe I've just been working too hard and don't remember where I actually left them.*

For a moment, he reminisced on times when he wasn't so busy. He mentally travelled to stage plays in the Humanities department at Cal Tech. He would notice small changes in the stage settings from show to show. Glasses would never be in the same place!

Who would move my glasses, I live alone! he thought.

He slowly planted his feet on the floor of his bedroom, touching the floor lightly first to make sure it was there. It was probably a smart thing to do given how his night was going so far. He slowly got to his feet, grabbing his glasses from the desk in the corner of his room. He walked to the window of his two-story rental house in Pasadena.

It was a chilly January morning. The central heating was blowing air through the vents—the whooshing sound was all that broke the silence. He felt slightly better, as if he had some company. It was a full moon that night. He scanned the sky and the streets below. Everything was very still, almost as if he was being challenged to figure out the secrets of the night sky. "Universe's poker face," he murmured. It seemed unreal, like a scene from a movie. The stillness of the moment was cracked suddenly by a large Post-it note falling from the wall. He was startled. He tried smiling at the eerie sensation he was experiencing. He put the Post-it note back on the wall.

Usually, Krish was calm and composed. However, tonight he was off his game. He walked down the stairs because he couldn't see the moon from his northeast facing bedroom window. He remembered the lunar eclipse that was due to occur that night and hoped he hadn't missed it. He tried to look for the moon from the backyard, but to no avail.

"Where has the moon gone?" he said. Finally, he saw it from one of the windows over the stairs. "Wow... look at that," he said. It was awe inspiring. The moon was partially—and then fully—covered by Earth's shadow. For some reason, the sight made him pensive. It authenticated the loneliness of his heart. He had written equations describing the universe with events separated by billions of light years. And here he was, face-to-face with a mere light-second distance. Krish found himself awe struck.

"Good reality check for the theoretician," he said under his breath. The vast distances, the big shadows cast by heavenly objects, made him feel small, isolated, lost, and lonely.

Suddenly, he saw a being come out of a big black hole in the middle of the shadowed street.

Oh shit... I'm going completely crazy, or did I just imagine it, he thought. He focused back on the eclipse unfolding in front of his eyes. *Is anybody else watching this or is the whole show just for me?* He closed his eyes tightly, then opened them again. The moon was still hanging in the sky. *Oh, thank goodness.*

The floor was hard and cold. He put on his slippers and a sweater. Warming up some water, Krish made himself a cup of tea. He sat on the couch in the living room. The aroma of the masala chai reminded him of home. The smells of spices cooking, mouthwatering street food, rush hour train rides, and the beautiful freshman, Prisha, at Bhabha Atomic Research Center (BARC) paraded through his mind.

As her name implies, she's one lustrous, gifted lady, he smiled to himself. Thoughts of her pretty face, long hair, and—what he could only imagine to be—soft skin took him to a happy place in his mind. The pursuit of the dry material universe, and the math that subtly controls it was invigorating, but felt empty without loved ones.

Krish delved further into time spent with Prisha. He remembered the day he had trained her in the use of a scanning electron microscope to observe nanometer scale objects for her research. During the training, he said, "After sample preparation, you load it in the chamber, apply vacuum, adjust the voltage, and obtain images at the desired magnification. You can also get an idea about the composition of the sample with its spatial distribution." Krish looked at her, hoping that she would be impressed with his knowledge and technique. She looked lovely in the white lab coat and the white hair net she wore. She shook her head gently, unimpressed.

"I see, but the software interface on this machine sucks. It's too cluttered. The instrument could also be designed better. It should send the electron microscopy images and composition information and combine it with optical images obtained on the microscope upstairs to provide a thorough sample analysis, seamlessly." It was Krish's turn to be impressed.

"Very good ideas!"

Prisha shrugged her shoulders and said, "I want to start a company that provides a great user experience in the lab. I like the business side of things more."

After that, they met in the cafeteria a few times for lunch. He particularly enjoyed their long walk to the cafeteria in the light drizzle of rain. They savored chai and poha together and rode on his motorbike around the neatly trimmed lawns and the beautiful campus overlooking the Sahyadri Mountains. Krish would be delighted when she rested her head gently on his shoulders during their bike rides together.

Prisha would come to him with queries about difficult scientific concepts—which, of course, he was glad to help with. She shared her dreams of starting a company, making big money, then moving on to another exciting and profitable venture. Krish enjoyed their different perspectives—science vs. business.

Krish stretched his arms and drifted back to the present, away from home. *I need to unwind a little this weekend*, he thought. Opening his web browser, he decided to see what the rest of the world was up to. The news was not any different than it was the last time he'd checked.

'18 Dead in Shooting Rampage, Women and Children Included': he shuddered at the headline. He read about grisly beheadings and carpet bombings of civilian areas.

"People are trying to outdo each other with violence," he observed sadly. Commentators summarized the state of affairs—with the theater of democracy hosting another rendition of elections, the rhetoric was sure to heat up again. Elsewhere, they didn't need election seasons to spew venom.

He shook his head dejectedly at the reality that these were the leaders they had to rely on. He hoped the business section would offer some better news. On the contrary, he was only met with the news of layoffs, foreclosures, people dying due to inadequate insurance coverage, leaders trying to manage the messy global economy, and greedy people milking the system just as much as the lazy people.

Math and physics sound better, he reasoned taking a deep breath. *Let me see who's going to the Super Bowl*, he thought, scrolling toward the Sports section.

"Holy crap!" he almost jumped out of his seat as he watched what was unfolding before him. He felt as if the furniture no longer existed. It was assembling from individual atoms right in front of his eyes. It was as if he had some special vision that allowed him to see the individual particles whizzing around in all possible directions, colliding with each other.

He suddenly remembered the van from 1975; the one he saw near Cal Tech. It displayed diagrams by a scientist, Feynman, to depict all possible histories to account for the way mass particles—fermions and force particles or bosons—interacted. This was a very important step toward understanding how our world works at an atomic level. As soon as Krish turned his gaze toward the chair, the particles assembled themselves as a chair. "What the hell!" he exclaimed.

He rushed to the mirror in the downstairs bathroom, examining his left, and then his right, eyeball. He couldn't see his eyes moving, even when he undoubtedly knew they had moved. This was normal. *All right, so my mind has not been completely lost.* His heart was still racing by the time he came out of the bathroom. The physicist in him thought that he was observing some strange atomic-level quantum effect in a big object, such as the chair. His mind wandered in that direction.

At the very least, the macro world of gross objects should have been left alone to obey the very intuitive and logical laws of Newton, he thought with annoyance. He imagined the good old days, before the confusing and non-intuitive quantum theories that didn't obey normal logic.

Nature does not determine the outcome of any event—even the simplest. All possibilities are probable. An electron can travel from here to the moon before it can travel from here to that chair, he tried to summarize some tenets of these strange theories, attempting to make sense of what was going on around him.

He continued, mechanically recalling concepts he had mastered as a prodigious high school student. *Objects are attracted to each other by a force that depends on the distance between them at that time. But, time is relative and depends on the observer as per special relativity. Maxwell's theory requires that time be constant in all frames of reference. Thus, time cannot be separated from three-dimensional space. Hence, the concept of space-time. And then, General Relativity describes that space-time is not flat, but curved, and distorted by the mass and energy in it. Objects move in geodesics—the shortest path on a curved surface. When space-time is not flat, the path of objects moving in space-time appears to be bent as if a force is acting on them. This is gravity.* He skipped over a few details in his head. *At an atomic scale, intuitive understating of the universe does not work. So, why am I seeing atomic level phenomena with my naked eyes? Am I hallucinating?*

He badly wanted someone he could hold on to, to keep him anchored emotionally and physically in *this* space and time. He fell to his knees and started sobbing. Uninterrupted tears flowed without restraint. He couldn't understand what he was experiencing or why.

Maybe I ate something bad… yeah that's it! He wanted so badly to wrap his mind around his reality with a simpler explanation. He gazed out of the window, clouds were passing by the eclipsed moon, giving it an even eerier appearance.

Is this the first time I'm seeing this? How many eclipses have I witnessed? Thousands? Is this Deja vu? he wondered. *Or is the vision of thousands of such events suddenly coming to me, quantum superposition?* He was puzzled and shaken. *Well…this is new terrain.* His mind took a deep dive within.

"Math! Mock theta functions from Ramanujan's lost notebook," he exclaimed—that was the answer. Ramanujan was a great mathematician. Krish started scribbling feverishly on a piece of paper he'd found. Then, he began writing equations from the notebook. Mathematics was the place in his mind where he felt most comfortable and safe.

Krish heard faint tweets outside. He looked up, realizing that the sun was about to rise. He got up from his chair, went to the window, and bent down to stretch his back. He had been buried in his math for a few hours. It was his comfort zone and made him feel like himself again.

The sky changed from dark blue, to faint pink, to orange. Slowly, the world revealed itself. The cloak of darkness was cast away, and the world around Krish was bathed in light.

Suddenly, his eyes lit up with possibility. What if all the things he had felt last night were indicators of the true nature of the universe, beyond what the current state of physics thought possible? It was an intriguing thought. He knew he had to pursue it further.

He took a quick shower. Even though he had barely slept, he was not tired at all. He was energized by the possibilities that lay ahead of him. He walked briskly to his office at Cal Tech. To his surprise, quite a few researchers and students were on campus this early on a Sunday morning.

"I'm not the only one hit the by the eclipse, I guess," he said as he passed by Professor Leonard Eagleman, whose hair looked unkempt. Leonard was from the marine biology department.

"You got that right, Krish. I'm studying some fish that were affected by the full moon and high tides yesterday," Leonard said smiling.

Krish walked rapidly passed the engineering department and toward the physics department. He opened the door to his office, sat at his desk, and started writing down everything he had experienced the night prior.

If anyone reads this, they're going to think I've lost it, he thought as he finished writing as much as he could remember.

Some time had passed. He shook his head to wake himself up as he realized he had slumped in his chair. The exhaustion was finally setting in.

He stopped by Ann's Coffee Shop to grab a small drink and a snack. Olivia, the barista with bright eyes and a pleasant smile, was serving drinks that day.

"Here you go, Krish," she said. Krish smiled back as he grabbed his coffee. The warm drink radiated comfort into his palms. He opened the cup to get a whiff of the latte, sipping his drink on the way home.

"Good morning, Mike," he greeted his burly neighbor who was just getting back from a jog.

"Howdy," Mike waved back. The mundane helped Krish stay grounded that morning.

Let me try to calm my mind with meditation, he thought once inside. Krish's parents were religious-minded. He grew up listening to magical stories from the ancient past and Sanskrit language hymns. *Maybe that's why I imagined that being coming out of the road, just like the stories I heard of other worldly creatures!* He was not particularly interested in mythological matters. He loved science and math. He had seen his father do some breathing exercises sometimes. He wanted to quiet his mind, so he sat to meditate for some time. He tried to focus on his breathing, but was not able to for long. He was too tired and there was too much going on in his mind. *This isn't working. I need to share this with someone. It doesn't make sense to e-mail Dave, unless I flesh it out more*, Krish thought to himself.

David Phinney was his research advisor. Dave was well known in his field of theoretical astrophysics. He was very egoistic and brash. Pushing beyond the current state of the art, based on some strange experiences of the night before, Krish knew exactly what Dave would say, 'Don't waste my time on half-baked ideas.' Dave brushed most of his students' ideas off as not worthy of his time.

Someone like Krish—with half a dozen highly cited publications in top-notch journals that made big news, and getting ready to defend his dissertation in a few months, all before he even celebrated his twenty-second birthday—would be considered borderline genius by most. But not Dave, who himself was the recipient of the MacArthur genius grant when he was twenty-three. His ego was as large as the galaxies he studied.

It's not too late to call Professor Neelkanth Tripathi, Krish thought as he calculated the time difference. Professor Tripathi, at IIT Bombay, had a lot of potential, but always thought of himself as an underachiever. He thought if he were at another famous university in the west, he would be well known. Krish used to discuss some ideas with him, as they were working in similar areas. There was a slight competitive heat between the two. Krish was not too worried about Neel developing his ideas first as, in recent years, Neel had focused more on applied physics and technology than theoretical physics. Funding pressure had forced Neel in that direction, but maybe that was why he jumped at any opportunity to discuss theoretical physics—his first love.

Let me figure out what I want to say, rather than just throwing the kitchen sink at Neel. Krish thought of calling home. *Mom and Dad won't understand what I'm going through. Plus, I don't want to freak them out,* he thought. He missed his home and family.

He lay in bed thinking about his name, his family, and his childhood. Krish's mother was a therapist at a military hospital. She had a philosophical outlook to life. Krish remembered an incident around the time when he was getting ready to graduate from high school. He was to continue his education at the university level at the tender age of thirteen. He knew he had a lot of potential and was hungry to learn more and work with scholars. He was also apprehensive about being, by far, the youngest pupil in his classes.

It had been a lazy Sunday afternoon. Krish was sipping hot tea in the backyard with his mom. She had added cardamom, ginger powder, and some mint to the tea. He still remembered the delightful aroma. His father was reading the newspaper. The hot summer had ended, monsoon rain had poured down, and it was almost spring time. Beautiful orange roses, yellow marigolds, white jasmine, and red hibiscus were blooming. There was a breeze blowing that afternoon. Sensing favorable conditions with plenty of food supply, the birds were getting ready to lay their eggs.

Krish and his mom enjoyed sipping tea while strolling in the backyard. On the branch of a small tree, a humming bird had built her nest. The eggs had hatched. It was amazing how the two baby birds and their mother fit in that tiny nest. But, it was getting crowded, and it would soon be time for the babies to leave. They were hesitant about their first flight. As Krish walked passed the nest, the baby birds felt threatened and finally had no choice but to take the leap to protect themselves from what appeared to be certain danger.

"Sometimes, fear of the unknown is necessary to overcome the known fears of life," his mom had quipped.

Krish's father belonged to the royal family of a princely state. His father and uncle didn't talk about their father much. Krish felt that this was a ghost best left buried. However, there were interesting pieces of information still floating around. Krish's grandfather was the Raja, or King, of a province. Krish remembered visiting the ruins of his ancestral palace and seeing a painting of his grandfather in the local museum. His grandfather's stern, proud face and big mustache made an impression on young Krish. His grandfather was wealthy and powerful. However, with the decline of the Maratha Empire, and advent of the British, his influence was shrinking. Then one day, his kingdom was annexed, and he lost everything—most importantly his pride. Apparently, he became depressed after that and died. The official version of his death was that he died of a sudden heat stroke, but under hushed tones, it was speculated that the proud man took his own life.

"Let us take him to the doctor, right now," Krish remembered his mother saying once; she was worried sick about her son. Krish would spend hours writing strange equations that sprang into his mind. Sometimes, he would get frustrated if he got stuck at some point. And, at other times, sad if he couldn't find a solution to an equation. His mother was worried that the depressive gene from his grandfather would affect her child as well. Her fears were strengthened when she caught Krish's uncle taking some pills and staring blankly at the sky sometimes.

Am I sick? Krish felt a cold chill down his spine as he considered the possibility that some dormant trait in his family was making an appearance in him. It could have been triggered by loneliness, being in a foreign country, adjusting to a new place, exacting standards of work, or the curse of brilliance. It was plausible. It was a scary thought, and a lingering shadow that hung over him.

Krish rolled over to the other side of his bed. He tried to brush aside the possibility that he was sick by wondering why he was named Krishnanujam. His father had told him the story once. His father had been interested in mathematics, but couldn't pursue it due to the sudden death of Krish's grandfather. Krish's father was fascinated by the life of the young mathematical prodigy, Ramanujan. Ramanujan read a book by G.S. Carr—a synopsis of elementary results in pure mathematics. It sparked his genius and he single-handedly figured out the collective discoveries of many scientists. Ramanujan came from a poor family and didn't have enough money to buy paper to write all of his workings. Entire fields of math have been created based on some of the ideas he described. *Obviously, my father had high expectations for me*, Krish thought as he drifted to sleep.

Krish got up from his nap. According to the clock on his wall, it was almost 4:30 pm. It was getting dark. He looked out his window and saw fog hanging over the hills. He felt confused. *What the hell am I on?* he wondered. He had a strong feeling in his gut that his ideas had a greater purpose, and that somehow, they would benefit this world enormously. *In what way... I have no idea*, he admitted, but he felt a calling, a drive to move ahead.

His gut feelings about his new ideas and work were spot on. Completely unknown to Krish, greater troubles were brewing for him. He was attracting the attention of governments and other powerful organizations—some that were peaceful, and some that did not want peace at any cost. The work he published had opened doors for newer weapons that could cause severe destruction; weapons that held implications for the human civilization as a whole. All by himself, he had no way of seeing the bigger picture. All this mind-bending work at such a young age had pushed his mental faculties to the limits. He was venturing further toward instability.

He looked at the street below and saw some activity at his neighbor's home. Mike's daughter was in the military. She was preparing to leave for duty, standing in her dad's doorway. Krish watched as Mike's shoulders dropped. His daughter, on the other hand, was standing in a relaxed posture. There was no hesitation in her movements. She appeared to have a clear mind. Unlike her father, and very much like her mother, she was a lanky, tall woman. She carried her heavy bag effortlessly. Hugging her parents, she walked to the cab and drove off, waving a confident goodbye. Krish liked the clarity of her thought and action. His own mind seemed to be the exact opposite.

By now, the sun had set; darkness and fog had descended on the entire neighborhood. He thought of the greater purpose of his life and work, and the possibility of a diseased mind. Everything was unclear and muddy. He decided to follow his instincts. He badly wanted to develop new ideas in math and science and to find out the truth about this world we live in, but still don't know much about. He calmly put on his jacket and headed to the lab.

CHAPTER 3
RAW POWER

~~~~~~~

Ancient India

~~~~~~~

Raw power torments.

IT WAS SPRING TIME. PAMPA LAKE IN THE KISHKINDHA REGION in south India looked as beautiful as ever. It had thousands of lotuses floating on the surface. The crimson, white, purple, and blue lotus flowers were blooming slowly, one petal at a time, until the sun showered its rays on them and they were in full bloom. Fish swam freely in the water.

Young Hanuman and his friends were swinging over tree branches and eating fruits. They threw half eaten fruits on the ground, dug up roots for food, jumped in the lake, and were frolicking merrily in the jungle. Their broad fingertips with wide nails, strong arms, long tails, and sturdy legs meant that climbing trees came naturally. Fear was unknown to them, especially in their own backyard.

There was bamboo, sandalwood, sal, banyan, and numerous other trees. The pleasant aroma of mangoes, bananas, and various berries was everywhere. All the bees, birds, and forest animals were busy getting as much food as they needed. There was plenty of water, food, and sunshine for everyone. It was a plentiful and happy place. A squirrel turned its head to see what was going on and ran away to climb a tree. An owl kept an eye on everything from high up in the canopy. The Vanara lived peacefully with the other inhabitants of the jungle.

Hanuman was the strongest among the Vanara youth. King Vali's son, Angad, was very quick on his feet, and Hanuman had a difficult time catching him when they were playing tag.

"You are very quick, Angad, but not as fast as me," said Hanuman playfully as he caught his tail.

"You are older and bigger, Hanuman, but nothing this prince cannot handle," said Angad proudly as he used his elbow to push Hanuman away.

"Jai Vanara—victory to the king of Vanara," shouted the kids in his group as they got ready for a mock battle with Hanuman's group. The two groups, numbering in the hundreds, were throwing stones, tree branches, sticks, toy arrows, and bamboo spears at each other. There was an awful lot of din.

"Hanuman, climb that tall tree to get a better view of the field and direct us," advised one of the other kids. Hanuman liked that idea. He jumped up the tree in no time and had a nice view of the forest. He looked at the playing field below. His group was doing well in the game, and he was not needed there. Hanuman's eyes scanned the rest of the forest. On the other side of the lake, he saw a man walking in an unusual way. He was curious to find out who this person was. Hanuman took a few leaps, landed on a tree and got closer to the strange looking man.

It looks like the man can hardly walk. His bones are all bent, and he can barely stand, Hanuman thought as he got in a good vantage position in one of the trees. *Is it safe for a man who can hardly walk to be here in the jungle by himself?*

The older man had a tuft of hair tied in a shikha- knot on his otherwise shaven head, a loin cloth around his waist, a stick for support, a wooden water jar with a handle, and a small cloth bag around his shoulder. He wore wooden sandals. The sacred thread that the brahmin-priests wore across their chest was noticeable. Both of his feet, hands, and knees—as well as chest and head—were bent. His gait was unusual.

Hanuman was an intelligent boy. *It is not appropriate to laugh at somebody's deformities. He must be a brave man to be in the forest alone,* he thought. Hanuman's parents had taught him to be respectful of the priests. The priests knew the scriptures, some possessed special powers, and some were always in an agitated state at a higher energy level than most people. They could curse you if you showed disrespect. Most of them were eager to share great knowledge and wisdom when approached respectfully. Some of the priests were great teachers. As a result, it made practical sense to show respect.

Hanuman jumped a good fifty feet from the tree and landed smoothly on his two feet. He landed on a sharp stone, but did not feel any pain. He slowly approached the bent-man. Hanuman folded his hands in the traditional 'Namaste' and bowed his head. As soon as he approached the man, he felt a sense of calm. He felt as if he was in the presence of someone extraordinary.

The mighty Hanuman instinctively put his head at the frail man's feet and was overpowered by emotion.

"Who are you, oh great Rishi? Please identify yourself," Hanuman asked in a shaky voice. The man looked at Hanuman with his piercing gaze, as if he was seeing something deep within the boy.

"I am Ashtavakra. I am a Muni, a philosopher-scientist. Who are you, Vanara?" He asked in a commanding voice not fitting his frail body.

Hanuman recovered from the spell of this man and answered, "I am the son of General Kesari."

Ashtavakra Muni smiled at Hanuman's introduction. It seemed he knew more about Hanuman than Hanuman realized.

"I am going to the great Agastya Muni's hermitage," the Muni said. Hanuman was drawn to this man with seemingly great intellect and power.

"May I join you?" Hanuman asked.

"As you wish," the Muni replied. The two of them started walking through the jungle toward the hermitage. Hanuman walked ahead to remove tree branches, thorns, and pebbles from the path. "You seem like a curious kid. Ask me any questions that come to your mind. Do not worry, I will not be offended. I can see that you are a special child. This is your opportunity. Go ahead," the Muni said as he warmed up to Hanuman.

Hanuman felt reassured. He had so many questions and curiosities in his mind, but did not know whom to ask.

"Firstly, why is your body bent?" Hanuman asked. He continued before an answer was given, "Do names have meanings? How come I don't get hurt when I fall? How come Vanara are stronger than humans?" Hanuman paused. "This is just a start, I have many more," he added with a twinkle.

"Good thing I walk slowly, and we have some distance to cover, then," the Muni said as they kept walking single file. "Uh, interesting questions. You may not see it, but your questions are inter-connected," the Muni said. He carefully shifted his weight from one leg to the other to take a step. The Muni spoke in a calm voice, "You see, diet, nutrition, and the lineage of your parents play an important role in a child's innate abilities. I was born bent in eight places probably because my father had bone problems. In addition, my mother's gotra, lineage, may also have contributed to it. Agastya Muni has written a book called Upchaar Samhita—that is, Treatment Compendium— and the ancient text of Rig veda describes surgery for attaching an iron leg. As such, Agastya and his students are great practitioners of medicine and surgery. I am visiting his hermitage in hopes of getting my condition treated."

The Muni was abruptly interrupted by a loud voice.

"I have not had human or tender monkey meat in a long time," roared a Rakshas, demonic being, as he jumped from a tree and blocked Hanuman's path. He rubbed his muscular hands with long, sharp nails over his bald head. His teeth were protruding out of his mouth, eager to bite. His seven-foot tall frame with raised hands looked immensely intimidating. He wore a necklace of human and animal bones. His blood shot eyes gazed at his lunch standing before him. He made a beastly, grotesque sound.

In a flash, Hanuman plucked a huge tree as if it were a blade of grass and threw it at the Rakshas like a spear. The Rakshas dodged it just before it hit his chest but lost his balance. Hanuman threw a huge boulder at him. This time, it hit him in the chest and he fell. Hanuman quickly jumped a good ten feet in the air and landed directly on the Rakshas' arm, severely damaging it. With one of his enemy's arms crippled, Hanuman placed his left foot on Rakshas' uninjured arm and strangled the Rakshas' neck with his right foot until he died.

Hanuman caught his breath after easily killing the man-eating Rakshas and said, "He looks old and seasoned, but became cocky because of our puny appearance. This gave me enough time to strike first. As soon as I saw danger, I felt a strange power inside me, and I reacted. I cannot control the power I feel. Also, I did not obey the rules of warfare. I did not give him a warning or a chance to surrender. I could have allowed him to get on his feet before attacking again. I want to be a great warrior like my father, not a killer." Hanuman felt some remorse as he moved the dead body aside.

"Victory to you, oh son of Kesari! You have a good head on your shoulders. This was an ambush, not a battle. Sometimes, use of brutal force is necessary to protect yourself," said the Muni. "I have witnessed the valor and high moral character that you display at such a young age. Let us continue our journey."

Hanuman and Ashtavakra Muni got over the interruption quickly and continued with their conversation.

"Getting back to your questions. Let me explain to you the secret of your birth and your powers. Great scientists and philosophers have long tried to create a super-human species by combining powers of humans and beasts together. In addition, we want this species to live for a long time." The Muni's eyes broadened as he revealed the ambition of the scientists.

"Let me explain. Our planet goes through times when the whole Earth, except a few places where the sun always shines, gets covered with ice. Entire knowledge bases are destroyed and humans must start from shunya, nothingness or zero. This land that we live in is fortunate to have ample sunshine, plenty of water, fertile soil, scientific and technological know-how, and as such, is one of the ideal places to start the rebuilding process after great catastrophes.

"Some scientists spent a lifetime studying the fetuses of humans and animals as they were available due to acts of war, natural, or other reasons of untimely death. Rig Veda and Atharva Veda have descriptions of how semen is formed and how man appears in the womb. In the beginning, they are only a few koshika cells in the fetus—some become eyes, some ears, and so on. Thus, the initial koshika can become anything: muscle, eyes, nose, etc. Similarly, in an adult, as koshika die, they are replaced by these special amar koshika that can become any organ as needed. So, if you ensure that amar koshika keep supplying fresh koshika, while the old koshika die off, you will have a human that will not age and live forever. There will always be a core of amar koshika available for whichever organ is dying and needs new koshika," the Muni explained.

"Diet, nutrition, and your way of living plays a vital role in maintaining balance between the supply of new koshika and the dying of old. The scientists came up with panchamrita, a mixture of potent foods, to be taken every day to maintain this balance. Scientists from eight major specialties—medicine, surgery, diseases of head, ear, nose, eye, and throat, pediatrics, psychiatry, toxicology, nutrition and geriatrics, and sexology—worked as a team to create immortal beings. But, of course, it is not that easy. A lot of volunteers gave their lives for this cause. Animals were also used for these studies. Most of them died due to too many amar koshika or too little. Only seven humans survived over hundreds of years of trial and error. And you are one of them!"

"Wow! Mother and Father never told me this story," said Hanuman with astonishment.

"You are their son, not just an experiment that worked out. They love you. They must be waiting for an appropriate time. But, we have a lot invested in you, and you still have a lot to learn. So, it is time you knew the truth. Due to the exceptional moral qualities of your parents, you have a very good sense of right and wrong. That is very important for someone with power.

"You are also blessed with spiritual powers of the mind and subtle energy that you have not realized yet. You had a spontaneous surge of such subtle energy that once, you could not control it. You jumped high and fell and broke your jaw, hence the name Hanuman, the one with an unusual jaw. Does that answer all your questions?" the Muni asked.

"Yes, but it raises even more questions in my mind," Hanuman said naively.

The Muni smiled. "Son, you have great physical powers and unshakable morality. In due course, you will acquire spiritual powers, learn all the Vedas that are compilations of knowledge, the art of warfare, and become a great warrior and spiritual master. Naturally, you have lots of questions in your mind. You will have to find the answers, and in some cases, realize the truth yourself. The Munis who live here in the ashram will help and direct you in your journey. And then you will live as long as you wish and help others in their journey for eons to come. That is our vision. That is the purpose of your life. May we all be successful in our mission."

Hanuman had a lot to digest. He walked in silence, processing everything he had heard. He was trying to piece everything together. He had learned enormously from the Muni. They reached a stream near the hermitage. The fourth prahar of the day had begun.

"Please sit here under the tree while I bring water for your evening prayer," Hanuman said politely to the Muni. As Hanuman was fetching water, he saw his reflection. He saw the years of work, research, and countless lives that had been spent to create his present form of a body and a mind as tough as armor. He was a combination between the best of humans and simians. He saw his simian face, his strong arms and legs, and his muscular body. Hanuman had all this power, but he was tormented. Who was he really? Just what he could see, or was there more? He developed a yearning to realize the truth. He then thought about the Muni. His body was weak, but he appeared stronger and wiser.

Clearly a weak body is not an impediment for one who is willing to seek and learn, Hanuman thought. All these thoughts were confusing to Hanuman. "Respected sir, please bless me," Hanuman went back and fell at the Muni's feet.

"Hanuman, you are more than your body and your thoughts. Slowly, you will realize your true identity and your goal." The Muni effortlessly read the questions in his mind. The Muni had closed his eyes in meditation. Hanuman sat down and closed his eyes too. The sun was close to the horizon. It was a calm evening. The birds were returning to their nests.

The somber feeling that the day was coming to an end inspired a disciple in the hermitage to sing the Sri Raga. The melodious notes filled the air, enhancing the mood of the savory moment. The Muni was lost in meditation and appeared to be one with the surroundings. He had dissolved into and become one with the scenery.

On the other hand, Hanuman's eyes were closed, but his mind was like the shallow water of the nearby spring, continuously running and jumping, flowing toward something unknown.

CHAPTER 4
CLARITY

~~~~~~~

Modern Day California

~~~~~~~

Intense experiences provide clarity of goals.

WHAT IS THAT NOISE?" KRISH SAID, SOUNDING IRRITATED. He had just fallen asleep after a long day at the lab when he heard a loud thud from downstairs. He was barely awake, but was sure he'd heard heavy footsteps, one after the other—quite a few of them—rapidly climbing the stairs. He also heard voices. Even before he could finish rubbing his eyes, and realize what was happening, he heard a bang as blinding light filled his room.

"Oh shit!" he was completely disoriented by the stun grenade. His ears were ringing, eyes blinded. He couldn't understand the shouts of the voices he heard. He tried to see what was going on. He was just able to make out the letters: SWAT. Krish covered his ears to try and stop the ringing. His eyes were trying to adjust back to the dim light of the lamp on his nightstand. His mouth was dry. He could smell that some of his papers were on fire due to the grenade. The fire was put out before it escalated.

The first thing he saw, when the smoke cleared, was guns pointed at his face and laser pointers all over his upper body.

"Show me your hands! Hands in the air! No sudden moves!" somebody barked at him. He followed the orders. The men who had invaded his space were armed to the teeth—every inch of their bodies covered in protective gear. Their fingers were on the triggers of automatic weapons pointed directly at him. He could barely see their faces through the helmets and safety glasses. Black uniforms added to their anonymity. Strangely, he could feel their nervous energy permeating through the protective gear, ready to pounce on him.

He immediately realized that one wrong move would leave him dead in a matter of seconds. He instantly calmed down. He knew exactly what to do. At that moment, he realized he had nothing to fear; he hadn't done anything wrong. But, if he acted nervously, it could appear threatening. It was in his best interest to bring the intensity of the situation down. It was necessary for his survival. He had everything to lose, and there was nothing he could do anyway.

Krish made eye contact with the person who appeared to be shouting the most. As soon as the thought of being calm flashed in his mind, his whole body relaxed. It seemed that everyone around him subconsciously read the message and their trigger fingers relaxed a bit. Krish turned around and somebody handcuffed him.

"Get out of the bed," he was told. He obliged.

Two guys thoroughly checked the room for any explosives and weapons.

It was Krish's turn to ask questions, "What's going on? Why am I in handcuffs?"

Another man, wearing a blazer—and by far the least armed man in the house—walked up the stairs.

"We have credible information that you are a mule carrying drugs from across the border," he answered.

"You can't be serious!" Krish said. He almost felt the need to laugh. "Credible information, really?" He could barely control his contempt; staying calm was going to be harder than he thought. He was shaking at this blatant falsehood. "I am a world-renowned physicist and a doctoral candidate. I don't have time for some government bull crap!" he shouted as he lost control of his temper.

Now that he was handcuffed, he posed no danger and the agents in the room were more relaxed. Krish could express his disgust without the danger of being shot. Adrenaline was rushing through his veins, causing his heart to pump rapidly. He had this unmistakable urge to punch somebody in the face—any one of these jokers would do.

"Sorry sir, I apologize for the inconvenience. I guess we got the wrong guy," the officer said. He motioned as if he had just received word in his earpiece. He relayed various codes to the other agents.

"What the hell are you talking about? You almost killed me by mistake?" Krish screamed.

"I apologize, sir, DOD informed us of imminent activity from this address… it was a mistake. We're just trying to protect our communities from the drug menace. I apologize once again," the officer said politely.

Krish sighed. He ran his tongue over his lips. There was no point in arguing. "What can I do about this? I need to complain to your bosses," Krish said, even as he felt his body flood with relief. "What about the door that you broke? I rent this place." His mind could finally worry about the small things. The officer thought, *only an innocent person could think of such things.*

"Please contact the city per Federal Tort Claims Act, FTCA. Come on guys," the officer said as he retreated. Krish saw the SWAT vehicles exiting his cul de sac. Some neighbors were peeking through their windows. He could only imagine what they must be whispering about.

Krish was still shaken by the whole incident when he got up the next day. He grabbed a cup of coffee on the way to work and said 'hi' to Olivia, the barista. He walked at a slower pace than usual to allow time for his mind to calm. He was taking in the greenery around him—the fresh air, the sunlight—to help ease the tension in his body. When he reached his office, he saw a note from Dave, his advisor: 'See me ASAP.' This was the first time Dave had left such a note. Krish could sense the urgency. Something was not right.

Krish walked to Dave's office not knowing what to expect. *Did I miss a deadline? Did the projects not get funded? Was there a particularly bad review for my latest paper? Did Mark or Kathy complain about me hogging time on the NASA Pleiades supercomputer account?* Krish was going through different plausible scenarios in his head, trying to decide what his explanation would be. He took a deep breath and knocked on Dave's door.

"Come in," Dave said.

When Krish entered the room, Dave was still on the phone with someone. The level of tension in the room could be cut with a knife.

"All right, I get it," he said, hanging up the phone. Dave scratched his nose and needlessly adjusted his glasses. "Close the door," he ordered Krish.

Krish took a deep breath as he waited for, what he was sure was, bad news.

"DARPA wants exclusive rights to your research on Quantum Communication. Otherwise, we're looking at a lot of problems—and not all of them academic. I just got off a call with them. They're responsible for sending that SWAT team to your home. This is how the government negotiates," Dave said flatly.

Krish was surprised to hear that. He felt betrayed and offended by the hostile takeover of *his* research. It was as if someone were asking him to give up the rights to his newborn child after having gone through the painful labor.

"The possibilities of QCOM are immense. How can we just give the rights of an emerging technology to one organization? And I know what they're really after—all the ways I screwed up before getting to the right approach—they understand the limitations of the system and use it as a red herring to misguide enemies," Krish said, anger invading his tone. He walked out in a daze. He didn't know what else to say.

Krish saw Mark, his lab mate. "Hey Mark, can I talk to you for a second?"

"What's up man, did you mess with Pleiades again?" Mark joked. Mark was an experimental guy. He thought all theoretical research was just empty promises.

"No man, I have a much bigger problem. Can we go for a walk?"

"Walk… this early in the morning? I have to get my laser started," Mark said.

"The government wants to hijack my work. They roughed me up last night," Krish knew exactly what to say to peak Mark's interest. Mark was a surfer dude who liked big waves, freedom, the wind in his hair, and most of all, he liked relaxing at the beach with all the ladies who were tripping over themselves to go out with him. He was a mythical and enviable creature in the graduate student community—popular and dateable, the hunk-scientist.

"I hate government bullshit," Mark said. "Let's go." Krish and Mark were soon walking down the stairs.

"Where you guys headed? Don't we have a group meeting?" asked Kathy, their third lab mate.

"Hi Kathy from MIT, also known as the Cal Tech of the east coast," Mark couldn't help pulling her leg. Krish thought Kathy liked

Mark, and that there was a little flirting going on between the two. Kathy was proud of her looks-high cheekbones, slightly almond shaped eyes, and glowing skin from her Asian mother—as well as the superb brains and dark, brunette hair that came from her Caucasian father.

Kathy was very sharp. She was working on interdisciplinary research for applying the mathematical tools developed for astrophysics to NanoRx. Her goal was to use devices the size of nerves to heal the human body as part of the President's Brain Initiative.

"If there's no meeting, I'll join you," she said. The three of them sat on a bench near the cafeteria.

"All right, here's the deal," Krish began. "One of the many applications to my research is in the field of secure communication. Quantum communication cannot be hacked. A photon from an entangled photon pair is transmitted over a distance. The very act of measuring it, changes it. And since it's part of the entangled pair, you have to know the properties of the whole system to decode the information. My research will increase the amount of information, and the distance over which it can be transmitted. The quantity and reach are important for any real-life application. My rough calculations show my constructs can transmit gigabytes of data up to 36,000 kilometers! That means they can be used for satellite communication—crucial for all military applications." Krish looked at his mates with excitement.

"Oh good," Kathy said, not impressed. "So, what's the problem?"

"DOD wants me to give them exclusive rights to the work, along with all of the mathematical models that didn't work!"

"Sons of bitches!" Kathy said.

"Oh, now she's fired up. Has nothing to do with my research," Krish said feigning annoyance. "Big brother has strange negotiating tactics. They almost shot me in my bed yesterday." For a moment, Krish thought that Mark and Kathy were jealous of him—that they also wanted their work to be important enough to be almost killed over. He was amused by that thought. He wanted some feedback and support from his lab-mates.

Mark thought for a moment before speaking, "With the government on the prowl, your computer is probably already hacked. I have written code to encrypt data that's very difficult to crack. Secure all your unpublished work through that. It will buy you some time. And stall Dave in the meantime. I don't know what else you can do."

"Good idea," Krish said. He gave a firm and warm handshake to Mark and Kathy. He felt like hugging them. He was all alone in this strange situation, thousands of miles away from loved ones. They were the closest thing he had to friends. But, he ended up not initiating the hug. The trio headed back to the lab.

Krish sent an e-mail to Dave, 'My mother is sick. I'm traveling home for a couple of weeks.' He took pictures of all his notes and equations, and encrypted as much information as possible using Mark's custom software, carrying it in a jump drive.

I'll do it the old-fashioned way. I can't trust anything on the web. No cloud storage, he thought. He destroyed all other copies. He burned the original copies in a chemistry department lab.

I need to have a proper meal at a nice restaurant to get over this shitty day, Krish thought as he walked to his house. French food sounded good at the moment. While walking home, he felt as if somebody was watching him. *I'm just being paranoid after last night*, he thought.

Krish picked up the pace, took the shuttle, and went home. The homeowner had called a handyman to fix the door.

"It will be ready by the evening," the handyman told him with a forced smile.

Krish was thoroughly confused. He didn't know who to trust. He was sure his house had been bugged. He scanned the house for anything important and took his passport out of the safe deposit box, just in case he needed it. He picked up his notebook—the one where he had scribbled a lot of formulae—and took it with him.

This is exactly why we need secure communication, or pretty soon we will be back to using paper for everything that you don't want unauthorized access to, he thought.

Krish drove to the French restaurant. The feeling of being followed persisted. He had a crepe and some wine to calm his nerves. *I still have some work to do,* he thought and ordered a latte. Krish was sipping his coffee when a customer at the next table got his attention.

"How you doing, Mr. Scientist?" the customer asked.

Suddenly, Krish saw a gun with a silencer pointed at him from under the table.

"What in fuck's name are you doing?" Krish shouted. He was about to react when he heard firecrackers inside the restaurant, near the entrance. He ducked under the table. Another guy with a gun began shooting randomly around the restaurant.

Krish had been sitting at the rear of the restaurant. The place was reasonably full, with at least twenty to thirty people. Krish saw a waiter throw an entire tray of food in the air and run in fear of his life. The terrified waiter was shot in the shoulder and collapsed to the ground in agony.

Chaos and screams filled the restaurant as people tried to duck behind a makeshift shield or run. Food and drinks flew everywhere; the loud echo of bullets was the only sound able to overcome the wave of screams. The firecracker sounds continued—*bang, bang, bang*—at a steady pace. The smell of death was everywhere. The fear of meaningless, sudden death at the hands of some pathetic loser gripped the once pleasant restaurant.

Krish was frozen for a moment. He didn't know what to do.

The waiter closest to him was probably shot from a bullet that ricocheted off the wall. He didn't seem to be in the direct line of fire.

He was young and probably only serving to put himself through school. He soon lost consciousness.

Krish tried to pull the boy's body under the table for protection. Krish wasn't sure if he just wasn't registering the gunfire anymore, or if it had actually stopped. He felt his pockets in search of his phone. Then, he spotted it on the tabletop. He tried to reach for it, but the gunshots started again. The gunman was shooting aimlessly, standing on a table across the room.

"Nobody moves and nobody leaves, got it?" the shooter said casually, as if he were explaining the rules to some sort of friendly game.

Raw power to kill in the wrong hands, Krish thought. The shooter rested his long gun on his shoulder. He changed the magazine, keeping a watchful eye on everyone.

"Some of you will live, and some will…" Before he could complete his sentence, a brave police officer barged in the front door to save the lives of strangers. He risked his life for his duty. He was in the direct line of fire. Krish cringed, preparing himself for the unfortunate fate of the young officer. At the first sign of resistance, however, the shooter shot himself in the mouth and fell from the tabletop.

Krish was stunned.

"Oh, screw you, you coward!" someone shouted at the gunman.

In the heat of the moment, the young cop also sent a round of bullets flying. One of the bullets stuck the original gunman, who was intent on harming Krish personally. He fell down bleeding, staring vacantly at Krish as he took his last breath.

There were broken pieces of glass, food, drinks, and blood everywhere. The fear that filled the place was palpable.

Krish got out from under the table and grabbed his phone. He carefully stepped on shards of broken glass and felt the slippery, crunchy sensation as he walked out of the building. He, along with a few others, got out the back door. They were asked by the police to raise their hands and remain still. Krish immediately got hold of a paramedic and told him about the waiter who was shot.

Krish sat under a tree away from the scene. Exhausted, physically and emotionally drained, observing it from a distance, Krish thought that everything seemed surreal. He had come face-to-face with death twice in twenty-four hours. Everything was happening so fast. He couldn't wrap his head around it all.

His thoughts went to the guy who had pointed the gun at him from under the table. *Who was he? What did he want? Was he partnered with the shooter? Or was he after me, specifically?* Krish wondered. As exhausted as he was, thinking about it all made Krish realize that he still had a reserve of energy from his fight or flight response. The mysterious gunman's accent sounded Eastern European or Russian. *Who was he working for?* Krish wondered. He was lost in his thoughts as a paramedic approached him.

"Are you all right, sir?" the medic asked. Krish was feeling dizzy and about to lose consciousness. In the chaos that ensued in the restaurant, his would-be assailant had pulled the trigger—either due to the sudden noise or by intent. The bullet had more than grazed Krish; he had been bleeding steadily and the shock to his body was finally setting in. He hadn't noticed the shot as his body was pumped full of adrenaline to survive.

The paramedic performed some first aid, put him on a stretcher, and sent Krish to the hospital. When he awoke, he inhaled the undeniable smell of hospital and looked around. He was surrounded by medical devices, tubes, flickering LED lights, beeps, and graphs.

"I need to talk to my parents," Krish told the cute blonde nurse on duty. "I'm a scientist at Cal Tech… figuring out the secrets of the universe," he added, making a feeble attempt at flirting.

"Very cool," she said politely, her ponytail bouncing as she shook her head. "I'm an intern, trying to figure out the secrets of the human body," she said with a smile. After the pleasant moment had passed, Krish was reminded of his sucky day.

"Please get my cell phone. I need to call my parents. The coverage of the shooting is probably all over the news. My parents will be worried." As an after-thought, he added, "How is my wound, anything serious?"

"You had a long day. The doctor will provide more details. The wound is superficial, nothing to worry about," she said in a practiced, soothing voice, touching him lightly to put him at ease.

Krish called his parents and assured them everything was okay.

They were relieved to hear from him. "Come back home, enough with your research," his mother said, the weight of worry obvious in her voice.

A strange thought occurred to Krish. *Was I shot by the crazy scumbag shooter or by that other douche bag who was pointing his gun directly at me? Was he real or a creation of my imagination?* He pressed the button by his bed to call the nurse.

Dr. Buzinsky answered from the nursing station. "Ma'am, I had a very rough day, and I cannot keep things straight. I need to see a psychotherapist or a psychiatrist to make sure I'm not losing my mind," Krish said plainly.

"I will arrange for that, sir," she assured.

It had started to rain. Krish had dozed off. When he opened his eyes, he could see that it was getting dark outside. He talked to the resident psychiatrist. She gave him a standard questionnaire.

"Krish, you're not schizophrenic based on your answers to the questionnaire. You have been through a lot of stress, and there are aggravating factors such as your doctoral research, loneliness, and homesickness. You should see a therapist until things settle down completely, but I wouldn't worry yourself too much." Krish nodded in agreement.

Krish couldn't help thinking how rudimentary it was to make such an important diagnosis based on a questionnaire. For any physical ailment, there were endless tests, but not for mental illness. *I hope Kathy's brain project makes some progress. I could use some help understanding the human mind,* he thought.

Krish was released from the hospital the next day. By the time he got off the bus, the rain had stopped. It seemed that springtime might come earlier than usual this year. Krish noticed that the evergreen pear trees had shed their tiny white petals all over the black pavement; they looked like snowflakes. All the tress looked clean and freshly washed from the rain. There were snails crawling all over the pavement. One bird's nest hadn't survived the rain and was lying in a helpless pile. The eggs couldn't be seen anywhere nearby, and Krish hoped they were safe somewhere. He was trying to enjoy the walk back to his house. There was a slight breeze, a wet leaf landed on his hair, and the water drops rolled over his face, startling him. He was obviously still a little edgy after having so many guns pointed at his face recently.

Krish noticed posters for the presidential primaries on the trees. Usually, California primaries didn't matter as the decisions were made well before it was time for the public to vote. But, this time, it appeared California's rich delegate count could make a difference. Plus, everybody always wanted money from Hollywood and the Silicon Valley. A poster advertised that one of the leading presidential candidates was making a stop in town that day and there was a debate being held. *I wonder what they'll fight about tonight,* he thought and kept walking.

Krish pressed the pedestrian crossing button at one of the intersections. The white walking man and audio signal came on. As he was passing the row of cars that had stopped for pedestrians, he noticed one car revving its engine and slightly crossing the stop line. He noticed a south Asian and an Arab man staring blankly at him.

He quickly crossed the street and turned right to be out of their sight. One of them got out of the car and started following him. Trying to avoid the man chasing him, Krish walked away from his house. He looked up and noticed a crowd nearby. He thought he might be safe there and made his way toward the gathering. The group turned out to be for the presidential debate. It had been a rough couple of days and he wanted to rest. But, given his situation, being surrounded by people seemed like a better choice.

The theater of democracy was on full display inside and outside the hall. 'Monkey,' 'liar,' 'Satan,' 'dumb,' 'stupid,' 'death to the president,' 'hang him,' references to men's and women's body parts, and various racial slurs were thrown around by both the supporters and the opponents outside the hall. The two sides were staring at each other angrily and throwing four letter words like flaming daggers.

Krish wondered if these people were truly this passionate about international politics, taxes, climate change, and education OR if they were just reacting to the words of their leaders. Maybe they were venting out their frustration over other parts of their personal lives via this public event. Some were clearly being paid to be there. Some were simply present to pick a fight for no reason in particular.

Inside the town hall, it was no different. "Go get them! Beat the daylights out of them. Who will hit the target?" said one candidate pointing to the crowd. "You, you, or you? Use your weapon, use it to fight back." Crosshairs painted on the pictures of opponents, chest thumping, subtle changes in tone, and language were all being employed to press the right buttons. There was a lot of anger in the people gathered.

Oh leaders, you're doing all this theater to get votes. After the election, you will move on, but this bad blood will persist inside these peoples' weak minds, and it will come out in the form of some mass shooting, child abuse, bullying, police brutality, or some other twisted way somewhere down the line, Krish thought.

On the other hand, the other candidate was advertising, 'free education, free health care, free retirement, free housing, free jobs, and the government will take care of everything, just give us your money.'

Well, it's just not going to work in the real world, sir. Plus, I have first-hand experience. I've lived in India during the socialist era, before the economy was opened. It was not good! Krish wanted to point out. *Same thing happens everywhere in the world, back home too. Leaders do the same thing at every level—from prime ministers, presidents, and dictators to executive managers, supervisors, down to foremen. People spread wrong, misleading information, create divisions, threats, anything really to maintain power.*

Krish leaned by a wall in the corner, thinking that it would give him a good vantage point for anyone coming toward him. He took position at the back of the hall, at a higher elevation. He had a wall behind him so he only needed to keep an eye out in front. Surprisingly, his lab mate Kathy was standing in the row next to him.

"The shooter at the restaurant was a bullied kid taking out his issues," Kathy said as she moved closer to Krish.

"I'm not a social scientist. I'm a physicist, but I thought…" Krish hadn't completed his sentence. Suddenly, his pupils dilated, his breathing became rapid, and his body felt warm all over. His ear lobes became red with excess blood circulation, and his sense of smell became more acute as his nostrils flared.

An invisible energy wave crashed into the crowd. Kathy broke apart into tiny particles. Slowly it spread to the rest of the crowd. The hall disappeared. Krish was standing there and around him the whole sky was full of tiny particles buzzing passed one another—moving randomly in all possible directions. Everything was swirling in an elliptical shape. There were trillions of super tiny particles, but most of the space was still empty, filled with dark matter. The dark matter was influencing the particles, but it could not be seen or touched!

The particles were moving through the Higgs field, interacting with the Higgs-Boson and acquiring mass. The forces of nature started acting upon them. The strong nuclear force formed protons and neutrons from quarks and held subatomic particles inside the atom. The electromagnetic force acted on charged particles, and they started interacting with each other and forming various molecules and complex biology. Some of the particles assembled to form Kathy and other humans, and some particles were still moving around randomly.

Out of all the probabilities of where the individual particles could end up, they were driven toward the formation of Kathy—because Kathy existed! This was the same anthropic principle that scientists used to explain the formation of this universe—out of the several universes that are mathematically possible, only the conditions favoring this universe dominate because this is the only universe we experience, and that's how this universe was created.

So, Kathy was converting randomness into herself. The probability amplitude distribution functions of the particles mathematically started looking like an arrow. They were converging toward something rather than nothing. Kathy was controlling the particles by her 'force'. However, she herself was still bouncing around randomly like the individual particles she was made of! The presidential candidates were now exerting their force on these randomly moving humans, including Kathy, and driving them toward a dark disk.

Krish thought, *humans are being driven toward a dark, bottomless pit, not a bright and enlightening goal, by corrupt and inept leadership.*

"All right, there you go… the debate is starting," Kathy's words abruptly brought Krish back from his hallucination to the hall where the normal back and forth political drama was currently going on.

Krish's breathing returned to normal. He thought he had stepped on something. He noticed an arrow lying at his feet. It looked just like the mathematical functions he had been thinking about. *Where did it come from?* he wondered.

He then heard the words, *"This arrow is powerful, like a thunderbolt. It is decorated with gold. Its wood is from the reed forest of Kartikeya. It has eagle feathers for fins toward the end, nodes that are very smooth, a tip that is extremely sharp, and its egress is perfectly straight."*

Krish picked up the extraordinary looking arrow. He didn't know what to make of it or if anyone else had heard the mysterious voice.

"This is messed up," Krish said out of frustration. "I don't know what's real or what's a hallucination."

After thinking about everything he had witnessed and felt over the last few days, and processing it through his scientific mind, Krish came up with some conclusions. He grabbed Kathy and walked toward a quiet corner.

"All the time that there is—past, present, future—is already here. We just interpret it linearly for our survival. There are multiple possible universes, and we create the universe we live in. Humans determine the outcome of Feynman's probabilities and probability amplitude, and the force that we exert determines the outcome of events from the subatomic level up.

"Just like humans' influence matter, when it comes to individual humans, the folks who apply 'the force' are the rich and the powerful. Leaders have power over populations, and they shape the population the same way that humans shape inanimate matter. People who have forgotten about their true power are easily misled. Additionally, if the leaders get degenerated and corrupted, the population degenerates and suffers as well."

Krish thought for a while before he continued, "The solution is for each individual to realize the power they have at an early stage in their life, so that they cannot be misled by leaders—the realization of the power to influence the outcome of all events and the universe itself. And, once you have been touched with the awareness of this power, you cannot go back to being lazy, corrupt, or warlike. Darkness cannot exist once there is light. And then, nobody needs to be taught to do the right thing. It just happens because you have felt 'the force'. You just need to realize your power! And I'll mathematically prove that this extraordinary power exists in each individual. I'll bring the force to everyone. That is my mission. This will be true democracy."

Kathy didn't know what to say. She processed what Krish was saying, staring at him blankly. This connection between science, mathematics, and societal function was unheard of. She finally looked at him with a twinkle and nodded gently. She was impressed. Kathy was a tough customer to win over. She lightly kissed his stubble-covered cheek with her tender lips.

"Good," she said. That was the highest praise she could bestow upon another non-MIT human. "Well, all this is just empty words without the math. Show me the math first," she insisted.

Krish knew she was right. He needed mathematical proof for what he had witnessed and conceived. For the moment, though, he was delighted. Krish defended his strange ideas, "A new idea is like a newborn baby—bloody, sticky, and helpless. Give it some time, and it will flourish." Happy with himself, he pumped his fist in the air and got ready to leave the hall.

An old woman standing next to Krish, looked at him strangely. "Lots of nuts here," she said matter-of-factly. Krish ignored her. As he walked toward the exit, he thought, *we're so preoccupied with the daily grind, that we don't pay attention to the big picture. The intense experiences that I had today blocked everything out of my mind's eye and drove me toward this insight.* The revelation was totally worth everything he had been through.

Krish was happy, he felt very light. He knew this was the right thing. This is what he had been looking for all these years. All those equations, and page after page of math that appeared in his mind from seemingly nowhere, were driving him toward this. *I wish Prisha were here,* he thought as he wondered about the one person he would like to share this moment with. He had an intense desire to hold this woman. He wanted to touch her beautiful, long hair, marvel at her sparkling, young eyes that were so full of energy and latent desire, and bask in the radiance of her beauty. He wanted to lay with her and make love to her. *Well, let us not get ahead of ourselves,* he cautioned himself. *I don't even know if she's interested.*

While Krish was lost in his world, the debate between the candidates concluded. Krish ascertained that he was not being followed any longer. He felt it safe to walk to home.

'I hope everything is all right... worried :(' flashed a message on his WhatsApp. It was Prisha. She must have heard about the shooting at the restaurant. That simple message brought a smile to Krish's lips.

"Good way to end a long day," he said as he continued his walk.

Back at the hall, the cleaning crew was busy at work after everyone had left. One gentleman was inquiring with them, "I lost an arrow for my crossbow. Have you seen it?" Kathy overheard their exchange.

She wondered, *was that the arrow Krish found? Where did it come from? His thoughts are extraordinary, fresh, and brilliant, but is his thesis correct or a figment of his imagination? Let math and experimental validation triumph above everything else,* she concluded.

CHAPTER 5
STANDING ON THE SHOULDERS OF GIANTS

~~~~~~~

Ancient India

~~~~~~~

Heroes emerge from the society's knowledge and expertise.

O
H! THERE YOU ARE, HANUMAN," HIS FRIENDS CALLED AS they finally found where he had disappeared to with Ashthvakra Muni. Prince Angad, Nal, Neel, and other young Vanara joined Hanuman near the hermitage.

"This gurukul's residence is a center of learning and exploration of various aspects of wisdom, as well as science of the physical world," said Ashthvakra. Hanuman looked intrigued and eager to learn more. On the other hand, Angad and some of the other Vanara were glancing at the young women helping to clean up after the evening prayer and lighting lamps at the gurukul, hermitage.

Angad was a handsome young prince. He wore a thick gold bracelet around the strong wrist that carried his mace. A gold necklace with a blue diamond pendant adored his chest. He had long hair held in place with a sizable gold chain tied around his forehead. He wore a short, deep-blue silk dhoti around his waist. His favorite blue color pigment for dyeing the dhoti was made from precious lapis stones. Angad took a sharp breath and walked toward the women with deliberate steps.

He approached one of the women of the gurukul. She had radiant skin, a slender body, and big, playful eyes. She held her neck and back erect, attracting attention to her slim midriff and navel. Her arms were toned, and one could tell from her movements that she had a flexible body due to the regular practice of yoga. She had long, black hair, wore a short, knee-length skirt made from cotton over her slim legs, and a cloth tied around her breasts. She also wore copper anklets. She appeared busy with her chores.

"Namaste," Angad said politely. His voice came out little hoarse. "I am Angad, a Vanara, the prince of Kishkindha," he continued.

"Namaste visitor. I am Savi, a student at the gurukul," she said in a leveled tone, pushing locks of hair behind her right ear. Looking at him, she continued, "Per my guru's instructions, we need to provide visitors with any help they may need. Do you need anything?"

"My friends and I would like to pay our respects to Agastya Muni," Angad tried hard to focus on the conversation rather than looking at her pretty oval face.

"He has not returned from his visit to the neighboring kingdom yet. You may see him tomorrow. It will be dark soon, would you and your friends like to rest in the guest quarters?" She pointed to the huts some distance from the main cluster at the gurukul.

The forest around the guest quarters was cleared, giving a direct view of the rooms, preventing any surprise moves. The guest quarters had a small wooden fence to protect it from beasts. The fence around the gurukul was much stronger and taller. The entire path between the guest quarters and the main gurukul was well lit with torches.

Angad was thinking about the offer when a Vanara came running toward him.

"Nal built a comfortable bed for the Muni. We have enough food and water. Prince Angad, let us have dinner," the Vanara informed him. "Unless you want to stay in the guest quarters," he added mischievously.

"Very well, we will see you tomorrow then," Angad said to the lady, trying to catch one more glimpse before turning away. His steps back to the Vanara camp did not have the same spring as before.

Back at the makeshift camp, everyone ate. One of the Vanara played flute by the bonfire. Another got his drum out and started playing a melody. The combination of the flute playing the softer, feminine raagini with a quartertone variation and the male raaga, conveyed a deeper meaning to the music.

Another Vanara told the story of a great warrior, Parshuram, who killed all the arrogant kings who mistreated the common man. The dancer employed skillful use of hand gestures, limb movements, movement of eyes and cheeks, speed, intensity, and patterns to convey the story quite vividly.

"You are good students of the Natya Veda," remarked Ashthvakra. A prahar period of three hours had passed after the sunset. Everyone was getting sleepy.

"I am too tired… going to sleep—not my turn to keep guard!" Neel said. "Everyone can sleep. Angad is wide awake thinking about the lady anyway. He will keep guard," he joked. Everybody burst into laughter.

"Be respectful, she is your future queen," a Vanara said.

"She looks like one," another commented. Angad did not protest the bantering as he was enjoying the thought of being together with the lady.

Hanuman was seated by the Muni. They were looking at the night sky. He wondered about the stars, the planets, the constellations, their movements, and how time was kept using these movements. Hanuman remembered his mother telling him about the extra month in that year.

"What is a leap month?" Hanuman asked.

The Muni explained, "There are thirty lunar days in a month. The moon takes 27.3 days to complete a trip around Earth, but the Earth also moves during this time. Thus, from Earth, the moon appears at the same phase, one new moon to the next, in an average of 29.5 days. We use twenty-seven stars, such as Chitra, or group of stars, such as Krittika, as a reference to describe the position of sun, moon, and comets. A moon-year is twenty nine and a half days time twelve, which equals three hundred fifty four and thirty six hundredths days.

"A sun-year is when Earth completes one round around the sun, and the sun appears at the same location as seen from Earth. That takes 365.25 days. Thus, the difference between moon and sun year is 10.892 days. In an average of two years and 8.5 months, this difference is around thirty days. Hence, we add a leap month every three years or so to bring sun and moon calendars in harmony."

"Wow! That is very elegant and smart," said Hanuman. He then remembered that it was his turn to keep guard. "It is my turn, please get some sleep, oh wise one," Hanuman requested the Muni.

Ashthvakra laid down on the bed that Nal had put together for him using the available supplies.

"You be careful Hanuman," warned the Muni.

The fire was dying by now. Hanuman added some logs to the fire to keep it going. He climbed a tree to keep guard over his sleeping friends. He noticed there were guards at the nearby gurukul too. Their torches were lit, and they were carrying bows, arrows, swords, and spears. Hanuman's thoughts went back to the man-eating Rakshas he had killed that day. The Rakshas' last breath left his body as his windpipe was crushed under Hanuman's strong foot—his eyes popping out.

The Rakshas had let out a beastly cry before he fell on the dusty ground below. There was regret in his eyes that he did not fight well.

Three more prahars had passed. Hanuman was resting as his turn for keeping guard was over. There was a cool breeze blowing. Everyone, including the guard, had dozed off. Ashthvakra was at the center of the camp. The strong Vanara, including Hanuman and Angad, were on the periphery. The smaller ones formed the inner circle. At pre-dawn, an arrow came whizzing from the direction of the gurukul toward the camp. It hit the tree above and fell, but did not land on anyone. Two more arrows were fired in the same way—one with fire on its head. The fiery arrow fell on a Vanara in the inner circle. He was awakened from sleep and suffered minor burns on his chest. He did not know what to make of it and decided to wake up Hanuman.

"Hanuman wake up, somebody fired this burning arrow!" the Vanara said as he shook Hanuman. Hanuman was up in a flash. He held his gada and looked around.

"Which way?" Hanuman whispered. The Vanara pointed to the gurukul. Hanuman woke up the guard with a whistle. He jumped on a tree and looked toward the gurukul. The gurukul was bustling with activity in the pre-dawn hour. Everyone was pointing toward the jungle.

The gurukul had fired a warning shot toward the camp to wake them up. The Rakshas' raid to avenge the death of their brother was underway. The Rakshas were always looking for an opportunity to attack the Vanara and hermits, both of whom always sided with the humans. In addition, whatever weapons and other technologies were developed at the gurukuls were always shared first with humans, giving them an upper hand. The Rakshas thought they were treated unfairly because of the way they looked and behaved—unkempt and uncivilized due to their consumption of human meat. They consumed abundant amounts of hallucinates, did not pursue the arts, used too much violence, and showed no apparent respect for females. They had no respect for the knowledge contained in the Vedas either.

In their defense, they didn't know there was anything wrong with their way of life, and believed there was no need to contain their basic instincts. The Rakshas in the raiding party were screeching and shouting. They were led by a female. She was known to be of unstable mind, but a fierce warrior. The Rakshas had their favorite weapons— hammer heads with sharp edges and large-bladed, saw-tooth swords. These were supplemented with big, sharp nails and extremely strong arms, useful in hand-to-hand combat. Some of them could jump high in the air as if flying.

At the camp, Hanuman woke everyone up. The Vanara had the stream behind them and the hermitage on one side. They were safe from those sides. Hanuman assumed the lead and Angad was assisting him. Nal and his friends uprooted some trees and placed them in heaps around the camp to force the hordes of enemy to break up. It was much easier to deal with individuals than with a group encircling the Vanara fighters.

The fighters from the hermitage came out and formed a defensive perimeter around the gurukul. They employed concentric, Asanhata formation. The senior, and most experienced, student fighters were on the outside. It was their opportunity to put the knowledge and skill they had acquired from their guru to practical use and defend their gurukul. Their teacher had not yet returned. A small stockpile of special weapons was in the center hut. The teacher's wife, and other female students, were stationed in the huts near the center. Female fighters with swords and daggers were guarding them.

One of the skilled archers from the gurukul fired ten arrows in rapid succession, two to three at a time, toward the Rakshas hordes. The arrows were meant to display the skills of the gurukul and serve as a warning not to mess with them. At the Vanara camp, Ashthvakra Muni was seated quietly at the center under the tree. The Vanara felt some kind of energy field around him. He could not be harmed. He closed his eyes for some time and visualized what was about to happen.

He called to Hanuman. "Bless you, oh brave, indestructible one. You and Angad take the fight to the enemy before they reach the camp and cause unnecessary deaths. These Vanara fighters are not trained soldiers, and as such, it is not their dharma. It is yours and the prince's duty to protect the weak. Use the narrow pass that the enemy must cross. Do not worry, you will be successful."

Hanuman and Prince Angad were fired up. They shouted the battle cry, "Jai Mahadev, victory to the Great God," and took a long jump from a tall tree. They reached the narrow pass just as the Rakshas were getting ready to cross. Hanuman directly engaged the female Rakshas commanding the hordes. Whoever crossed the narrow pass was mercilessly slaughtered. Both of the young Vanara attacked with such ferocity, and broke skulls with such speed, that the Rakshas were stunned. The two Vanara were hitting the pressure points with force and precision, and the Rakshas were dying instantly. Between the two, they were moving methodically to block the enemy.

The female leader realized she was losing troops. In a desperate attempt to break the line held by the two Vanara, she jumped high and landed her sledgehammer directly on the young prince's head. He managed to dodge the full force of the blow, but not completely, and broke his nose, gashed his eyes, lost his balance, and fell on a boulder with her on top of him. He broke his shin bones as well.

Hanuman noticed this and landed a fierce blow to the female's head, knocking her unconscious. Her troops flocked around her, lifted her, and retreated in a defensive formation. Hanuman lifted the prince in his arms. "We saved our friends," the prince said smiling.

"You fought like a prince. I am privileged to fight by your side," Hanuman said as he carried Angad in his arms back to the gurukul for treatment.

The entire gurukul saw the valor of the two Vanara. "Jai Mahadev!" they welcomed the young heroes. Angad was taken straight for treatment. He could not have chosen a better place to break bones. The gurukul was well known for medical know-how.

"Tie clean cotton cloth to stop the bleeding," Savi shouted. In the absence of her teacher, she oversaw medical care. "Check for poisoning from the weapon, clean the wound, prepare for Nasika Salya Tantra or rhinoplasty using a forehead flap." Then, she turned her gaze to the prince. "So, you are very fond of reckless adventures, are you?" Gone was the polite student from the evening before—here she was the surgeon in charge of her patient.

"Just doing my duty," Angad replied, trying to hide his pain. His wounds were excruciating as the adrenaline of the battle subsided.

"Well, your nose is a mess. I need to fix it. Another surgeon will fix your broken shin bones. The good news is, you will not be completely blind, just one eye is damaged," she said flatly.

Savi was nervous about performing her first solo surgery, but tried to put on a brave face. "Do not worry, you are in good hands. I have practiced this procedure many times."

"Go over the procedure with me," requested Angad.

"I will measure the portion of your nose with a leaf, cut the nasal stump with a knife, cut a piece of skin from your forehead in the desired shape, cover the nose with it, and a small pedicle will still be attached. Then, I will apply stitches and put tubes of castor oil plant in your nose. I will sprinkle lycorine, red sandalwood, barberry, cover it with cotton, then apply clean sesame oil," she continued and recited the entire procedure.

Angad took a deep breath. She looked bewitchingly beautiful as she recited the procedure. He loved the hint of worry for him in her voice, and the nervous energy due to her first surgery. He slipped his hand around her waist, pulled her close with a strong jerk, and held her. She leaned forward to keep her balance. Her breasts were touching his chest. He kissed her lips even as her hair covered his face. He heard footsteps approaching.

"Everything will be fine," he said changing the subject as she got away from him. Neatly arranged, clean surgical instruments were brought in.

"There are 125 types of instruments described by our guru. We will only use a few on you," joked another surgeon who entered the room.

The team of medical practitioners got to work. Hanuman kept an eye on the proceedings from the window. He stayed near Angad for some time. Everything seemed to be going smoothly so Hanuman wandered around the gurukul. *This place is wonderful, so much to learn here. The guru and the students are a repository of so much knowledge and wisdom. Why do the Rakshas want to destroy this?* Hanuman wondered as he sat at the Muni's feet.

"Son, it is very important you understand the answer to your question. Listen carefully. Hundreds of students are helping with transferring the knowledge accumulated at such places of education in writing for future generations," the Muni said as he brushed his tuft of hair with his fingers. "There is a lot of work on mathematics here, too. Do not forget that mathematics is the language that this universe speaks. One of the greatest breakthroughs achieved here is the representation of the largest to the smallest values using just ten numbers—shunya, ekah, dvau, tryah, catvarah, pancha, sat, sapta, asta, and nava. There are numerous other aphorisms to do with shapes of objects, areas, relation between the diagonal and sides of squares, fractions, etc."

The Muni paused. He looked at the sky and closed his eyes. "Philosophy, yoga, mathematics, and science are nurtured here side-by-side. They have benefitted from each other and pushed the boundaries of knowledge. The aim of all fields of study is to understand the workings of the universe, including the human body, and use it to improve the living conditions in this world." Hanuman was listening intently.

"The ultimate aim of this endeavor is to realize and experience the true nature of the universe and function in this world in a free, liberated state. Function in the world, not as a slave to your desires or the desires of others, but to enjoy life as the master. You will never achieve this goal if you follow the Rakshas path of slavery to your uncontrolled instincts. This is the major difference between the two approaches. Violent force is necessary to keep order and to destroy those who are more interested in using power for their own dominance rather than creating an environment where everyone can realize the true nature of the universe and their own power as humans. If these forces are not destroyed, they can change the direction of human development completely. That is not acceptable and will not be allowed to take place at any cost," The Muni spoke in a steady and assured voice.

The Muni looked straight at Hanuman and said, "You have an important role to play in influencing the outcome of these events. You are of great physical strength, tremendous mental capacity, and outstanding moral character. In addition, you are not influenced by carnal pleasures and other senseless enjoyments. You are the result of a lot of hard work and good fortune. Everything has come together nicely in you. The timing is also appropriate for a decisive war to determine the course of human development on this planet."

Hanuman felt the weight of those expectations on his shoulders. He had goose bumps all over his body. There was a mixture of anxiety and elation in his heart. While maintaining his composure, he said in a slightly skeptical voice, "I feel proud that you and others show so much faith in me and my abilities. But, will I be able to fulfill these tall expectations all by myself?"

The Muni smiled at the young boy's hesitation and doubts. "You will have all the support you need. You will have partners and a leader.

Do not worry, you will also get a lot of training for handling special weapons and for protection against deadly weapons. We are with you. Equally important is that you will train in yogic sciences and understand the philosophical and mechanistic aspects of the universe. You will help us win this war and sustain the results for hundreds of generations to come. The stakes could not be higher. May you be successful in your mission. Jai Mahadev!"

CHAPTER 6
QUEST FOR PROOF

~~~~~~~

Modern Day California

~~~~~~~

Hurdles test the intensity of fire within.

KRISH WAS AWOKEN BY THE BUZZ OF HIS PHONE. HE READ the text message that flashed: 'Good morning. I'm downstairs, open the door.' It was Kathy. *Why is she here? Is it Dave?* he thought to himself as he went downstairs to open the door.

"I brought you some coffee," Kathy said as she entered the house. She was in her faded blue jeans, light berry-colored top, and a black cardigan.

"Thanks! That's really nice, but...um, what brings you here?"

"Just came to say hi," Kathy said. "Let's look at that mathematical approach you want to take for your hypothesis. I'm curious. I hope it's okay," she added.

"All right, have a seat. I'll get ready," said Krish. Just then, there was a knock on the door. Krish saw a young lady standing in his doorway. She was tall, with a bony, square face, wearing a dark suit;

her eyes scanned the surroundings. She wore small earrings, and her blonde hair was tied in a ponytail.

"Hello sir, I'm Agent Brooke Craig. I'm responsible for your protection," she introduced herself, flashing a badge. "You've been busy lately," she continued.

"What? Wait, who are you again?" asked Krish, as Kathy watched in puzzlement.

"You were almost killed… twice. We can't take any more chances. I'm the bureau's liaison to DARPA, protecting high value scientific talent," she said, looking at Kathy. "I'll make sure you stay safe."

"Oh great! That should help with my thinking and research," Krish said, a touch of annoyance laced delicately around the edges of his voice.

"Dead people don't get to think or do research," Agent Craig shot back, without looking at Krish. She was already busy getting a feel for the layout of his place and memorizing all possible exits. "You carry on with whatever you need to do. Let me look around once, then I'll be waiting outside…sir," Agent Craig said as she started checking the house.

I guess I don't really have a say in this. Might as well get on with my work, Krish thought as he sipped some coffee and closed the door behind her.

Kathy and Krish were discussing ideas over coffee.

"Let's look at it from first principles. Nature does not determine the outcome of the simplest of events. All possibilities are probable. Nature just roles the dice every single time," Krish said. "For example, outcome of experiments with sub atomic particles is affected by the act of observation. The observation at present time can affect the past behavior of the system. Shinning photons on a beam of sub atomic particles near a screen downstream affects whether the particles travel through one or both slits upstream! The past is uncertain until you observe it!" Krish was laying the groundwork for the ideas pouring out of him. He was encouraged by the fact that he'd managed to hold the attention of the extremely intelligent Kathy. He immediately noticed how beautiful she looked when she listened intently.

"Scientists also apply a mathematically dubious tool, called normalization, to make sense of phenomena. For example, to obtain a finite charge and mass value for an electron that matches our observation, normalization is employed to cancel the positive and negative infinite, and leave a small value for mass and charge that matches our expectation!

"We scientists do all kinds of non-scientific things. We 'believe' in the existence of particles that cannot be seen or observed. We believe in their existence because these particles explain certain anomalies in data and predict the behavior of other particles. A common example of this is the quark-based model to explain properties of photons and neutrons in the atomic nucleus. Another example is the electron.

"Scientists use model based reality to explain everything. If a model explains what we observe and makes predictions for the future that matches our measurements, we accept the model! Observations feed into the model, and the model predicts the observations. It is, in essence, a circular argument! A very useful one, though, because it helps us deal with our reality as we experience it."

"I didn't need a lesson in fundamental physics, but I do see your point," said Kathy.

"I was just stating the basis for my hypothesis," said Krish. "So, there is enough basis to say that the model we use to make sense of the universe around us can, and I would say must, be improved."

"Makes sense, but what about the mathematics? Without experimental or mathematical proof, it's just a conjecture," Kathy was fulfilling her duty as a critical devil's advocate.

"New mathematics needs to be conceived for that."

"What do you mean?"

"I mean, I have a strong hunch that this new mathematics will come from Ramanujan's work." Krish took a sip of his coffee. "Did I mention he's dead?"

"Who is Rama…what?" asked Kathy incredulously.

"Ramanujan was a self-taught mathematical genius. He was a Fellow of Royal Society and Fellow of Trinity College. He came up with complex mathematical formulas without proofs. Cambridge mathematics professor, G.H. Hardy, once said about him, 'The formulae he came up with must be true, otherwise nobody would have the imagination to come up with them.' A lot of development in number theory in the twentieth and twenty-first century was based on his work. Just to give an example, there are nearly 3.9 trillion ways of partitioning—the ways you can write a number as a sum of other integers—the number 200. He came up with an answer within 0.004 of the correct answer. Such precision is unheard of, even to this day!" Krish said excitedly.

"He died young in 1920. Mathematics just poured out of him in the last year of his life, but it was lost. Some of it was captured in the famous 'Lost Notebook' which came very close to being burnt after the death of another mathematician, G.N. Watson. The notebook was found just before being incinerated, and it contained mathematics that helped us understand black holes! The mock theta functions are described in it!"

Kathy was just as fascinated by the life of this extraordinary genius as his mathematics.

"Ramanujan wrote a lot more formulae on papers that were scattered around his bed when he died. Those papers were lost. There could be mathematics on them that will help me describe the effect of an external force on the outcome of a whole system, rather than a particle. In short, I want to develop on Feynman's approach that explains how we get from quantum particles to the macro-system that behaves per Newtonian laws." Krish was developing his ideas even as he spoke about them. Kathy's beauty and brilliance was the ideal fuel to help him push the boundaries of his thoughts.

"Feynman's approach is the well-known 'sum over histories' or 'alternate histories'. That means the current state of the system, at the time of observation, is described by the sum of all the histories that could have led to that observation. 'Past' and 'future' are an infinite spectrum of possibilities until we 'observe' them. I want to study the effect of individual human beings influencing 'smaller', quantum particles and leaders—military, economic, political, spiritual—influencing 'systems' made of individual humans. To take it a step further, 'quantum democracy' would be when individuals realize their power and truly shape the world, and the universe, around them. I want all individuals to realize this power. I want to lay the mathematical foundation for such a force using mathematics pioneered by Ramanujan. We found the lost notebook, but now I need to find those lost papers."

"That's ambitious and risky! What makes you so sure of the hypothesis? You could be totally wrong. Even if you're right, this kind of work would normally take decades and at least ten PhD students," cautioned Kathy.

"I have these moments of inspiration sometimes, where these models of physics and reality flash in front of my eyes. I actually experience them," Krish said matter-of-factly. Kathy looked at him quizzically. "And the psychiatrist told me I'm not losing my mind," he added with a smile. "I also feel a strange force is guiding me toward an outcome. And then, there's this arrow," Krish pointed to the exquisite arrow he'd found at the hall during the political debate.

"If I hadn't seen your skills in physics and mathematics, I wouldn't believe you. But, I have, and I hope this works out for you. It's a very risky endeavor," Kathy said.

"I feel confident about it. It's our job to explore new ideas."

"All right then, if that's what you want to do. What's the next step?"

"Penn State, Professor Goldstein, member of the National Academy of Sciences—he's the one who discovered Ramanujan's lost notebook. He may have clues about the lost pages," Krish answered.

Just then, Agent Craig walked in to perform a periodic check.

"Let's have lunch, then you can get ready for Penn State," Kathy said.

"Agent Craig, please join us for lunch," Krish invited.

The three of them had lunch at a Thai restaurant.

"I love the iced tea and fresh herbs this place uses," Krish said, trying to start up a conversation. "Agent Craig, do you have any interesting stories from your line of work?"

"I do actually. One comes to mind. I was once working with the Secret Service protecting POTUS. This was during the time when the president ordered the daring raid that killed a prominent terrorist leader. During that tense period, the president stepped out of the Situation Room for a moment. A stealth Black Hawk helicopter was down. Time was running out for the SEAL team. He was outwardly cool, but anxious from within. He reached into his pocket and took out a small statue of a monkey and pressed it in his hands. I think he said a silent prayer. His eyes were closed and he took a deep breath, then went back to the Situation Room." She paused as she explored the memory again. "As you know, the raid was successful."

"Very cool," Kathy and Krish said together. They were looking at Agent Craig with a newfound respect and honor. She had something else on her mind, though.

"I saw a similar monkey figure in your room, sir. What is it? If you don't mind me asking…"

Krish tried to guess what Agent Craig was talking about. Nothing came to his mind, until suddenly, it just clicked. "I think you're talking about the figure of Hanuman. He's one of the gods in India. He's well-known for his courage and strength," Krish said. "My mother gave me that statue for good luck and protection," he added sheepishly.

The two ladies laughed. "Mr. Scientist is a Mama's Boy," Kathy teased.

"I am here for your protection, sir," Agent Craig chimed in. They all laughed. It was a good icebreaker, and the three seemed more comfortable with one another now.

"Please call me Krish," he said to Agent Craig.

After lunch, Kathy went back to the lab. Krish drove home to pack some research material and clothes for his trip to Penn State. He slipped the small statue of Hanuman into his pocket.

Krish and Agent Craig were riding in a cab toward the airport. As they passed over a hill, Krish saw the red sun glowing from behind the clouds. Its rays were shinning down from the empty patches in the sky, taking the form of bright beams of light pouring down. *There are so many clues about the vastness of this universe, everywhere around us. And yet, we're so busy with our own, tiny lives that we don't even notice the spectacle unfolding every day,* he thought.

"So, what exactly do you do?" Agent Craig asked, looking at Krish who seemed lost in his thoughts. Krish looked back at her. He thought she was trying to understand who he was, to help her with the job of protecting him.

"I'm a researcher, a scientist. My research has applications in secure information transmittance over long distances, and weapons application as well. It's a game changer. That's why the government, and other rogue governments apparently, are after me. Some want me dead, and some want me alive," Krish explained. "But what I am, myself, most interested in is understanding the true nature of the reality we experience. You see, physics uses a model-based approach to understanding our universe. A well-constructed model will create its own reality. I want to break free of this model-dependent reality and experience the world as it is, in its true nature, then explain it mathematically," Krish elaborated.

His passion for his research was evident by the way he spoke. Agent Craig listened carefully. There was silence in the cab. The cab driver's head moved slightly toward his passengers, indicating his interest in the conversation. Agent Craig looked out of the cab's window. She adjusted her sunglasses, taking everything in. Krish felt a connection developing between the two as she appeared to have grasped the essence of what he'd said.

"I'm impressed. I guess I have a special person to protect. Call me Brooke," she said with a smile. As she smiled, her bright white teeth illuminated the attractive shape of her mouth. Suddenly, the teeth were replaced by ones and zeros. Her entire physical form was replaced with ones and zeros arranged in her shape. The cab, the road, buildings, clouds, the sky, everything was ones and zeros, or otherwise bits of information. The fundamental particles of nature were bits of information—ones and zeros.

Krish felt like he was inside a computer-generated reality—the Matrix. He was being driven deeper and deeper inside the Matrix. Line-after-line of computer codes that represented the mountains, sky, clouds, and humans went whooshing by. As he dove deeper and deeper into the Matrix, the computer programs got shorter and shorter. Finally, he came face-to-face with the super program, which was almost like the 'God' that controlled everything. It was less than ten lines! The whole universe could be compressed into ten lines of code! That meant there was no randomness; randomness cannot be compressed. Everything was programmed and predetermined.

The super program was allocating run-time to numerous other sub programs representing matter, humans, clouds, mountains, cars, etc. Krish lodged himself in one of the programs; that program was part of the worldwide web. As he was traveling at light speed with the ones and zeros, he noticed some ones and zeros being dropped, leading to an error. But, lo-and-behold, when the information reached the target computer, the errors were corrected and everything worked just fine! There was no error. This was due to pieces of code that fixed the errors. He saw similar error-fixing codes in the interaction of the fundamental particles.

Aha! These error-fixing codes are the secret of the stability of the Matrix! Krish was delighted to see them in action.

"We're almost at the airport," Brooke tapped on his shoulder to bring him back to reality. Krish was snapped out of his hallucination instantly. As they got ready to get out of the cab, Brooke took off her sunglasses. Her blue eyes locked with Krish's deep, thoughtful eyes. She was looking at the man who had a brilliant mind, fire in the belly, and guts to follow his calling and risk his life doing so. The two of them seemed to have some things in common.

"It has been good getting to know you, Krish," she said. "Let's roll."

Brooke and Krish walked into the Ontario airport for their domestic flight. It was a small airport. Brooke was on her guard. She briefly spoke to her leading officer to find out about the other passengers and any threat potentials.

They settled into their seats, near the middle of the plane. Brooke took the aisle seat. She checked the gun in her holster and made sure she had several rounds available, just in case.

Soon, they were at cruising altitude. Some passengers were getting up to use the restrooms. The air hostesses were serving peanuts and juice. Suddenly, some commotion could be heard from the front.

"People arguing over bathrooms?" Krish asked the air hostess with a smile.

She shrugged her shoulders, "Don't know."

Brooke was up in an instant. She had a bad feeling about it. In her line of work, such situations could escalate rapidly and she had learned to trust her instincts without hesitation. "You stay put, let me check it out," she said to Krish. Her right hand went toward the holster. The air hostess took a step back as she got a glimpse of the gun.

"Ma'am..." Brooke flashed her badge to calm her down. She walked toward the front of the aircraft to investigate. Some passengers were blocking her path.

Krish followed to see what was going on. She turned back to look at Krish. "I asked you to stay put," she said sternly. He was standing on his toes and looking past her.

"I'm just...smoke?" he said.

Brooke turned around in a flash, took out her gun and badge, and took charge of the situation. "Federal agent, get down," she shouted as she pointed her gun toward the lavatory from where the smoke was emanating. Suddenly, everyone got out of the way. Leaving just Brooke and Krish standing in the aisle, a few steps away from the lavatory. A tall man came out with his pants partially on fire and smoke from near his waist.

The girl sitting near the restroom screamed loudly, "Ma'am... he's on fire!" She closed her eyes and covered her ears expecting an explosion. Panic spread quickly.

Amid the chaos, Brooke was laser focused on the man, with her gun pointed directly at him.

"Don't shoot, or I will blow up the plane," he said with a deadpan face.

"You already tried that. Everyone stay calm. I'm Federal Agent Craig. Stand down, now!" she shouted.

"We just want him," the man said pointing toward Krish.

"Then why blow up the plane?"

"We didn't know about you," he screamed at Brooke, pulling out a knife and charging forward.

Brooke had a few seconds before the man would be too close for safety. She had her gun pointed with fatal accuracy. She wanted to make sure she didn't miss or that the bullet didn't ricochet and hit another passenger or the plane. Her preferred shot would have been in the head, but this was a very confined space with screams and panic all around. She had to neutralize this person to protect Krish and the other passengers. She knew she was the only one standing between certain mayhem and the killer.

Brooke fired three shots at the man. They all met their target in his chest, but he kept moving toward her.

He suddenly stumbled on something in the path and lunged at her. The stumble startled her for a second, but it also brought him closer in an erratic manner. Instead of the head, she put three more bullets in his chest to make sure he was dead. She didn't have time to take evasive action to protect herself. He fell on her; his knife puncturing the delicate skin of her neck and cutting the carotid artery.

She fell on Krish, gushing blood.

Krish supported her back and shoulders, making sure she didn't have a hard fall. He kicked the assassin's body away from her and tried to apply pressure to her neck to stop the bleeding. Krish could see pain rising in her blue eyes and her resolve to fight it. Eventually, the life was sucked from them completely, and she could no longer keep them open. The knife had done its damage. Within a minute, Brooke was no longer moving or breathing. She sacrificed her young life in the line of duty to protect Krish and everyone else aboard that plane.

Krish shuddered to think about what would have happened if Brooke had not been there to be the hero. He was overwhelmed with guilt and gratitude simultaneously.

The other passengers were thankful to the young lady as well. Some were sobbing, crying loudly, and covering their children's eyes to prevent them from seeing the horrible scene. All were glad that it was over. There was smoke, blood, and bullet shells all over the scene. The plane turned toward the nearest airport for an emergency landing.

Krish sat near Brooke, holding her hand. "May God bless your beautiful soul, Brooke. Salute to you for your courage under fire. You will always inspire me. A lot of people owe their lives to you." He touched her forehead to bless her with the Hanuman statue he carried with him. "I pray that her sacrifice is not wasted and that my research does not fall into the wrong hands. I hope this science saves more lives than it takes," he said with a shaky voice, utterly heartbroken.

CHAPTER 7
AN EXEMPLARY LIFE SHOWS THE PATH FORWARD

~~~~~~~

Ancient India

~~~~~~~

Life lived is the best example.

A FEW YEARS HAD PASSED; HANUMAN WAS AN ADULT VANARA now. He had grown to be a fine young person in every way. He was physically formidable, mentally stable, and agile. He always sided with the truth, and was not attracted to senseless pleasures, wealth, or power. Following in his simian father's footsteps, Hanuman had become a great warrior, one of the greatest wielders of the mace, an expert swimmer, a great jumper, and a natural leader of the troops.

Having been initiated, coached, and trained into yogic sciences by the experts living in the hermitages, he had experienced the subtle forms of energy and could calm his body and mind down to the extent that he realized the subtler, and even subtler, forms of his own self and his own being. He had discovered there was as much to know inside oneself, as there was in the entire universe. He had developed the ability to observe his mind and body as they are, without any engagement on his part. These forays and dives deep into his own self had revealed extraordinary insights and capabilities. He had become a master yogi. This particular power had catapulted Hanuman among the greatest warrior-yogis of all time.

The sweat, blood, tears, and sacrifices by several generations of scientists, and countless humans and apes, had come together spectacularly in Hanuman. His immortality would be a boon to society, as was hoped by his creators. Hanuman, though, was not satisfied with all these extraordinary accomplishments. He was still not sure what he was supposed to do with all these supreme powers and capabilities. He had a yearning for something unknown—something he had not discovered yet. Hanuman thought, *this is akin to numerous chariots, thousands of elephants, hundreds of thousands of fighters arranged in perfect battle formation, but with no king to command the forces and direct them!* Something profound was missing. His quest was unfulfilled, and it was not clear to him what he was chasing.

One such day, Hanuman sat on a large rock in the mountains. He wore a short silk dhoti around his waist and tail. His jaws were swollen like that of an ape, a thick solid gold bracelet adored his mighty wrist, and his silver anklet shone in the sun. He wore solid gold ornaments around his huge biceps, it was intricately carved with human and ape figures and decorated with uncut diamonds. The dome-shaped shirstran that protected his head was engraved with an image of an ape in the middle of a jump—when he was completely horizontal, he appeared to be flying.

Hanuman sat cross-legged, with a straight back, and instantly went into a meditative state. He felt a surge of energy. He experienced a meditative bliss. His subtle energies rose higher and higher, but he could not reach the highest peak of realization that lay just out of reach! He knew intuitively that there was something more, but he could not get to it. He felt frustrated by such a block in his consciousness.

Just then, he heard the sound of the alarm call ring through the air. It was repeated three times by the patrol party on the outskirts of the hill, indicating a non-friendly presence in the vicinity. From the intensity and urgency of the call, it was apparent that they had spotted something potentially dangerous. Hanuman rose slowly with his mace as he came out of his meditation.

Sugriv, the younger brother of King Vali, came out of his cave, resting his mace on his shoulder with a worried expression.

Sugriv said, "Hanuman, I am fortunate you sided with me. You witnessed the injustice my bullying older brother bestowed upon me. He took away my wife by force, and instead of sharing any wealth at all, he kicked me out of the kingdom. And now he wants to kill me!"

Hanuman said, "Dear Sugriv, I respect you as my king. You are a brave and righteous Vanara. A person who steals his younger brother's wife is morally corrupt and justice needs to be delivered to him. I will always back you."

"My brother will not let me live in peace. Since he cannot come to this hill, because of his feud with the powerful Rishis, he sends mercenaries to kill me. That sick ape…" Sugriv muttered.

"Two humans are approaching our area," reported the guard that had sighted the intruders. Without catching his breath, he added, "We are not sure if they are warriors or hermits. They are wearing coarse jute clothes and their long hair is tied in a bun similar to hermits, but they carry quivers full of arrows and very special looking, gold decked, shiny swords. They have strong, muscular bodies. Their bows are six feet long, with a strong grip in the center and two curved arches on top and bottom."

The guards knew the importance of their finding and wanted to protect their leader.

"Hanuman, ask the spies to follow the humans closely without being noticed, and you go to the hermitage to inquire if anything is known about these mercenaries," ordered Sugriv.

At the hermitage, the Muni was overjoyed as Hanuman described the two powerful humans.

"That sounds like Ram, the prince of Ayodhya. We are extremely fortunate to have such a powerful, great soul in our presence," exclaimed the old, learned, stern-looking Muni with childlike excitement. "I need to make detailed astronomical and seasonal observations for posterity. Hanuman, make no mistake, we are witnessing history as it is being created. This is our good fortune. Let me tally my astronomical observations with the data from the time of his birth.

"Ram was born in the month of Chaitra on the ninth day. Rahu, the point of intersection between the moon's orbit and sun's orbit, as seen from Earth, was near the sixth Nakshatra Ardra—associated with the star Betelgeuse and in the vicinity of Punarvasu; the brightest stars in the constellation of Gemini—Castor and Pollux. Nakshatra, as you know, is a group of stars used to describe the position of heavenly objects such as the sun and moon in the sky. The sun and Mars were together near Uttara Bhadrapada (corresponding to γ Pegasi and α Andromedae). Five astral bodies were in an exalted state—the sun, Mars, Saturn, Jupiter, and Venus. Jupiter was setting on the western horizon as the moon was rising on the eastern horizon.

"Hopefully Ram's decedents, thousands of years from now, will be able to trace back the time when Ram walked on Earth based on these observations. And I hope they will follow his ideals. A great sage has taken up the responsibility of compiling all this information in the form of a poem. It will be transmitted orally—that is the best way of preserving the information, for thousands of years, with the greatest accuracy."

The Muni paused in thought for a moment. "In this hot and humid climate, it is difficult to preserve monuments and books can be destroyed during wars. But not poetry. That is etched in one's mind and soul. As long as humans live in this nation, history will be preserved as poetry and passed from generation to generation."

It seemed that the Muni had found the purpose of his life—to document and capture minute details of Ram's life to help with preserving them for generations to come. Hanuman was jealous of the clarity in his purpose, but was also impressed by the foresight of the Munis that planned for thousands of years, not decades or centuries.

They measure time from microseconds to a trillion years. With that in mind, thousands of years sounds about right, Hanuman thought with a chuckle. Hanuman also realized the significance of this great human being—Ram. Great pains were being taken to record his movements for the annals of history. Hanuman was determined to find out more about this important man. *Is he a threat to Sugriv or can he be an ally? What skills and power does he bring to the partnership? What is he doing in this forest?* Hanuman had a lot of exploration to do.

Hanuman tried to get as much background information as possible from the Muni. "Who is Ram?"

The Muni stopped writing and looked up. "Why do you ask?"

"He is in our territory and approaching the hills where my leader, Sugriv, lives. Sugriv is under constant threat from his brother, Vali. I need to know what Ram's intentions and capabilities are. And what he is like as a person. Can he be an ally?"

The Muni walked away from his writing desk and sat with his legs crisscrossed under a banyan tree nearby. He ran his fingers through his matted hair, smiled, and looked intently at Hanuman. He closed his eyes for a few minutes and sat in a meditative state.

After some time, he opened his eyes and said in a calm, deep voice, "Dear Hanuman, oh powerful one! Ram is the heir apparent of the prosperous kingdom of Ayodhya to the North. He is the best archer in the world today. He has killed powerful demons single-handedly. Pleased with his bravery, the Great Seer, Vishwamitra, gave him access to all the powerful weapons, including the Universe Missile, Brahmastra, which destroys all forms of life for many years. He is also a very popular prince. He has complete support from his citizens. He is respected and loved by his brother, Lakshaman, and wife, Sita." The Muni observed Hanuman's reaction.

"From your description, he seems like a powerful prince. Should we be ready to fight him? Why is he here, so far away from his kingdom?" asked Hanuman.

"I will tell you more about Ram, then you can make up your own mind. Let us fetch some water from the stream…come along." The way to the stream was along a curvy footpath, between trees laden with fruits and flowers. Parrots tweeted in the tress. A deer heard their footsteps, raised its head—ears standing erect and moving in the direction of sound—but went back to grazing once it saw these two beings were not a threat.

The Muni proceeded once they reached the creek side, "Ram, being the eldest and the most eligible heir to the kingdom, was scheduled to be coronated king by his aging father. On the very day of the coronation, a political coup was orchestrated by one of his stepmothers in the name of her own son! The situation was delicate. Ram's powerful brother, Lakshaman, the prime minister, the representatives of the common citizens, and the clergy all supported Ram. Ram had the power to claim the throne by force. Single-handedly, with his handheld shastra and astra missile, he could have imprisoned his elderly father and annihilated the city his stepbrothers resided in.

"Ram, alone, was powerful enough to win the battle, but to add the support he had from all the centers of power, the crown was his for the taking. It seemed the coup was ill advised. But, Ram's father was caught in a political web and cornered into supporting the coup," the Muni paused, again resting his eyes upon Hanuman. He wanted the Vanara to consider the situation, to completely understand Ram's true nature.

"What did Ram do? How did he end up in the jungle?" Hanuman asked.

The Muni's chest swelled with pride; his eyes full of respect and honor. He gazed into the sky and said, "Ram went to his father and informed him that he would leave for the forest the very same day. This would ensure that there would be no further political instability. He vowed to take his brother and wife with him! The kingdom, the power, the wealth, the royal life meant nothing to him. The palace and jungle were one and the same to him. Such equanimity is unheard of. Yogis cannot attend such equanimity with even hundreds of years of practice."

The Muni stood tall. His hands locked behind his back. "Hanuman, I want you to realize the significance of Ram's actions. History is full of instances of innocents being killed over kingdoms and wealth, but there are only a handful of examples where a man realized the significance of the moment and seized the opportunity to show the righteous path to the population. He inspired people to rise above the material considerations of wealth and power. He inspired them to keep their word at any cost, honor their father's orders, and most importantly, be equanimous in all situations! An action is better than a thousand speeches. Ram is laying the foundation for a materially, morally, and spiritually prosperous society. And he is leading by the power of his actions. Ram is on his way to being called the avatar of Vishnu-the protector and guide of society."

Hanuman listened to what the Muni had to say. He helped the Muni fill a pitcher with water. They headed back to the hermitage. The sun had set. Darkness was spreading in the forest, blanketing everything. The full moon looked splendid and calm, reflecting gentle, peaceful light. An image of Ram was forming in Hanuman's mind—that of a brave, powerful, righteous, poised being who would sacrifice his self-interest for the well-being of society. Ram appeared to be a powerful, but fair and kind soul who faced hardships himself. Regardless, he gently showed the righteous path to others, not unlike the moonlight showering down on the forest that night.

After obtaining the information he desired, Hanuman decided that he wanted to meet Ram in person.

The next day, Hanuman looked at Ram from a distance. He was a tall, muscular, dark colored man with a peaceful gaze and a cool sense of detachment from everything around him. He had a six-foot-long bow, a quiver full of arrows, and a gold decked, spotless sword with him. His brother, Lakshman—who looked equally as strong—walked a step behind. He was of lighter complexion and appeared to be a warrior you didn't want to challenge. In fact, it appeared it was best not to engage, or even cross paths, with this man at all. If Ram's persona was cool like the moon, Lakshman's energy was hot like the blazing sun.

Hanuman jumped from a tall tree at some distance and walked with folded hands toward Ram. Hanuman did not carry his powerful mace with him. The gesture was the traditional Namaste, but also served the purpose of announcing that he came in peace.

"Who are you crossing into Vanara territory?" Hanuman asked in a slightly rude tone to get firsthand experience of Ram's even temper.

Lakshman did not like the forest-dweller speaking to his elder brother in such a tone. He answered in a polite, but firm and slightly condescending manner, "This is Ram, the heir apparent of the great kingdom of Ayodhya! He is reputed to be of one word, one woman, and an archer who hits the target every single time. Need I say more?"

Ram smiled gently at the pride his brother felt in him. He was observing Hanuman's reaction.

Hanuman felt very calm in Ram's presence. He also felt an extraordinary power. Ram had a strange effect on Hanuman. Hanuman kept his face expressionless. "I see. But, what are your intentions behind crossing into our territory?"

Lakshman again interjected, "We are here in search of the noble, virtuous, and brave Lady Sita."

"Who is Sita?" Hanuman asked. "Please provide me with more details and background so that I may understand the nature of your travel. I need to know if you are a threat."

"I understand your intentions. Let me elaborate. Lady Sita is my elder brother's wife. She is an extraordinary lady. She is a princess born by a non-uterine birth—naturally gifted with subtle yogic powers. She is an exemplary and devoted woman. She is ideal in every sense, and I respect her as I respect my mother. As you may have heard, there was a coup in our kingdom. Once Ram decided to live in the forest, leaving Devi Sita alone was not safe, as her life could be in danger from the power struggle. Being with the brave Ram appeared the only safe option for her. Or so we thought…" Lakshman paused.

Various emotions appeared distinctly on Lakshman's face—anger, sadness, helplessness, and determination. He clinched his bow tightly. "That fateful day, brother Ram did not return from his hunt for quite some time. Back at the hut where we lived, I was guarding my sister-in-law. We grew worried as the sun was about to set and there was still no sign of Ram. A pride of lions had been sighted near our hut the day before. Suddenly, we saw monkeys and birds frantically fleeing an area in the forest—the same direction Ram had gone in. Then, we heard a cry for help. It could have been another hunter or the jungle playing tricks on our minds. While I knew my brave brother was more than capable in any circumstance, emotions got the better of Lady Sita. She ordered me to help Ram.

"I was hesitant to leave Lady Sita alone, but she insisted that she could take care of herself. To convince me, she reminded me of times when I had seen her swordsmanship, her footwork, and speed. Her specialty was using two swords—one to defend and one to attack. She also reminded me of her recent killing of the mountain lion that had attacked her. On her insistence, I left her alone, trusting that she could protect herself in case of an encounter with a beast. I left my special double-edged, straight-blade sword with her in addition to the Asi dagger. Unfortunately, brother Ram and I took a long time to return that day, due to the elusive hunt. By the time we came back, there was no sign of Lady Sita."

Lakshman took a break. His anger was rising. "It was not a beast that took her as there was no sign of blood or tracks. We did see human footprints, however. Tribals told us they saw a flying machine, possibly transporting a lady inside, flying southward. My suspicion is with the demons, as my brave brother and I have killed scores of them. We have bad blood with them, and we are a major impediment in the northward expansion of their king, Ravan's, territory."

Lakshman turned to Ram. "There are a lot of rich kingdoms in the North, and Ravan wants to expand his territory. It is possible that it was a trap, and Ravan's helpers drove the hunting game away so that my brother and I would be gone long enough to allow them the opportunity to take Lady Sita. In addition, that lustful, loathsome demon, Ravan, has an extraordinary flying machine that can fly long distances from his island in the ocean to the south."

Lakshman appeared physically exhausted from recounting those painful events. From his voice and expressions, it was clear that he was being eaten alive with guilt.

Hanuman listened carefully and with compassion. He said, "I completely understand. You and Ram are brave and righteous, and a lot of injustice and bad fortune has come your way. The same is true of my leader, Sugriv. If we work together, we can help each other succeed and accomplish our goals."

Ram listened, nodding his approval. For Ram, it was important to get help in his search for Lady Sita. Hanuman needed allies for King Sugriv against Vali. With their interests in alignment, this strategy could prove to be a powerful alliance.

Ram, Lakshman, and Hanuman walked toward the mountains where King Sugriv resided. Hanuman had arranged for Ram and Sugriv to meet.

"After hearing about your valor, admiring your powerful weapons, and access to missiles, I feel confident you will end my misery by destroying my brother," Sugriv said to Ram as their meeting concluded. "Members of my million-strong army will look for Lady Sita throughout this land and reunite her with her great warrior husband as thanks for your loyalty and alliance."

The two leaders had laid the foundation of a warm friendship. Sugriv hugged Ram and Lakshman. Hanuman also embraced Ram with the affection of a friend. As soon as Ram touched Hanuman, the Vanara had an exceptional experience. The normally formal and polite Hanuman could not control himself. He felt as if tremendous energy had been transmitted into his body. All of a sudden, he was overwhelmed with emotion. Hanuman understood on a soulful level that he was in the presence of a spiritual man.

Ram possessed exquisite skill, high moral standards, and a spirit of sacrifice. Additionally, Ram was also an accomplished yogi. The epitome of energy that had eluded Hanuman was activated inside him due to Ram's influence, and he was bathed in supreme bliss. The true nature of time and universe was revealed to him. He stayed in this state for two days, without moving an inch. He was bursting with energy and was shaking. *Shree Ram*, was fixated in his mind. Hanuman's quest for a supreme spiritual teacher was over. Ram was the one to guide him on his spiritual path, without uttering a word—just by his actions and kind touch.

Ram's spiritual guidance fit Hanuman's quest like lock and key. He helped sooth Hanuman from his meditative state. Hanuman realized the true nature of matter, this universe, and the human life. With Ram's grace, Hanuman had reached the pinnacle of his internal exploration and had become a complete and accomplished yogi. Hanuman could not distinguish between his physical body and the universe around him. He had transcended his physical body and become one with the universe. The yoga, union was complete.

Meanwhile, Sugriv was growing impatient. "I cannot stay in this jungle for another moment," Sugriv said to Ram, as he was eager to kill his brother and reclaim his own wife, kingdom, and freedom. Sugriv could no longer stand to be restricted to the hills, away from the capital city.

After careful consideration, Ram said, "I will kill Vali from a distance—while hiding behind a tree, similar to a hunt." Everyone was surprised to hear these words spoken.

One of Sugriv's army captains said, "We believed you to be a powerful and righteous person, killing someone by subterfuge is not befitting of a warrior."

Lakshman was offended by this captain's disrespectful comment.

Before Lakshman could release his temper, Ram spoke up again. "I have killed several powerful demons in face-to-face combat, but Vali is a special circumstance. In addition to being very powerful, he is cunning and inventive. He has defeated the mighty King Ravan. He has strong armor—the best among all the warriors. Vali is a morally corrupt person. He has been unfair to his brother and is always looking for a chance to kill him. He has degraded to the extent of stealing and sleeping with his younger brother's wife. Moreover, if time is lost, this disagreement between the brothers could turn into a battle with the loss of thousands of lives. I also do not want to use powerful missiles, which would cause widespread destruction, for the annihilation of just one person. Thus, there are ethical and practical reasons behind killing the brave Vali like a hunter—draw him in with his arrogance, and kill him in one clean strike with no chance to escape."

The captain was not convinced, but decided to keep quiet in the presence of Sugriv.

Sugriv understood the strategy and agreed to it. He knew Ram's assessment of Vali's strengths, weaknesses, and the possibility of thousands of casualties was real, accurate, and not worth the risk.

Vali himself was aware that the great warrior Ram was present in the region. He was also aware of Ram's meeting with Sugriv. Nevertheless, he was confident in his ability to deal with Ram in a one-on-one duel. He never suspected a surprise attack.

As per the plan, Sugriv lured Vali in for a duel, making sure to remind him of the warrior's oath not to deny a challenge. Vali's wife saw the trap, and tried to warn him, but Vali refused to see it—drawn into the trap by his arrogance.

Sugriv took the brunt of the beating from Vali as the duel began. Fists, nails, trees, and boulders were making relentless contact with his weakening body. He was near to losing consciousness from the attack when Ram, hiding behind a tree, saw the opportunity he was looking for. Vali was separated from Sugriv as he attempted to lift a huge boulder to throw at his brother.

Vali's torso was clearly visible as the special armor and chest plate shone brightly. Ram decided that he had a clear shot. He had prepared meticulously like the skilled archer he was. Since it was mid-afternoon, Ram located himself such that he was shooting to the east. His mind was calm and motionless as he locked onto the target. The wind direction was favorable. Ram had moved as close to Vali as possible to get a minimum loss of velocity. His feet were planted firmly a foot apart and did not move. He pulled the bowstring until it was about to break—the maximum tension in the bow would result in greater speed. He had selected arrows that were heavier at the bottom for greater range and higher penetrating force. For releasing the arrow, he placed the top of his thumb on the tip of his forefinger in the kakatundi, or the mouth of a crow position. Ram's head was still and centered as he aimed the bow perfectly. He used two quivers with different types of arrows for this special mission.

He shot six armor-piercing arrows in rapid succession, with elongated points and flattened heads, at the exact same spot on Vali's chest. Vali's armor cracked, exposing the flesh of his mighty chest. Ram only had one chance before Vali would either take a giant leap and disappear behind a protective cover, or ferociously attack Ram with his heavy mace. In a flash, Ram shifted the bow to his left hand. He took out a broad headed arrow from the second quiver and fired it directly at the opening in Vali's armor. The arrow struck exactly in the hole created by the earlier arrows, broke Vali's rib cage, and pierced his heart and lungs. Blood gushed from the wound as Vali held his chest and fell to the ground.

Ram was as calm as ever. This was not the proudest moment of his life, but he had a job to do and he had done it successfully. Vali lay fatally injured on the ground. As he lay bleeding, waiting to die—now surrounded by his brother, Hanuman, and Ram—several thoughts occurred to him.

"Why deceit?" he asked.

Ram plainly explained the reasons why he had to attack from a hidden place. The warrior Vali accepted the matter-of-fact explanation and made peace with it as he prepared to take his last breath. The moment of death was fast approaching. Vali realized his physical power, wealth, kingdom, weapons, family—everything he had fought so hard to attain—was useless when he needed it most. He was feeling life at its most intense and raw form as he was about to die!

Vali was finally beginning to realize that he was more than his physical and mental body. He could feel the vastness of his spirit, but the lifetime of baggage—in the form of old thinking patterns, attachment to his mace, his pendant, his crown, gorgeous, lusty females, the joy of killing, condemnation for his brother, worry about his son, and arrogance of power—was holding him back. At that most delicate moment, as the last few breaths were leaving his body—his heart had stopped beating, and he was treading between the freedom of spirit and bondage of body and mind—Ram touched his head gently, subtly reassuring him as he crossed over into freedom.

Ram knew what Vali was going through. He helped Vali along the right path, saving him from being trapped in the creation of his own mind. Vali died fully satisfied, liberated, and free.

Although Vali got a raw deal in the manner of his death, Ram ensured that he received the ultimate realization of his true nature. As per the scriptures, Vali could have spent several lifetimes deluded by his physical power before realizing the true nature and vastness of his own being and spirit. But, thanks to Ram, he realized the supreme wisdom that had been hidden in plain sight his entire life and gained everlasting freedom!

CHAPTER 8
DISTRACTIONS OBSCURE GOALS

~~~~~~~

Modern Day California

~~~~~~~

Twists, turns, and hidden treasures.

KRISH WAS WAITING TO MEET PROFESSOR GOLDSTINE OF THE mathematics department at Penn State University. There was a small pond near the department building. Krish admired the placid pond surrounded by Amur Maple trees and watched the ducks swim amongst the lilies. The trees reached for the crisp blue sky like green skyscrapers. Neatly manicured lawns and curvy paths presented a feeling of calm to all who passed by.

Krish sat down and polished the lenses of his glasses. His mind kept going back to Agent Craig's sacrifice and how much his life had changed in the last few days. He was entering a new phase in his life. For a moment, Krish thought about quitting and going back to his normal, predictable life as a researcher. He could just brush everything he had experienced aside and write it off as shenanigans of his overactive mind, let the government deal with his research work, put his head down, and go on with life. With a doctorate from Cal Tech, and his achievements in mathematics and physics, he would get by just fine in his profession. The path he had embarked on was full of uncertainties and dangers. His career could be sabotaged by the powers that be, and he could even lose his life. He wanted to delve deeper into that thought and consider everything carefully, but his reflections were interrupted by a phone call.

"I'm Louis Sessions, Director of the FBI," the voice on the other end said. "My agent is approaching you as we speak. Get in the car with him. We need to talk."

In a few moments, Krish saw a tall, bald African American man walk up the stairs. His well-fitted grey suit drew attention to his muscular physique. He stood erect, flashed his badge and said in a polite tone, "I'm Special Agent Brown. You're Dr. Krish Bhat, is that correct?"

"I am," Krish said.

"I need you to come with me to the FBI field office. I assume Agent Sessions has already made contact?"

"Yes."

"Let's go," Agent Brown ordered. Agent Brown drove Krish to the field office in State College, PA and arranged for a video call with the director.

"One of my best agents died protecting you," Sessions said. "Innocent lives are at stake here, Mr. Bhat. You have too many enemies. I know you scientists don't trust the government, and probably with good reason, but don't forget, Brooke was also part of the government. I urge you to consider sharing as much of your research with DARPA as possible. It will be used for the greater good, and I'll be able to put more resources into protecting you. We have full cooperation from the Indian government, whose passport you hold. Also, we will coordinate strikes on enemy scientists to send a message that you are under our protection and that there are costs associated with harming you. I'm confident the rogue governments will take the hint. At this point, you can't honestly still believe there is any way to play this game by yourself. You need us, and we need you. Let's make a deal."

Krish heard everything patiently. "I need some time to think this through."

Krish walked out of the conference room and was directed to an empty office. "I need to consult with my colleague."

"This is a secure line," said Agent Brown, pointing to a telephone.

Krish lifted the receiver and dialed Kathy's number. "Hey, how's it going?" He asked casually—as if he weren't surrounded by the FBI.

"Doing all right, what's up? I heard about the situation on the plane. Thank God you're okay."

"Brooke saved all of us," Krish said. "This absolutely can't continue. I can't keep cheating death like this. I'm with the FBI now. Here's the situation—I'm more interested in developing my research in the direction of fundamental physics, but my life is being threatened due to its technological applications!"

"And what exactly are those technological applications again?" Kathy asked.

"Well, it all started when a soldier was killed as he kicked opened the door to a building in a war zone. This started a conversation around personnel safety in the twenty-first century urban warfare scenario— particularly when soldiers are put in vulnerable situations. Various designs for exoskeletons with Iron Man-like capabilities are being tested. Other areas of grave concern are electronic attacks on satellites. Cyborgs-cyber organisms-that connect human brains directly to computers are in advanced stages of development. There are many such crucial projects. A commonality in all these projects is the need for assured, resilient networks with calculated stability and security. The fruition of all these projects will be tremendously accelerated by

QCOM. I have achieved secure signal transmittance ranges up to 36000 kms using QCOM. To be able to hack these signals is literally against the laws of physics. Other countries and rogue entities also realize the tremendous significance of this technology. They want to eliminate me to slow down the progress of the US government on these crucial projects. The US wants exclusive rights to take the research out of the open academic arena and place it under wraps. And I'm caught in the middle of all this!"

"The bottom line here, Krish, is that you cannot deal with these threats on your own," Kathy stated plainly. "As much as I distrust the government, I know they have a tremendous amount of resources needed for your protection. So, the logical choice is very simple... sell out to the government. If you can't beat them, join them. And believe me when I say this, you won't be able to beat them on this one."

"I know, but it's just so unfair and wrong," Krish whined.

"Oh, man up already! You're smart. You'll make many more breakthroughs. I have no doubt about that. This will also give you some freedom to explore Ramanujan's work and develop your ideas of quantum democracy." Kathy paused for a moment. "It pains my ego to admit this, but many great scientists, including Einstein, visualized impossibly crazy ideas in their heads first, developed mathematics to prove it, and years later, these ideas were verified experimentally. The so called 'God Particle' and detection of gravitational waves from black holes that merged a billion years ago by LIGO being prime examples. Just get these dangerous thugs out of your way!"

"Did they threaten you or something?" Krish asked, as Kathy seemed to be singing the government's tune.

"Come on Krish, be practical. You need the stability, protection, and the money!"

"I know, I know. All right then, let me at least try to get a good deal with these people. After all, it is our taxpayers' money," Krish said jokingly.

"Yep, it's your right to take every penny you can from them," Kathy laughed.

Selling his research would buy him much needed time and security to focus on the research that really mattered to him. Reluctantly, Krish informed his advisor, DARPA, and Cal Tech of his decision. At the end of the day, he breathed a sigh of relief that he would have constant government protection, and would no longer have to look over his shoulder.

After meeting with the FBI, Krish was back at Penn State University. He had re-scheduled his appointment with Professor Goldstine.

"Professor Goldstine will see you now," a student informed Krish. Krish walked into the professor's rather spacious office.

"Hi Krish, come on in. It's very nice to meet you. I saw your e-mail and heard about the tragedy that unfolded on your way here," the professor said warmly.

Professor Goldstine was a man in his mid-sixties. He was preparing to address a symposium later that day. He wore a classic two-piece suit. He had white hair, white eyebrows, a wrinkled, clean-shaven face, a hunched back, and an aged, but scholarly appearance. Krish was impressed to notice that the professor's tie had Ramanujan's photo printed on it. Behind him, on the wall, the logo of the American Mathematical Society (AMS) was framed. He acted as president of the association. The logo showed Ramanujan's photo looking from the clouds, the Indian summer sun, and a city skyline. It was clear, Professor Goldstine held a deep-seated respect and appreciation for Ramanujan's work.

"Yes, it was unfortunate. Thanks for your concern," Krish replied, his eyes falling to the floor for a brief moment. He went on to describe his research, his recent experiences, and his search for Ramanujan's lost papers.

Professor Goldstine offered Krish the kindness of patiently listening to what he had to say. He closed his eyes while he listened.

After a minute or two, the professor admitted, "I found the lost notebook by chance, when I was visiting Trinity College Library in Cambridge. You're seeking out the lost papers. There's a difference here. The notebook I found came very close to being destroyed. Nobody knows for sure if these lost papers even exist, let alone where they could be. I have no idea." Professor Goldstine paused to observe Krish's reaction. "However, from my experience with Mr. Ramanujan, I wouldn't be surprised if he has a treasure trove of mathematics hidden somewhere that could solve several mysteries of the universe. I almost think he did it on purpose!" he chuckled. "Like the elusive lover! He has enriched my career and my life and has moved mathematics and science forward in unimaginable ways."

Krish was a seasoned doctoral researcher, dead ends were nothing new to him. He was not disappointed hearing Professor Goldstine's verdict. It would have been too easy if he had gotten the answers he was looking for on the first try. On the other hand, he was heartened by the professor's journey of accidentally stumbling upon the notebook. Krish's active mind saw untapped potential, not a dead end.

Krish attended the professor's lecture later that day. He felt reassured that if Professor Goldstine, and many others, could benefit from Ramanujan's work, so could he. *I trust my hunch about Ramanujan. I'm sure he has the mathematics I'm looking for.*

Back at the hotel he was staying in, Krish observed the night sky. Stargazing was his favorite activity. Mars was approaching closer to Earth. It was the brightest red object in the sky. It appeared to be a shining red beacon, attracting attention, urging the imaginative mind to speculate about it—not unlike a seductress, tantalizing and setting the imagination of the onlooker on fire.

He realized that he was enjoying the sense of adventure and discovery in this endeavor he had undertaken. The next logical thing to do was travel to the place of Ramanujan's origin—India. With everything he had been through, going home sounded exactly like what he needed. He could use a little moral support from his family. Plus, he would finally get to see Prisha after all these years.

The thought of Prisha brought a smile to Krish's face. He was eager to hold her delicate, young body in his arms, kiss her, make love to her and share his exciting research with her.

Krish landed in Mumbai, India. The heat and humidity made him feel immediately at home. He began thinking about the implications that his research and philosophy might have for India.

The brand-new airport terminal was world class. Krish was impressed to see stringent security, even at the perimeter of the airport, far away from the gates. The hospitality of the venders, the genuine smiles of people, and surprisingly helpful immigration and customs officials made him feel welcome.

Krish treated himself to his favorite chai-tea, samosa, and spicy pav-bhajee, thick gravy topped with melted butter. It really hit the spot after such a long time. He was truly glad to be home. He seamlessly transitioned into his mother tongue, Marathi, as soon as he got an opportunity. It was a warm embrace of familiarity that acted like a soothing balm on his wounded mind and soul.

At the food court, a sturdy young man with cropped hair, short, thick, chevron mustache, and wearing a khaki safari suit walked up to Krish and said assuredly, "We will protect you discreetly until you get back to America. Please continue your activities without any hesitation. We are proud of your research. You make India look strong among developed countries."

He then disappeared into the crowd without hearing Krish say, "Good to know…thanks."

Krish stepped out of the airport and walked toward the line of waiting cabs.

"Please use this cab, sir. I am a poor farmer who had to take up driving to feed my family," one of the cab drivers pleaded.

He had heard about the hardship of farmers due to the heat and lack of rain. The parched land and the farmers were literally dying for rain. Increasing population, poor crop choices, single sources of livelihood, lack of water management, political apathy, and predatory money lending at exorbitant interest rates had combined to create a deadly trap for farmers who were committing suicide by the thousands—all due to a single failed crop!

Krish hired the cab. He had dozed off during the ride home. The tremendous force of jet lag had overpowered the adrenaline rush of seeing his family and Prisha again. He was woken up by a knock on his car window.

"Roll down the window, sir," a young boy, less than ten years of age, urged Krish as he dangled a small string necklace made of jasmine flowers. "For your girlfriend or mother maybe." Women wore such flower strings in their hair for ornamental purposes.

"How much?" Krish asked, rubbing his eyes. He didn't need the flower string, but the boy was urging him, pointing toward a lady with a baby sitting by the roadside—apparently his mother. The boy's livelihood depended on it. Instead of studying and going to school, he was thrust with the responsibility of being the breadwinner for his family at a tender age. Krish could only imagine the exploitation that family must be facing from the police and local thugs.

There was something ironic about the situation, a kid who was innocent like the flowers, was eking a living by selling them—even as big hoardings and loudspeakers blared about religion and powerful politicians made promises about housing, clothing, and food over and over again during the democratic elections. All only to be forgotten for the next five years until the elections were due again. The dance of democracy!

"Ten rupees, but for you... I will make a deal in five," the boy said, trying to make a sale. "Three for ten... it is a good deal, take it. Fresh flowers and very good smell, sir."

Krish smiled kindly, "All right, three please."

The boy handed over three flower strings to him through the half-opened window. As Krish reached into his pocket to get the money, the signal turned green and the car started moving. The boy's heart skipped a beat. In a flash, his eyes were a mix of emotions—fear of losing money, helplessness over the car driving away, betrayal if Krish didn't pay on purpose, possible consequences for his family if he lost the goods, possible hunger and beating!

Krish couldn't bear to see the boy's helpless face. He tapped on the driver's shoulder to slow down, the driver shook his head indicating he couldn't slow down due to the traffic. The boy ran with the car to get the money. Finally, Krish managed to get a fifty rupees bill from his wallet and almost threw it out the window to the boy. The boy got the money and flashed a smile that spread from ear to ear. He touched the bill to his head and said, "Thanks, sir!" as he got out of the way of oncoming traffic. The boy had risked serious injury for a very small amount of money.

Krish's sharp mind analyzed the situation of the farmers committing suicide and millions of people living in squalor. *These are hard working, industrious people. In this country, solutions also exist for these problems. The situation is similar to the US—with its terrorism, economic, and social problems. If only individual humans could be made aware of their power, they could influence their reality and live the way they want as the free individuals they are! In such a liberated and free state, there cannot be corruption and there cannot be a man creating problems for other men just to make more money for himself. I cannot wait to prove this mathematically!* Krish fantasized.

Krish was enjoying his stay at home—sharing stories of recent events with his parents, eating fresh homemade food, and simply relaxing. It was the healing environment that his mind badly needed. He was also very eager to meet with Prisha. He called a mutual friend, Jia, to find out how was Prisha doing.

"Why do you want to know?" Jia asked him. Jia worked as a lifestyle coach. She was a close friend with a strong personality—very confident and funny. She was dark-skinned, medium height, with short, black hair. She wore thin glasses with a trendy red frame. She carried a few extra pounds, but dressed smartly to attract more attention to her ever present, genuine smile, sharp nose, and pretty, round face.

"I've known her from the time she worked on a research project at BARC. I was just curious what she might be up to these days."

"Well, while you were gone, she got married and had a baby," Jia answered flatly.

"Married? Wow, so soon?" Krish tried to hide the disappointment in his voice.

"Oh! Was she supposed to wait for her knight in shining armor? She found a decent guy and got married. That's what her parents wanted too," Jia added as if she were stating something that should be obvious.

"Well, she didn't strike me as the homely, obedient type, but I guess I was wrong," Krish said. He was crushed. He really thought they had something going between them, but then again, with women you never truly know what they're thinking. He swallowed his bruised ego, the pain of rejection, and being passed over, and tried to get ahold of his emotions. He calmed down within a few moments.

"Are you there?" Jia was trying to find a reason for the silence on the other end of the line.

"Yes, yes, bad cell signal," Krish lied. "I'm delivering a plenary talk at IIT Bombay next week, please come," he said in an attempt to change the subject.

"Oh yes! I haven't slept in a while. I'm sure your lecture will help with that. I'll be there with bells on!" Jia said playfully. "If babies are allowed, I'll see if Prisha can come too," she added mischievously, fully aware of the chemistry between her friends.

Krish looked confident and relaxed as he got ready to present his work. He stood with a laser pointer and remote control in his hand, presenting his findings to a room full of researchers from diverse fields.

"He's so cute, love his confidence," one student whispered to her friend.

Krish wore a dark suit and shiny black shoes. His rimless glasses adding a scholarly touch to his sharp look. He was in the perfect zone, presenting his highly cited, groundbreaking work that had applications in defense to communication, and if expanded, could help understand the nature of the universe. He fielded several queries from researchers with varying scientific backgrounds. He engaged in a lively debate with them, answering questions and raising new ones. At the end, he received a standing ovation from the room. Every single researcher present was inspired by this young man, his work, thought process, and ideas.

Krish was busy packing up his presentation materials after the talk. From the corner of his eye, he noticed a tall, muscular man, who didn't look like a typical scientist, observing him and walking toward him rapidly.

Before he got too close, he was stopped by a man in a safari suit who caught him from behind by the waist, called for help, and contained the situation without causing a disturbance.

Krish shook his head and thanked his stars. He packed his laptop in his leather bag and was about to leave when he was pleasantly surprised to see Prisha and Jia approaching the dais.

"Hey Krish. Excellent talk… it's been a long time," Prisha said with a tinge of humor and emotion. He could see right through her even as she confidently shook his hand. She was an extroverted, self-assured young lady.

Krish blushed and his heart raced. It felt surreal to have the woman he had been dreaming about for so long within a few feet of him. She looked so beautiful. He couldn't stop staring. He honestly couldn't be sure that he had blinked at all since she'd walked up. She wore formal black slacks and a silk, cream-colored blouse that covered her delicate shoulders. Her thin neck stood tall above the collar of her shirt, her long hair tied neatly, her pants hung seductively from her hips, covering her long legs. She brushed against him, looking directly at him as she needlessly adjusted her hair to further reveal her perfectly oval face and soft pink lips. They would have made an impressive couple.

"What have you been up to?" Prisha asked.

Krish was woken out of his dream state by her words. "Nothing much, just research. How is everything with you, married life, kids?" he asked as he looked at Jia. He didn't notice any jewelry on Prisha that indicated marriage. Wearing a wedding ring was not part of the culture in India, and the traditional necklace indicating the status was not generally worn in a professional setting by women.

"Oh God! Really? That's the first question you ask?" Jia interjected. "Mr. hot-researcher, you can ask her that when I leave. In fact, I have to go now. I have a meeting at the other end of the city, see you later," Jia smiled. "Beautiful slides, steady voice, clear thought pattern, enough excitement and energy, deep knowledge of subject matter… good job overall! I have a lot of questions about your research, some other time," she added. She then whispered in Krish's ear, "Enjoy! I can tell she wants you too!" Jia winked mischievously and left the conference hall. Krish smiled at Jia's words.

"Have a good time dear," she said to Prisha as she strode away.

Prisha drove Krish to a highly rated restaurant at a 5-star hotel in the city. They sat at opposite ends of their booth. As they placed their order, Prisha moved closer to Krish, brushing against him. Her freshly washed hair had a pleasing, light sage-sandalwood smell.

"Well, I'm not married. Jia was just pulling your leg," Prisha said, concealing her laughter as she gently touched his shoulder with her hand.

"Oh that brat!" Krish said, faking anger, but feeling relief.

"After you left, I cracked into the Indian Institute of Management, Bangalore. They have a 1% acceptance rate—one of the lowest in the world," Prisha said proudly. "Then the entrepreneurial bug bit me, and I got together with some friends and started a company in the area of the Internet of Things, IOT, connecting various devices in our homes seamlessly for security, comfort, and convenience. I'm the VP of Marketing. My philosophy is: retire early, retire rich."

"Wow! Congratulations! Awesome job!" Krish was genuinely happy to see his woman so successful, smart, and sexy at the same time. He had never been so impressed.

Their outlooks on life were different. He was a mathematician, and a physicist who wanted to understand the true nature of life and the universe. He was a deep thinker, philosophical, and a little shy when it came to things other than science. She was a go-getter, extroverted; she liked to take charge. She was happy with the world as it was and wanted to generate wealth, grow a business, make money, then go ahead and do something else. Very entrepreneurial. He enjoyed their totally dissimilar viewpoints. He loved her for being so independent and successful.

The next time Krish and Prisha met was at a party at a friend's farmhouse. She wore a dark Kanchivaram silk saree with kalamkari motifs and a sheer, backless, modern blouse—a perfect blend of traditional and contemporary. They hugged lightly as they met, grabbed a glass of fine red wine, and went to the garden in the backyard to lounge on the grass.

Dark clouds hovered over the grey mountains. Perhaps inspired by the scenery, she loosened her saree pleats held together over the shoulder by a pin and playfully covered his face with the garment. He inhaled her enchanting fragrance.

In the white moonlight, the flowers appeared gentler and softer. The yellow seemed more vivid, the shades of pink near the bottom of the petal appeared darker, the bright red looked more pleasing. Krish looked at her intently. She smiled. Her lips looked softer, darker, and more inviting than ever. He grabbed her wrist and pulled her close to his chest. He slid his hand around her waist, resting it on the small of her back. She gently swung into him and put her head on his chest. He was eager to look in her eyes, but she had closed them in this peaceful embrace.

He tenderly massaged her back and shoulders, enjoying the feel of her against him.

She suddenly pulled away, looked him straight in the eye, and grabbed his neck, kissing him wildly. She pulled him toward the grass and rested her body on top of his. The woman who had occupied his dreams from years on end, was now—in every way—his reality.

Krish and Prisha enjoyed casually dating. Cooperation between the US and Indian government meant that Krish could focus on his personal life for a few weeks without worrying too much about people hell-bent on causing him harm. Krish wanted to search for Ramanujan's lost papers. But, he was newly in love and did not want to be away from his sweetheart. He ignored his yearning and decided to enjoy his time with Prisha, at least for the time being.

After one particularly enjoyable dinner-movie date, they returned to Prisha's apartment and were snuggled up in a blanket with some hot chai tea and bhajia, making plans for the future.

"What better place for entrepreneurship than the Silicon Valley and the San Francisco bay area? We could live in California."

Prisha thought for a moment before agreeing, "Yep, we can make that work."

Prisha's parents, however, did not approve of her lifestyle. She had received a nasty e-mail from them saying, 'You are on your own now. Don't expect any support from us. You face the consequences of the decisions you made without our consent. Good bye.'

Prisha's independent decision making about her career and romantic choices did not go over well with her parents' conservative thinking. While they supported her education, they felt they were being sidelined, and that she didn't have enough experience to deal with so many facets of life on her own. Tradition and age were locking horns with newfound independence and confidence. The result was the cold shoulder, taunting, and negativity from her parents. Prisha felt lonely and abandoned. Dating without commitment was raising eyebrows from Krish's parents as well.

"Oh boy, this situation is getting complicated, especially with the parents," said Krish.

"Let's meet with Jia and see if she has some advice. She's good at understanding such family politics. She is a lifestyle coach after all. We can pay her," Prisha suggested.

"Let's do it," Krish agreed.

Krish and Prisha met Jia over dinner. Jia listened carefully.

"Similar stories are unfolding in one way or another in my other friends' and clients' lives too. The power of capitalism unleashed after opening up the socialist Indian economy to the world is creating unprecedented opportunities and wealth on the one hand, but also conflict and rivalry on the other hand. That's why my business is flourishing."

"Understood," Prisha said, sounding annoyed. "Your theoretical analysis does not help with our situation. Do you have any advice for us?"

"Okay, sorry. I digress," Jia said. "Let me ask you one thing, how committed are you? How sure are you about your relationship?"

Krish and Prisha looked at each other. They almost spoke at the same time, "We love each other and are very compatible."

"That's a good sign," Jia said. She lowered her eyeglasses over her nose, looked Krish in the eye and asked, "Do you see yourself getting old together?"

"I see where this is going," Krish said. "This is too soon. Whose side are you on, ours or our parents?"

Prisha agreed, "We have been dating for just a few weeks. It's too early to think about marriage."

"We live in India, Prisha," Jia reasoned. "Live-in relationships are frowned upon, especially in middle-class families. Both of your parents already contacted me and asked me to be the intermediary. If you want their approval, you should get married soon. Plus, Krish may have to travel back to the US or other places for his work. He cannot leave you hanging after having lived together."

Krish and Prisha were caught in a complex web of family issues, emotional blackmail, and the norms of culture and society. A lot of their friends were in similar situations and had to hasten their marriage plans. Against their best judgement, they decided that getting married truly was the most reasonable solution to the conflicts they were facing. Even though it was sooner than they would have liked, the couple believed in the love they shared.

After rushing to the altar, Krish and Prisha traveled to cooler resorts in the Himalayas for their honeymoon.

"Let's go water rafting," Prisha said excitedly. Water was Prisha's favorite element. Krish, on the other hand, preferred walks, treks, and hikes. But, Krish agreed to her suggestion.

As he probed his bag for his waterproof watch, he came across the Hanuman statue his mom had given him and the arrow he found in California. He had completely forgotten about it since coming to India!

Krish and Prisha were walking toward the spot for rafting. He sat to rest by a fresh water lake that had been formed during the spring due to melting snow. The Hanuman statue rested safely in his backpack. All of a sudden, he experienced a strange feeling— like a bolt of energy was running through his body. He felt joyous.

His eyes were closed, but he was smiling with uncontrollable bliss. He experienced a spontaneous meditative high and lost awareness of time and his surroundings. He was completely focused on the energy surging inside him. The legendary mountains, where great souls were said to live, the lake, and the fresh air were triggering something profound within him.

Within a few moments, he was again conscious of his surroundings. Krish had experienced a glimpse of something extraordinary. He did his best to describe the occurrence, but Prisha didn't understand what he felt. He explained to her about his prior experiences and the hallucinations he'd had in the States. He showed her the scar from his bullet injury from the shooting at the restaurant.

"What did I marry into?" she said jokingly. "Krish, I'm proud of you." She kissed him in a way that made him feel loved.

"You're quite a trailblazer yourself," he said as he pressed her hand in his. He put her head on his chest, and they relaxed by the lake. The union of the two bodies, their hearts, and minds was complete.

The spontaneous meditative experience reminded Krish of his mission to find Ramanujan's lost papers. Upon returning from his honeymoon, Krish wasted no time in traveling to the Southern Indian state of Tamilnadu, where he would visit Ramanujan's home. He couldn't put off his mission any longer.

The feeling of being followed persisted within him. He felt that, in the background, hidden from him, was a constant struggle going on between the security forces and his enemies. *I'm caught in this cat and mouse game between my enemies and my protectors. Who knows, they may get to me one day, I need to find these papers and move onto the next step in my research quickly*, Krish cautioned himself. *But, I won't let this constant threat terrorize me, or let it change my outlook. I'll still enjoy my life and mission.*

As he travelled in a bus, he noticed that South India was completely different from the Western part of the country, where he came from. He enjoyed watching the tall coconut trees and magnificent temples as he travelled. He delighted in the delicious sambar, rice cakes, red, green, and white chatnees, and the extraordinary dances and music. He also noticed that the people were crazy about their movie stars. It was another world altogether.

Krish found Ramanujan's wife's, Janaki's, address and met with her.

Janaki was more than one hundred years old, with dark, wrinkled skin. She wore a traditional white sari worn by widows, thick glasses with a big frame, and her thick, slightly unkempt grey hair was loosely bound with a clip. She spoke loudly—probably because her hearing had been affected by age—as a result, she sounded angry when she spoke. You almost didn't notice she had only a few teeth left. Being a widow, she wore a black tika on her forehead, unlike the red worn by married women.

The old woman said, "There were a lot of papers scattered by my husband's bed as he died. His friend, Chidambaram, may have some of them. People still come inquiring about him. They write books, make movies. I'm blessed to be his widow. I'm well taken care of."

Krish followed up on the lead. Chidambaram, who lived in the neighboring village, had passed away.

"Here is a box. See if you find something," his son said as he handed Krish a worn wooden box.

Krish sat for a moment on the front steps of Chidambaram's household. He carefully glanced at each page, silently praying for the outcome he desired. As soon as he saw the mathematics contained in the first two pages, he realized it was of the highest level of complexity and development. Flipping the fourth page over and beginning to read the fifth, Krish believed that his heart had stopped beating in his chest. His eyes grew wide, then filled with tears. He put a hand to his mouth and tried to swallow the lump that had lodged itself in his throat. *My god...I've found them! This is it!*

Krish was overcome by emotion, his entire body was covered with goose bumps. He touched his head to the ground out of respect, "This man, Ramanujan, is beyond words, superb! What a genius, really! I'm humbled." Krish remembered what someone had said about Ramanujan's theorems, "They must be true because, if they were not true, no one would have the imagination to invent them."

Chidambaram's son looked on curiously, as he didn't understand what was so special about these papers—the very ones he had almost gotten rid of.

Krish continued digging through them. Unfortunately, most of the papers were so worn out that they were unreadable. It was a setback, but the pages that were legible were the answer to Krish's prayers and the key to unlocking profound understanding.

"What is this?" Krish asked as he opened another stack of paper from underneath the lost pages.

Fortunately, the wise Chidambaram had copied all the pages by himself! Word for word! He didn't understand a single thing about what he was copying, but he trusted Ramanujan's ability, and his gut told him of the value captured here.

Finally, half the battle had been fought and won. Krish had found Ramanujan's lost papers. Now, his task was to deduce the theorems written and see if any were applicable to Feynman's probabilities. After relationship distractions and numerous complications of life, the quest for knowledge had resumed in earnest!

CHAPTER 9
LIFE AFTER TRUTH

~~~~~~~

Ancient India

~~~~~~~

Tough situations test mettle.

PRINCE ANGAD, WHO FOUGHT ALONGSIDE HANUMAN AND drove the demons away in his early teen years, had kept in touch with the beautiful lady surgeon from the hermitage—Savi—throughout the years. In the last few months, however, he was too preoccupied with his father's death and the political instability that followed.

After Vali's death, Angad had made peace with his uncle, Sugriv. He was now the heir apparent of the kingdom. Ram's strong and formidable presence, and his alliance with Sugriv, had been a stabilizing hand in silencing any dissenting acts from loyalists of the old regime. Angad had wholeheartedly embraced Ram and his uncle; they were fair, transparent, and represented the future. A new era of spiritual, moral, artistic, and scientific development was beginning.

Angad was ready to move on with his life. The monsoon rains had started, and as the dark clouds thundered and poured, new plants, animals, and life forms were being created everywhere. Angad's heart was filled with new sensations and the energy of youth. He strongly desired female companionship. He could not wait to be with the beautiful Savi and was looking forward to enjoying her company. He had found out that Savi was the princess of the neighboring kingdom. She had completed her studies as a surgeon at the hermitage and returned home. He journeyed toward her palace.

As he reached the city of Ahobilam, the sun was appearing on the horizon and the light was slowly replacing darkness. The morning dew had condensed on surfaces and made everything—the stones, trees, grass—appear in a darker shade; everything was wet with freshness. Walking on the grass provided a pleasant sensation to Angad's feet. The mist settled delicately on the green trees. He saw a splash of green, the mist, and then the grey sky above it. It was a cloudy, misty, romantic morning. Angad imagined the warm, soft presence of his lady next to him on that wet morning.

"Namaste Prince Angad," Savi said, not hiding the joy she felt at the sight of him. She blushed, looked down, and shook her head a little to bring herself to her senses—a reminder to her own mind about what it was imagining. The warmth she displayed pleased Angad. She wore a bright green, short dhoti and a body hugging cloth around her breasts. She was getting ready for a horse ride. Her freshly washed, fragrant hair was tied in a bun—a small dagger tucked near her waist encased in a golden, intricately carved sheath. She stood close to Angad, with her almost bare back toward him. She could feel his eyes on her skin.

Angad thought, *in such a short period, Savi has changed. She is a grown woman now. She fits the image of the beautiful women described in the scriptures. I adore her plump breasts, round thighs, ample pelvic girdle, and slender waist. I cannot wait to be with her.*

She was also burning with anticipation of what was about to happen.

Angad pulled her close to him and pressed his mouth possessively against hers—claiming everything that she was willing to give.

They made love in the mists of Ahobilam that morning.

Later that day, the young prince and princess roamed the city together. They saw well-manicured gardens blooming with various kinds of flowers and fruits.

"Savi, the wilderness appears more lively than these well-maintained gardens. The raw force of life cannot be captured inside a garden. The wilderness is where it is expressed best."

"You are right, Angad, but mostly wild flowers and beasts flourish in the wilderness. The delicate roses, jasmines, tulips, and lilies are best grown in a garden. Raw force is, well… raw. Delicate, evolved, advanced expressions of life in the form of art, food, clothes, and even science need tenderness and security to flourish." She was very sure of her thoughts and did not wait for an affirmation from Angad. She continued, "Let me explain the finer details, layout, and symbolism of this great city as we stroll.

"The part of the city we are in right now is the lowest part, where all the people live. There are two main streets that go from east to west and north to south. All the palaces, offices, and markets are located on these two streets. Parallel to these two main streets are several other streets forming square shapes, within which are zones for houses, performing arts, galleries for painters, brothels, food places, sculptors, jewelers, and small shops belonging to various artisans and workmen. In other words, this tier has everything you need to live and enjoy life. There are also several places of worship for various gods—water, fire, rain, mountains, oceans, trees, animals, planets, the sun, etc.

"As we walk up to the next level, you will see a huge, pleasant lake built by our king. Let us cleanse ourselves in this clear lake." They first washed their feet in the crisp, peaceful waters. They splashed the glorious water upon their faces and ran damp fingers through each other's hair.

Looking into each other's eyes, Savi continued, "There is just water here, no trees or any other structures surrounding the lake. This conveys that, as you enjoy the pleasures, and finish your family and societal duties, at the lower level, you need to rise up and cleanse yourself at this level. Cleansing is intended to slowly wash away all the good and bad impressions that you invariably acquired on the slate of your soul as you lived your life at the first level. Water is an excellent choice for cleansing.

"As you trek to the third tier, you see a splendid Vishnu and Mother Devi temple. Vishnu is the one who protects and leads us. Devi is the power and inspiration to the Vishnu. They are both very human looking. You pray to them at this level. While being confined in your physical form, you explore what lies beyond the physical at this level."

Angad was trying to imbue the essence of what Savi was talking about. For the next stage, there was a glimpse of the hilltop, but no clear path forward. The path was blocked by wilderness and boulders.

Savi looked at Angad and asked, "What do we do now? Can you figure it out?"

Angad put his weapon down, jumped on a tree, walked around, and tried to make his way through by pulling down some trees, but he could not get ahead. He finally got tired and sat under a tree as Savi watched him mischievously. As he sat and rested for some time, he heard the faint sound of a stream just beyond the big rock in front of them. He smiled at Savi, as he got the point.

"You have to sit quietly, with a calm mind, and it will come to you," he said. Savi nodded and smiled at her handsome, young friend approvingly. They followed the stream and continued to trek higher into the hills. They reached the top and saw a small temple.

"This is the highest point in the city. The temple is for Mahadev in the form of a cylindrical shaped lingam, its is a symbol of power. This conveys that one's purpose in life is to realize this highest, formless level and achieve freedom. At this stage, you realize aspects that are beyond your body." She paused and looked around, pointing to the curvy path they had travelled. The path completely disappeared sometimes.

"Once you realize this level, you can go back and guide others along the path, or choose to live in this state continuously."

Angad was deeply impressed by the depth of Savi's character and intellect, and the wisdom of the people who built this great city. Angad had known Savi as a princess and a surgeon—here, he saw her as a teacher and a yogi.

There were very few visitors to the hill that day.

Savi sat on a rock nearby. She was immersed in the view of the city below, the setting sun, and the cool breeze. As she sat, soaking in the silence and the peace she felt. Her breathing slowed and she quietly slipped into a meditative state.

Back in the mountains of Kishkindha, it was a cloudy day. The sun could not be seen due to the cloud cover. It was muggy, and everyone was waiting for the rain that wouldn't come. It was a very unpleasant day.

Hanuman had changed completely since Ram's blessing of the supreme yogic experience. Sometimes, he appeared to be lost in meditation, even when he was fully engaged in his day-to-day duties as the new general in Sugriv's administration. Although, he was not yet at the highest yogic level where he could be in a meditative state all the time without effort.

Ram was having troubles of his own. The anguish, frustration, and guilt of losing his dear wife was becoming too much to bear. She had trusted him by leaving the palace and living in the dreadful jungle, and he had failed her. It tore him apart to think of what Ravan could be doing to her. How was Ravan treating his beautiful, young wife who was completely at his mercy? Ravan had kidnapped scores of women and made them slaves or queens.

Sita's thoughts never left Ram. She was a princess, the epitome of gentle, feminine energy. She was born of a non-uterine birth, outside the human body. She had a tall, slender frame and glowing complexion the hue of wheat. Her long hair and brown eyes were uncommon and gave her an exotic appearance. She always wore a gentle gaze, which hid her steadfast resolve and strong character. Sita was an accomplished yogi and also had the arms training necessary to defend herself if the situation arose; swords and a dagger were her weapons of choice. She was raised as a princess who had learned to handle palace politics.

The first time Sita and Ram met, he completely swept her off her feet with his muscular body, mighty bow, and a calm, gentle smile. And Ram could not take his eyes off her slender, shapely form. Sita had looked at Ram and playfully gestured as if to say, 'what are you looking at?' She always teased him about that.

Thinking about Sita put a smile on Ram's face. But, the realization that she was not safe caused him anguish beyond compare.

"Brother, I have single-handedly defeated thousands of demons. I have weapons that could destroy several planets. You and I can march today and rescue my dear Sita from the clutches of that evil spirit right now, but—curse my fortune—I cannot do that!" Ram said in a steady, controlled voice, despite the anxiety that dwelled within.

"This is a great teachable moment for society," Ram continued, "How to be an ideal leader, to obey the rules of warfare, to motivate society to fight for a just cause, and to obey the rule of law under all circumstances. This is an opportunity to demonstrate how to establish a just and fair system for all. I cannot lose this opportunity. But, personally, it is too painful, and I cannot take it any longer."

It seemed that there was a volcano boiling under Ram's cold, steely exterior. Lakshman could not see his brave, courageous, powerful, elder brother in this heartbroken, devastated, and despondent state.

"The learned people have started calling you the avatar of Vishnu, the Protector, the Leader," Lakshman said. "You are only the seventh person to be bestowed with that title in thousands of years of history! Personally, I don't care about titles. I will go myself and get Lady Sita back. I have not slept a single moment since that awful day. I will rain so many missiles down on Ravan's city that it will be fried, and each and every soul will repent the day they were born under the demonic rule of their evil king. I will kill each and every one of his sons, brothers, commanders, generals, soldiers, and then Ravan himself. I am itching to put an arrow straight between his eyebrows and shatter his skull into a thousand pieces. The brain that came up with the idea of touching such a pious woman will be spilled on the unholy soil of Lanka and fed to the vultures.

"The arms that touched my brother's wife with evil intentions will be uprooted from their joints and thrown into the sea. I will fire the Great Universe Missile at that city and obliterate it from the face of this planet. Even if Lord Mahadev wants to save him, He will not be able to do so. Every bird, animal, human, or demon living in that city and supporting such evil will be skinned alive. Shree Ram, I beg you," Lakshman pleaded as his temper and voice rose. "Please order me without delay. I don't need any monkeys or apes. I will march right now, at this very moment, and not show my face to you again until I bring Lady Sita back."

Lakshman was shaking with anger; his eyes watery and full of enough furry to destroy the planet in-and-of themselves. His heart beat rapidly in his mighty chest, and sweat trickled down his broad forehead. His bicep bulged with excess blood as he lifted his heavy bow; his entire body taut.

Ram realized the situation was getting out of hand. His words of discouragement were like daggers ripping apart his loving, powerful—but volatile—brother's heart. All the pain and humiliation the two brothers had felt was finally boiling over. The best that humanity had to offer, the equanimous, the supreme yogi—Ram—was wavering in the face of tremendous, barbaric, and animalistic provocation by Ravan.

Finally, Hanuman tried to placate them. "Oh virtuous princes of the great kingdom of Ayodhya, please control your emotions. I suggest we take a walk and visit the hermitage. I heard the great Agastya Muni is visiting. He may be able to advise us."

There was an almost audible sigh of relief in the cave. Just the mention of a walk away from that hot, humid place defused a potentially explosive situation. The princes supported that idea and were eager to receive the great Muni's guidance.

As if on cue, it finally started to rain—further helping to cool things down emotionally and physically. The brothers were soaked—both hoping that the rain would permeate their bodies, extinguish the lava in their hearts, and calm their souls. Luckily, their tears were cleverly camouflaged by the sympathetic droplets of rain.

Ram, Lakshman, and Hanuman walked toward Agastya Muni's ashram. As soon as they saw the cluster of simple huts from a distance, they felt the positive vibrations. Older students, studying at the ashram and responsible for guarding the outskirts, were observing the three powerfully armed men as they approached. Ram was keen on not wasting time with any unnecessary misunderstanding. As such, it was conceited to visit a Muni of such stature with this vulgar display of arms.

As the trio approached a large banyan tree—that appeared to be a few centuries old—Ram said, "I suggest we keep our weapons by this tree to put the student guards at ease. As such, we are visiting the Muni to seek his guidance." Lakshman and Hanuman nodded in agreement.

"Somehow, I feel that these powerful weapons are completely useless in the environs of the ashram anyhow," Hanuman confessed. "I feel a very peaceful calm. At the same time, I also feel an otherworldly, disarming, and awe-inspiring presence emanating from the ashram. I feel as if the weapons will not work properly as we come near, or there may be such a swift and overwhelming reaction to any misadventure that it is pointless to even think about using them here. These simple huts are peaceful and dreadful at the same time.

"All the animals and birds roam around fearlessly, as if they don't have the least bit of worry about their predators. I think they can feel the protective energy. The cows, goats, deer, peacocks, hares, and squirrels wander freely. There are plentiful fruits, vegetables, and flowers. There is a patch of land for agriculture. Hundreds of students go about their activities and perform the chores at their schools of study. It is such an idyllic environment—perfect for all encompassing education, development, and healing."

Ram just smiled at Hanuman. It seemed that Ram's mood was slowly beginning to improve. They walked toward the ashram with folded hands, to further quell any doubts about their intentions.

The Muni eagerly walked out of his ashram as he saw Ram. Agastya had a long beard. His hair was coiled in the center, and he had a slight pot belly. He wore a coarse, cotton white dhoti and wooden sandals. He radiated compassionate energy and appeared to have a secret spring of blissfulness flowing inside him.

Agastya was a multi-talented man and considered an authority in theory, as well as in the practice of, weapons, missiles, medicine, and the yogic sciences and literature.

"Welcome Shree Ram, a great prince and the seventh avatar of Vishnu, the Protector," the Muni said with a warm smile. He tried to hug Ram, but instead, Ram bowed down to touch the Muni's feet. "I completely understand your state of mind, and that is precisely why I have traveled here to be near you, to help you deal with this extremely difficult situation," the Muni said.

Ram was surprised by the Muni's insight. The Munis maintained their own spy networks—helping them to stay connected with the world even though they resided deep in a jungle. It also helped them determine who to support in the event of a battle—who to share weapons and knowledge with. Select warriors, like Ram, were given access to powerful missiles stored in secret locations. The missiles could be accessed with short notice, and it was always better to have advanced warning so that all could be prepared. Special hymns recited in a particular order and manner were used to ascertain identification and access to weapons. Stealth and secrecy were almost as important as the weapons themselves.

The Muni held Ram's hand and walked with him to a special hut where they wouldn't be disturbed. Hanuman and Lakshman stood guard nearby.

The Muni looked at the despondent Ram. His task was to help Ram get mentally energized for the tough battle ahead. Once the Muni had a strategy in his mind, he said, "Nobody can mistreat Lady Sita, not even a powerful king. She is safe." Ram and his companions were uplifted by this news. "Ravan is an ego-maniac and a self-preservationist. His city, Lanka, and the powerful kingdom he founded are his proudest achievements. He has amassed tremendous wealth, power, and weaponry. He will not do anything that jeopardizes the very existence of his kingdom or power.

"He knows about you and your power. He knows that you have killed thousands of demons using special weapons. Your recent killing of Vali has labeled you unpredictable, showing that you can bend the rules of warfare if needed. Ravan was afraid of Vali. He knows that you have the support of all the human kings. You have also earned the support of the powerful Vanara.

"We, Rishis, are always on your side because of your virtuous nature. Ravan's spies will surely report our meeting. I will give you access to flying machines similar to Ravan's. I will also share knowledge of building a bridge in the ocean with your new Vanara friends. Ravan will not do anything to invite an all-out war on himself from all sides, led by a living legend such as yourself. He will not threaten his own existence, I assure you."

The Muni's words soothed Ram's heart and gave him back his confidence, which had waned. "Further, Lady Sita is a brave, self-respecting person—very loyal to her husband and aware of his power. Her interaction with Ravan was an opportunity to test Ravan's character. It was an opportunity to see how he would treat someone who is physically less powerful than him, when no one was watching. He has failed this test of character miserably. She put up a brave fight with Ravan when he abducted her. If pushed into a corner, she could kill herself and cause tremendous ill will and shame to Ravan. Ravan has gotten himself into a precarious situation where there are too many ways for him to lose power, get killed, or both. He will proceed with caution. My spies are keeping a close watch on the situation. Do not worry, Sita is safe."

Ram breathed a sigh of relief. It felt as though he was finally releasing a breath he had held since the moment he left Sita's side.

Ram and his companions stayed at the ashram for a few days. He was finally at peace, nourishing his soul in the presence of the Muni and nursing his mind back to health. Ram was also practicing yoga with the Muni.

On the day Ram was scheduled to leave, he joined the Muni in a private meditation session. The Muni presented a special arrow to him. Ram bowed his head, respectfully and graciously accepting the arrow.

"This is a special arrow that will always remind you of your true nature. You seem to have forgotten, being trapped in the vicious cycle of events and locked within your emotions. Now, let me guide you toward the experience of your true self again."

In a few moments, Ram was lost in meditation. He felt light, weightless. He then transformed into tiny particles, and eventually, acquired the form of energy that was not limited by his body or mind. In the energy form, he saw himself shooting an arrow. He arranged the particles of matter in the shape of a target, even as the arrow travelled toward it. Thus, he became the one who hit the target every single time.

While in energy form, Ram saw an Asura—the most malicious of the demigods—attacking his brother from behind. A deer, standing near his brother, ran away in fear. This action immediately alerted his brother of the attack, and he swiftly retrieved his sword, killing the Asura. Ram used his energy to mold the matter, humans, animals, and situations as he guided them on the right path. Thus, he became one who always kept his word. He always transformed his words into reality.

In travelling as a cluster of energetic particles, Ram ventured to where Sita was being held.

"Sita, marry me or I will kill you!" Ravan threatened. The female guards Ravan had stationed nearby nodded in agreement—swords drawn, encouraging Sita to obey. In one smooth and decisive motion,

Sita grabbed a sword from one of the guards, and with practiced ease and not a moment of hesitation, cut herself superficially over her arm. Blood dripped from her wound.

Seething with anger and shaking with contempt, Sita erupted, "You call yourself an erudite scholar, but don't know how to respect the feminine form that nurtures and cares. You only understand raw, masculine power. So, I will teach you in a language that you understand. You dare come near me, and you will be shattered into a thousand pieces by me or my powerful husband—you worthless, pathetic, imposter of a king. I don't care if I die in the process of killing you. You have set in motion events that will lead to your complete annihilation. But, you already know this to be true, don't you?" Sita shot the question at him with such ferocity that Ravan dared not come any nearer. Without another word, he left her chamber.

Ram was proud that Lady Sita had realized her own yogic strength. He now understood why she could never be harmed. The fearless and righteous are always safe. Ram, thus, became the one who only had one woman in his life. Sita was that woman, and she played her role in helping Ram lead society down the right path. Ram—one word, one arrow, and one woman.

Ram came out of his meditative state—nursed back to peak mental health. He was completely in touch with his true self and the subtle powers he had forgotten. He was assured of his wife's well being, and that brought him immense serenity. He bowed at his teacher's feet for bringing him back to the right path, even as he himself was tasked with showing the righteous path to the people.

CHAPTER 10
HURDLES IN THE QUEST

~~~~~

Modern Day India

~~~~~

Closest relations hurt the most.

A S EXPECTED, THESE MODULAR FORMS SHOW SUPER symmetry. They reveal their original form when Moebius Transformation is applied to them. But, look at these other seventeen gorgeous, deceptive, beauties. Their coefficients get larger when written as an infinite sum—like the modular forms, but without showing super symmetry!" Krish exclaimed. He was explaining Ramanujan's mathematics as he studied the lost pages.

"This mathematics was used in string theory. The mock modular forms were used to describe the entropy of black holes a hundred years after his death! To put that in perspective, can you discover an answer to a question that will be thought almost hundred years from now?"

Krish wore a white T-shirt and black jeans. He sat at his desk and sipped herbal tea from his favorite yellow Peet's mug from California. He took a sniff of the tea and enjoyed the aroma of cardamom, dry ginger, nutmeg, and cloves. A dash of honey added a tinge of sweetness to the brew. Krish had been in India for four weeks now. So far, the Indian security forces, with help from the US, were keeping him protected and giving him time and space to explore his research while enjoying his private life as much as possible.

Prisha sat near him, absent-minded, gazing at the Arabian Sea. She wore red silk pajamas, sitting back in her recliner, sipping coffee from a mug of her own. Krish and Prisha were in the sea-facing penthouse Prisha was renting in a Mumbai high-rise.

"I just launched a product that measures the amount of sunlight and rooftop solar output. It controls air conditioning and water heater temperature in five star hotels," Prisha said proudly. "We operate in a totally different space, don't we?" she asked after a thoughtful pause.

"That's what I love about us, sweetheart," Krish said. "I do all the crazy research, and you pay for it. Aren't we made for each other?" He winked mischievously.

Prisha dragged him onto her chair, pushed the lever, and reclined the chair completely backward. She took off his glasses, put them on the desk, and looked lovingly up at him. As the sunset and the pleasant, early winter breeze caressed them, Krish noticed the changing mood in her eyes. She moved her eyes away and ran her long fingers through his chest hair, trying to gauge his mood.

Krish slid his arm around her waist and pulled her closer. She turned on her side to face him. They were cozy in the recliner, pressed against one another. She placed a hand around his neck, playing with the hair that rested along his nape, and looked away, suddenly feeling shy. He tilted her chin up slightly and offered a passionate kiss.

"Oh no, it's getting dark! I want to show you something," Krish said.

"Let me guess... something interesting about the sky?" Prisha said with mild sarcasm.

"Nope, a surprise for you. Let's go," Krish said. He took her down and showed her the brand new, red Tesla Model S in the garage. "From one entrepreneur to another, Prisha, Elon Musk sends his regards," Krish beamed.

"Wow! This is amazing! So very thoughtful, Krish. We need to go up and finish what we started. You will get extra special treatment today," she murmured seductively, grabbing his hand.

After a moment, a question mark appeared across her face. "How did you pay for this?"

"I got a royalty check for my patent," Krish explained.

"That is so cool!"

"Let's go for a drive." As they took the slick machine for a spin around the part of the city with less traffic, darkness was setting in. Prisha opened the panoramic moon roof. The Tesla was whizzing through the evening like a ball of fire. It was surrounded by darkness on all sides. Krish felt an invisible force affecting the car's movement; instead of traveling in a straight line, the car was being pushed to the right slightly. *Just like how the stars and galaxies are affected by the dark matter that surrounds them!* he mused. *We can measure the effect of this material on the movement of stars, but we have zero idea of what this dark matter is!* Krish laid back in the passenger seat and looked at the sky above.

Krish was hallucinating—actually experiencing the problems he was tackling in particle physics. It was as if he had become the so-called 'God Damn Particle'—Higgs Boson. He saw matter acquire mass as it moved through the Higgs field. The dark matter also had mass, as seen from its effect on other bodies. But, it was difficult to figure out if the dark matter was interacting with the Higgs field or not. *How does the dark matter acquire mass then?*

"Damn it!" Prisha yelled. Krish was woken from his hallucination. "When will people learn how to ride bikes?"

A motorbike rider with his headlights off had cut in front of the car. Whatever was going on in the darkness surrounding the car had appeared smack in its path and profoundly affected it. That sparked an idea in Krish.

I think I have to go back to basics. There are a lot of things that are not known. I need to look at the fundamental particles that make up matter to really get ahead in this problem, Krish thought. He immediately pursued that thought.

When it came to dark matter and the fundamental particles, the first name that popped into his head was Anton Kimble. Krish took out his phone and Googled Professor Anton Kimble at Cambridge.

Professor Kimble was disabled and confined to a wheelchair due to an accident he was involved in when he was twenty-two, but nevertheless, he had continued his breakthrough research in physics and mathematics, becoming a celebrity scientist. His lucid writing made science interesting for lay people.

Toward the end of the drive, Prisha grabbed a spicy snack from her favorite street vendor, then turned around to head home.

"I wish I could show the car to my parents and invite them over for dinner tomorrow. I haven't seen them since the wedding," she said.

"Sure, let's do that. And your sister too," Krish agreed.

"Wow! Nice apartment. It must cost a fortune. Look at the sea view too! We hope that our second daughter will at least help us a little bit," Prisha's mother fired the opening salvo. Her conservative parents were unhappy with Prisha due to her independent nature. They didn't hold back any punches.

Krish's impression of Prisha's parents was not very positive. *They seem like mean-spirited bullies. We got married to make them happy, yet still they're pissed,* he thought.

Prisha's father piled on, "Be careful, or you will lose everything. What if you develop a disease or get fired? It's all too common in these new companies and big cities. No guarantee of a wife when you come home and no guarantee of job when you go to work. In India, it's becoming all too common, just like the west. Hope you two don't get divorced! You guys are quite modern and westernized, not traditional like us and your sister."

Receiving such unkind words as soon as they entered the home set the tone for the rest of the evening. Krish was at a loss of how to react. After all, these folks were his wife's parents.

In their minds, Prisha was too focused on success—more than their egos could tolerate. They wanted her to fall on her face so as to teach her a lesson.

"So Krish, do you have a job or is she feeding you? Are your parents okay with you not working? Did they instigate you to marry her so that she could pay for your hobbies—research, I believe you call it? Did you create all this misunderstanding between us? Prisha was not like this before she met you. You changed her with your western ways. What kind of a man are you? I'm not even sure you are a man," her father fired missile after verbal missile. They were taking turns humiliating the newlyweds.

"Be careful when you do it. You don't need another mouth to feed when you don't have a job. If we're interrupting your intimate time, we will leave. I know you are newly married. You must be like bunnies!" Prisha's mother added. "You have put on some weight. Your size looks bigger," she twisted the knife into the wound just a bit deeper to make sure the damage had been done.

"Are you going to take her to the US, or do you have somebody else there? You spent some time together, you know, the 'love them and leave them' culture!" her father winked menacingly.

Prisha was almost reduced to tears by the barrage of insults from her own parents. They were pressing all the buttons to make her pay for her perceived mistakes, independence, and success.

It pained Krish to witness the attacks on his wife and himself. They had even insulted his parents. This drama, and the ruthless jabs from people so close to them, was a major storm rocking the boat of their young marriage.

Although not completely unexpected, the savagery and sleaziness of the attacks was creating a very toxic environment. Marriage, career, and life in a large city was stressful enough as it was. Prisha needed emotional support at this delicate juncture in her life. Instead, what she got was extremely personal attacks at close range. It enhanced the sense of abandonment and lack of moral support she had been experiencing.

Krish thought, *just like the leaders who influence people and their actions, parents also have a major impact on a person's life. People who have not realized their true power are most vulnerable. I need to double down on my work so that I can prove the true power humans have—make Prisha realize it, and free her from her helpless state.*

The bad blood created by Prisha's parents spoiled the fun the couple were having in the honeymoon phase of their marriage. As a diversion, Krish focused on his research. He contacted Professor Kimble of Cambridge University and informed him of the findings within Ramanujan's lost pages.

"I found eighteen new functions described. Eighteen! These are special cases of mock modular forms that show super symmetry only at certain points—unlike the mock modular functions that don't show super symmetry at all. I need to test these functions and generate some experimental data and new particles," Krish explained.

"Try the Compact Muon Solenoid at CERN, the European Organization for Nuclear Research, in Switzerland. I saw data gathered from millions of images taken per second as particles collided at almost the speed of light. There is a treasure trove of data and new sub atomic particles being generated every second!" the professor suggested.

Anton also introduced Krish to a senior staff member at CERN who would arrange for his pick up from the airport and help plan experiments he needed. Krish was ready to get away from Mumbai and put some distance between him and the family theatrics.

Krish touched down at the Zurich airport. The Swiss Alps made for a pleasant backdrop befitting the beautiful country. It's as if the mountains were welcoming everyone and providing a glimpse of the natural beauty awaiting exploration in the rest of the country. Krish saw a tall man in uniform holding a board with his name on it.

"Welcome, sir. I'm Finn, let me get your bag. There will be a short flight to Geneva from here," he said. Finn was burly, six feet tall, with blonde hair and brown eyes. He wore a dark suit and black sunglasses.

They would leave for Geneva the next day out of a private airport.

The next morning was crisp, sunny, and beautiful. Krish enjoyed his ride to the airport. He had the car's sunroof open as he drove past the mountains—fresh air in his lungs and stunning views of the Swiss Alps to adore. He remembered his drives in California, with views of the blue ocean interspersed with inviting sandy beaches as his driving companion. But, despite the tranquility of this moment, he had a feeling something bad was about to happen—in some unexpected way, some screw up somewhere. He had learned to recognize nature's way of setting you up by starting the day in a great way, then ending it with a disaster—only to make the sting of disaster hurt more.

Krish boarded the flight to Geneva. The flight arranged by CERN was practically empty, with just one other passenger and Finn on board. The other passenger was a South Asian looking man who was busy reading his newspaper. The warm towel the air hostess offered felt fantastic on Krish's face. Ten minutes into the flight, the hostess returned to serve drinks.

"Orange juice please," Krish said. He looked at her to make sure she understood his half-Americanized accent. Finn, sitting in the row behind Krish, got up in a flash and strangled the unsuspecting air hostess—leaving her body in a heap on the ground.

"Time to die, Mr. Scientist," Finn said, landing a powerful blow to Krish's nose.

Krish was dazed as his nose started bleeding profusely.

Finn moved toward the pilot's cabin to hijack the plane and kill the pilot.

The tall man sitting a few rows behind Krish ran toward him. He grabbed Krish by the collar of his shirt.

"Friendly. I have been watching you and your would-be assassin. Let's go before the plane goes down or he comes back. Feel like skydiving?" He took two harnesses out of his backpack, handing one to Krish as he stepped into his own. He joined the two harnessed by clips, opened the exit door, and dove from the airplane with practiced precision and speed.

Before he could even recover from being punched in the face, Krish was in the middle of a free-fall at 120 miles per hour.

"Not your first time, I suppose. I fancied skydiving, but not like this," Krish shouted, not sure if his savior heard it. Krish tightly hugged the man from behind as they plummeted. "I hope you have a parachute. Otherwise, thanks in advance for breaking my fall."

"Stretch your hands, stop strangling my neck!" the man signaled as Krish desperately tried to hold on to him.

Feeling the immense pressure of the wind as it hit his face, Krish could barely keep his eyes open. Even though he was clearly speeding toward the ground, he found himself wondering if gravity was real. He suddenly noticed a huge net stretching all around him from the airplane above to the Earth below. The fishnet was made of three-dimensional space and time. He had become just a point weighing 155 lbs. There was no gravitational force acting on him. He was just passing through this net that was curved due the presence of mass and energy. As he passed along the curve, it appeared that gravity was acting on him.

Wow! I'm feeling gravity in my bones! Amazing! Feeling the force is much better than writing an equation for it! Krish thought. The recent news about LIGO, Laser Interferometer Gravitational-wave Observatory, came to his mind. *Recently, gravitational waves from two black holes, that collided more than a billion years ago, were uncovered by LIGO detectors located in Louisiana and Washington. Displacement of the order of one-ten-thousandth of the diameter of a proton was measured. In the future, instruments that are similar to the kind used at LIGO will be so sensitive and accurate that every gravitational wave—such as the one generated by this fall when I hit the ground—can be detected. Imagine what that would mean. The world can be experienced in high resolution. That would be so cool! What else could it mean?*

"Legs in an L-shape, bend down, start jogging soon," Krish heard somebody yelling.

His hallucination was broken. Krish was brought back to terra firma by his savior as the parachute was deployed, and they approached the ground and landed.

Krish was caught in the crossfire between government and rogue nations who wanted his research. The enemies felt that he was an easy target as soon as he left India. If they couldn't have him, they were ready to kill him so that the other side couldn't have him either. Krish knew there was not much he could do about the recent attempt on his life.

His work at CERN was progressing rapidly and his experiments were generating terabytes of data to be analyzed. He studied the effect of subtle and focused external force fields on the collisions of particles and their self-assembly into bigger particles. Using Ramanujan's newly discovered functions to predict the outcomes of these experiments, he was working with a great sense of urgency on his complex and passionate research.

Krish hadn't called Prisha since his arrival. He was missing her and wanted to share the progress and recent events with her. He set aside some time to connect.

"Hi sweetie, how's it going? My work is progressing well," Krish said, trying to update his better half without causing too much panic. "How is your work?" Krish asked.

"They fired me from my own company! The company that I started! They took away all my projects—projects that I conceived. They fired me via e-mail, an e-mail with acknowledgment of receipt to sender!" Prisha raged.

"Oh no! What? They can't do that!" Krish couldn't believe what he was hearing. "Go to your mom and dad's to feel better," he said instinctively. Krish realized that being booted from the company that she co-founded would be really hard for her to cope with. It would be equivalent to losing a baby for her. She had put in a lot of sweat and tears into the venture.

"My parents told me not to step foot in their house," she said coldly. She couldn't hide the disappointment in her voice even as she tried to mimic her father's stern tone. "So, what was I saying… yes, the Olympics. The black athletes—don't ask, don't tell, development of navigable waterways," she paused. "Oh boy, man landed on the moon. Oh, I can see the man on the moon! Or is it the sun? I think man landed on the sun. Did you eat? I'm hungry. I got to eat shit, bye. Don't fuck with a hot Swiss chick, you cheater! Don't put your head in that fucking long collider machine or it will get smashed. Ciao!" Prisha abruptly disconnected the phone.

Krish had no idea what she was talking about. He assumed that she was just in shock due to her unceremonious loss from the company she had given life to. *This could also be psychosis—incoherent thoughts and speech. These could be early signs of something serious. I'm really worried about her. This is a cry for help!* This was not an ideal time to be stuck in Switzerland. But, he couldn't leave. With the tight schedule he was working at CERN, and scientists from all over the world lining up for experiments and data, he was lucky to have found a spot in the agenda. The director at CERN had custom built parts and software to conduct the experiments Krish had proposed. Everybody knew these were great ideas that would advance science by leaps and bounds.

"I'm not sure when I'll get access to another collider if I miss this opportunity. My advisor and Professor Kimble have put their word in to get me a spot on the schedule. I can't waste it. I can't leave until all these experiments are finished," Krish said to his collaborator.

Prisha would have to fight these demons on her own for now.

By the time Krish left work, it was evening. It was the beginning of the spring season. He saw colors everywhere he looked. The vibrant green trees in full bloom, lush grass, the velvet Bougainvillea—the purple and pink flowers—were complemented magnificently by the ever-changing colors of the evening sky.

Krish was driving east. He could see glimpses of the colorful evening he was leaving behind in the side and rear view mirrors. On the other hand, the sky in front of him was dark blue, leaning over rugged, stony mountains. Slowly, the darkness of the evening encroached upon the superb display of colors and painted everything black.

For the last month, Krish had enjoyed his wife's company, finding Ramanujan's lost papers, and working at CERN. But, the path ahead was tortuous. With Prisha's health issues and the constant threats to his life from rogue organizations, Krish sensed obstacles that would severely test his focus and commitment in his quest for knowledge.

CHAPTER II
THE TEACHER REMOVES DOUBTS AND GUIDES

~~~~~

Ancient India

~~~~~

Truth removes fear.

MEETING WITH AGASTYA MUNI HAD COMPLETELY rejuvenated Ram.

"I feel energized, and in my mind I see myself victorious in the battle with Ravan. I am sure of success. Now, it is time to make this mental image a reality," Ram expressed to his brother.

Ram's positivity had rubbed off on Lakshman, Vanara King Sugriv, and Hanuman. Ram and Hanuman's friendship had blossomed into a student-teacher mentorship.

"Shree Ram, you have helped me along my yogic journey. Whenever I say your name, I instantly come in touch with the subtle energies within me and attain a meditative state. I am indebted to you forever," Hanuman said with heartfelt gratitude.

The monsoon rains were over. Sugriv and his comrades had indulged to their heart's content in females, booze, food, sleep, and other physical pleasures throughout the rainy season. They had lived in the forest for too long and were enjoying the luxuries of city life.

One such evening, the Vanara were enjoying a beautiful dance recital as musicians played sensuous music. The sweet smell of roses and smoke from hallucinogens filled the assembly halls. The halls were decked with different varieties of flowers and an abundance of fruits, honey, sweets, meats, and milk available for enjoyment. The floors were covered with thick rugs and the walls with tantalizing paintings and carvings.

"The curvaceous dancer and her gentle mudras remind me of the curves and bends of the jasmine laden with fragrant flowers," said one enthusiastic Vanara as he sipped his beverage from an hourglass-shaped, golden cup.

Each noble Vanara sat on a comfortable, low-lying bed with a cotton mattress fitted in silk sheets and plenty of soft, cylindrical pillows for support. A small wooden table, with intricate carvings and curved legs, was placed in front of the bed. A red, silk cloth decorated the table.

"I need one more drink. Come sit next to me and serve," said one noble Vanara to a hostess.

Scantily clad ladies made sure the gold cups constantly overflowed with alcohol using their long, delicately handled, silver containers with an elongated, curved spout. There was an excess of food, alcohol, hallucinogens, male and female escorts, dance, and music for everybody's enjoyment. Plenty of experts, trained in the art of enjoying and giving sensuous pleasures, were at hand to enhance the guests' experience.

The royals, enjoying their evening, were shaken out of their slumber by the sudden sound of loud, warning drums beating within the palace.

"The drums warn of an emergency. What the hell? My mood has been spoiled," complained one noble to his hostess.

The loud beating of the drum was followed by a thundering sound that scared the assembly senseless and destroyed any remaining effects of the alcohol in their systems. Everyone sought to seek cover.

Guards came in panting, barely able to speak, "Maharaj, a missile has been seen flying over the city. An arrow with a message attached to it landed just outside the palace. It came from the mountain region where Prince Ram has been reportedly living. It has a terse message: 'Be here tomorrow at sunrise. Preparations begin now.'"

The entire assembly understood that Ram and his brother had fired a warning shot. The time for indulgences was over, and the time to prepare for battle was upon them!

The next day, after some apologizing from the Vanara for their indulgences and delay, the meeting commenced.

Ram addressed the assembly of thousands of Vanara, "Warriors, get ready to embrace glory and defeat the evil Ravan. Achieve permanent protection of your southern borders. Obtain advanced weaponry. Protect the way of life that stresses enjoyment, but also freedom, justice, culture, and the pursuit of higher, spiritual goals. Har Har Mahadev! Victory to the Great God!"

"Har Har Mahadev," the Vanara roared back.

"Enough of this drug-induced slumber," King Sugriv said to his army. "It is time to fight as warriors for our motherland—for a just cause. Let us sacrifice today to lay the foundation for stability and prosperity for generations to come!" He used both arms to lift his heavy mace over his gold crown.

"Long live the brave king!" his men shouted as they raised their weapons high above their heads.

"I will discuss strategy with your leaders," Ram said. "You will get orders and details from them."

All the leaders walked to a large cave in the Kishkindha Mountains. They sat on stone seats.

Ram wore a coarse cotton white dhoti. His hair tied in matted locks. Heavy metal armor protected his muscular chest. He held a tall, double curved bow in his right hand, two quivers full of arrows tied to his back, and a short sword hung by his waist for close combat.

Ram was a warrior by birth who had become an ascetic to keep his father's word. Lakshman and Hanuman stood by his side.

King Sugriv wore a short red dhoti tied around his waist and tail. His mighty, hairy arms balanced a heavy mace, while a dagger hung by his waistline. He wore thick gold bracelets around his wrists, a pendant with a blue jewel on his chest, and a heavy gold crown studded with a red ruby in the center. He sat attentively, eager to get on with the battle preparations.

Trusted guards protected the entrance and kept an eye out for spies.

Ram stood up from his seat and addressed the assembly of brave men and seasoned warriors. He spoke with a steady, assured, and confident bravado.

"Har Har Mahadev! We are here to strategize about our attack on the island of Lanka. There are several factors that need to be planned meticulously. But, before we get into the details, I want to assure all of you that victory will be ours, because truth and righteousness always win! Jai Mahadev!" Ram paused for a moment. He wanted his allies to reflect on what he said and internalize it. "I can clearly see the red-yellow sun banner of Ayodhya and the flying-ape flag of the Vanara on Lanka."

He walked over to the sand model of Lanka they had built and placed their flags on the highest palace tower that belonged to Ravan.

The military leaders were astonished by this bold assertion, particularly from Ram who was always measured in his words and well controlled in his actions. After all, Ravan was a formidable enemy, especially in his own homeland.

As if reading their minds, Ram continued, "I am not saying it will be easy. It will undoubtedly be hard fought. Some of us will sacrifice our lives, but we ultimately will prevail and annihilate Ravan! That is my word. Agastya Muni has built special weapons and missiles, arranged for a flying machine and chariots in anticipation of this war. They will help us."

Ram observed everyone with a steady gaze. "With the assistance of millions of Vanara, the great warriors assembled here, the great Muni's support, and the power of truth and righteousness, we will be victorious!"

The military leaders finally bought into his vision and sounded a loud battle cry, "Victory to Ram! Victory to the Vanara! Victory will be ours!"

Sugriv said, "My lord, myself and my entire army is at your command. I formally announce you as the commander-in-chief of this war!"

Ram folded his hands and respectfully accepted the role of commander-in-chief. Ram had aligned his team's vision and set a clear goal. "Here are the major tasks and responsibilities. We don't have much time, as I don't know how long Sita can hold off Ravan on her own. She needs help. Hanuman, swim the ocean and travel to the island of Lanka. Locate where Lady Sita is being held and obtain military information such as how the city is protected, defense installations and weapons, important enemy leaders, their specialties and weaknesses, and most importantly, study any divisions to be exploited within the enemy camp. Pick your team and leave right away for your task. Report back in one month."

Hanuman adored Ram as his guru and friend. Now, he also witnessed Ram as a skilled military leader. Hanuman touched Ram's feet in reverence and said, "My Lord, I will leave at once and bring you good news about Lady Sita's well-being." Hanuman knew Ram could not rest for a moment being so worried about Sita. He also knew that one month wouldn't be long enough for the task.

Ram continued, "We will follow the art, science, and principles of Yudh Shastra, the Book of Warfare. Sugriv, make sure we are secure from behind as we march forward. Sign treaties and make peace with friends, and crush Ravan's allies before we move forward. Call all of your troops stationed in different locations throughout the country. Arrange for food, water, and supply lines along our path to the southern ocean. Send advance parties to ensure safe passage."

Sugriv nodded in acknowledgement of the task. He got up, put his heavy mace by his side, and said, "Shree Ram, I will start working on it right away." Sugriv paused for a moment. "One important aspect is the supply of medicinal herbs found in the Himalayas, thousands of miles away. These herbs are short lived. They will be needed to fight Ravan's missiles, radiation, venomous weapons, arrows coated with paralyzing oils, and injuries from maces, spears, harpoons, and axes. I have asked my garrisons stationed to the north to use mechanical devices to cut and transport big chunks of the hills from the Himalayas and bring them all the way over to the ocean to the south. This way, the herbs will be preserved until we need them."

Sugriv brought his experience and knowledge of the land's geography to the preparation strategies.

"Brilliant thinking my friend Sugriv. Excellent! With leaders like you, our victory is assured!" Ram walked up to Sugriv and patted his back. Sugriv folded his hands to show respect. "Another crucial hurdle is building a bridge to cross the ocean to the island of Lanka," Ram said. "The distance is around 100 yojanas, and we will be under attack from Ravan's strong ships, likely firing missiles while we build.

We will deploy a flying machine made available by Agastya Muni for protection. But, we must finish building the bridge in four to five days' time."

Ram looked at the Vanara Nal, and said, "Send Nal to study the tides and survey the ocean for a suitable place to build the bridge. Employ tools made from steel, copper, and diamonds to cut and transport trees and stones that will be needed for construction. Get help from the Muni in locating the ridge that connects to the island. That will serve as a platform for the bridge."

Ram had planned everything out. And, following the Yudh Shastra, he had considered the smallest details that could be decisive in a war against a powerful and malicious enemy.

Ram moved close to Lakshman. Ram said, "Lakshman, you are responsible for the missiles. Transport all the missiles under the cover of the night. Make sure all the Signature Arrows are carried in a special metal covering for protection against radiation. Start working on the transportation immediately. Select five hundred of the bravest Vanara to help you guard the missiles and five thousand to help with the movement. Remember, you will have to do most of the work at night. Stealth and the element of surprise are as important as the missile itself."

"I agree brother. I will coordinate with the Muni and get access to missiles for transportation. We will have a few of the Muni's disciples with us to help operate the weaponry as well." Lakshman cleared his throat and addressed the Vanara as a whole. "I will keep the specific Signature Arrows coated with the same radiation material as the missiles—secure and protected from leaking radiation. When the Signature Arrows hit the target, and produce a small explosion of a particular color and intensity, the technicians will know which type of missile to fire and what the target is." He wanted to be sure that they all understood the procedure. "Only Ram and I have access to these missiles."

All the military personnel felt their confidence levels rise a notch higher.

Hanuman said, "These demons know several tricks to change their appearances, and even in conjuring up fake forms. We need tighter control to make sure the powerful missiles are not misused or fall into the hands of the enemy."

Lakshman nodded in agreement. "In addition to the fact that only Ram and myself have access to the Signature Arrows, as a secondary verification we have to recite a specific hymn in an exact manner and diction to authenticate our identity every day the war goes on. The rendering takes a lot of practice and cannot be mastered in a short time by an imposter. Every morning the hymn is selected randomly from more than a thousand that we have had to memorize for this particular war.

"The missile user, in turn, also verifies the identity of the technicians responsible for launching it. Now, a word about the deadly Universe Missile that is filled with extraordinary radiation. There are additional verifications for the Universe Missile, and only Ram has been taught how to fire it. He is required to do it himself. Before using this missile, that is the messenger of death and misery, he has to say a prayer to take all responsibility for the consequences of firing it. Once it is fired, there is no turning back. The island could be completely destroyed and rendered uninhabitable for hundreds of years as a result," Lakshman concluded.

Everyone was awestruck by the power of these incredible weapons. As the meeting came to an end, a feeling of awe and worry was taking shape in the minds of some of the warriors.

One of the old generals from the Vanara army, colossal in size at seven-and-a-half feet, stood up and declared, "I respect my King Sugriv and his decisions, but the mission we are embarking on is the greatest in scope that I have ever seen." The general was nervous to be speaking against Ram, but felt compelled to express his worry.

His throat clenched, and he said in a hoarse voice, "The scale of the war—the distances, the technology, the mighty enemy—is unheard of. There is no doubt that thousands of Vanara lives will be lost. If we lose the war, our entire race and kingdom will be wiped from the face of the earth—as the demons will surely destroy us completely after their victory. And for what? To find Ram's wife? To thank him for killing Vali by subterfuge? We are happy the way we are. We don't want this gamble."

Some of the other generals nodded in agreement. The whole assembly was stunned by their dissenting voices. Nobody said anything.

The silence proved to be too much for the fiery and volatile Lakshman. He said, "My brother and I don't need your help! We are fully capable of fighting this war on our own. And, speaking of annihilation, we will destroy your kingdom before we leave from here! Remember, your king was roaming around in the jungle when he asked for our help. Your people would have killed themselves anyway due to this fight between the two brothers. Put your tails between your legs and get lost! You are cowards, not warriors!"

King Sugriv was in a precarious situation with a rebellion on one hand and antagonized allies on the other. Sugriv looked to Ram for guidance.

Ram took a deep breath and said in his ever-steady voice, "Please do not mind Lakshman's words. It is his love and devotion to me that came out so aggressively. You are correct General. This is a high risk—high reward situation. Your people could be completely destroyed or permanently secure and prosperous for thousands of years. You have to decide if you are up to it. I can take care of securing my Lady Sita with or without your help. But, you have to decide what kind of society you want to live in—one that is brave and righteous, or one that settles for the way things are, and is always on guard for the next attack. You are encircled by demons from the south and north. And, as long as they have the island as their base, you will never be secure. You decide what you want to do and let me know. There will be respect for your decision no matter what you choose."

Hanuman watched the proceeding quietly before he stepped forward. "We have given our word to Shree Ram. We swore an oath to him when he helped us against former King Vali. Does our word mean nothing?" His reflection appealed to the moral side of his fellow Vanara. After a pause, he added, "In addition to the future security of our kingdom, there is another big reason why you should walk this path with Shree Ram…" Hanuman looked squarely at the dissenting general. "You have these doubts in your mind because you don't know your true nature. By Ram's grace, I have realized the true nature of life. Let me help you do the same, and all your doubts will be destroyed."

Hanuman took a few steps from his seat. He took off his metal helmet and placed it on his seat. He walked bare footed. The silver anklet around his right foot sparkled in the daylight. He walked on the hard floor with a steady gait. He approached Ram, bent on one knee, and touched Ram's feet with his fingers. He ran those fingers through his long hair, depicting that Ram had blessed him.

Ram smiled gently and gave him a special arrow. Hanuman took the arrow and passed it among the leaders sitting along the cave wall. After all the leaders had handled the arrow, Hanuman took it in his hands again, and sat in a meditative state. The leaders followed his example. Hanuman guided them along their meditation.

In a few moments, the leaders experienced an extraordinary energy inside them. Their experience was beyond the physical dimensions. Some, who were more spiritually inclined, had tears rolling down their faces. Everything became clear to them spontaneously. It was a very simple and straightforward realization once they stopped the constant buzz of their minds.

Hanuman spoke gently, "We have to perform our duty as warriors, and everything else will follow." Hanuman looked around at his fellow Vanara and smiled. I know you cannot express what you just experienced. Let me help with that."

He thought for a little while, then said, "Energy is constantly flowing, and we see its effects in the world around us. The effects we see and feel in our world are—day follows night, water flows from the top of the waterfall to the bottom, wind blows from higher nipida, or pressure, to lower nipida, planets go about moving in their orbits, etc. These are all results of energy flow. These physical objects don't do anything as such. Similarly, you simply must be the instrument for the energy to manifest. That is all. Follow your duty as warriors to the best of your abilities, let the energy work through you, then you will have the ability to create the future you want. Just say 'Ram' whenever you want to get in touch with your true nature. And your true nature is that of the creator of the world around you. Jai Mahadev!"

The warriors felt completely recharged by Hanuman's lucid explanation and their extraordinary meditative experiences. The dissenting general was overwhelmed by the realization of this simple, yet profound, truth. He said, "Hanuman, you have shown us our true nature. We have realized that we are beyond this physical body. With a yogi like you on our side, we realize that death is just related to this body. We will do our duty and not run away from it to protect this puny body and mind. We will perform our duty as warriors, and because we are righteous, we will create a world where we are victorious. Jai Shree Ram!"

"Jai Shree Ram. Victory will be ours!" Hanuman cheered.

The chiranjeevi, or long-lived, Hanuman became a guru to others on their journey toward truth. Ram smiled gently at Hanuman. In addition to being a great warrior, a long-lived Vanara, and yogi, Hanuman had also become an excellent guru.

Ram's faith in Hanuman's abilities and character was not misplaced. He thought, *Hanuman appears to be an excellent choice for the task of staying on Earth for a long time—potentially, thousands of years—to guide others!* Ram kept his thoughts to himself for the time being. Everybody got to work on their assigned tasks with renewed energy and urgency. There was little time to lose and a tremendous amount of work to be done!

CHAPTER 12

DESPAIR: HUMANS ARE BEYOND HELP

~~~~~~~

Modern Day

~~~~~~~

The pearl.

WOW! LOOK AT THESE PARTICLES SMASHING INTO EACH other at light speed. And they're revealing their components while generating new particles in the process. We need the data from the Compact Muon Solenoid. We also need results from the High-Luminosity Large Hadron Collider. This data will provide boundary conditions, constants, and inflection points for Ramanujan's equations. This is tremendous—worth ten research papers at least! What a facility!" Krish said to his colleagues at CERN. He was beyond excited about his experiments and the work being done at CERN.

"I'm particularly interested in seeing the results of run 16256, where we changed the detector setting downstream to see if it influenced the behavior of particles up stream and 16300 where we applied an external force," Krish could barely keep his excitement, curiosity, and anticipation under control. "Thanks a lot Anton. I'll send you my results for review," Krish said to the great professor.

"I hope the 'God Damn' particle does appear in your work, for verification of earlier results. Otherwise, we will have to conclude that it just appeared once to tell us not to keep looking," Anton said with a deadpan expression.

"I need to slice and dice the data. I'll have to connect with my graduate advisor, Dave, and lab mates, Kathy and Mark," Krish said.

"I'll join you, and will just have to tolerate the sunny Southern California weather and beaches. I must say, I'll miss the cold, cloudy weather tremendously. Now that we're not part of the European Union, we're truly an island," Anton said referencing his homeland of England. He moved his wheel chair in a circle, depicting the island.

"Sounds good professor," Krish chuckled. "See you at Cal Tech."

Krish analyzed the data at Cal Tech with his advisor and colleagues using NASA's Pleiades supercomputer. He had all the mathematics and data in front of him—several research articles in top rated journals with very high impact factors. But, Krish thought that some pieces of the puzzle were still missing.

"In all this work, I can't figure out what could be bigger than the sum of the individual parts. Something is hidden in plain sight, and I can't see it," Krish said to Kathy, placing his head in his hands. Kathy nodded in agreement. They dove silently into further data analysis and mathematical proofs.

Krish invited Prisha to be with him in Pasadena. She was busy getting the visa and other paperwork arranged. From his conversations with her, it was clear that her psychosis was getting worse. Krish wanted the two of them to stay together so that he could support her through this.

It was a cool, cloudy day in Pasadena. Krish was enjoying a relaxed Sunday afternoon at his home. His neighborhood was very quiet. He closed his eyes and took stock of all the progress he had made in the last couple of months. He looked at his exquisite, ancient arrow.

As he sat, he slowly started noticing his breath and could feel his lungs expanding and contracting. Then, he noticed his individual heartbeats. He was feeling very relaxed and in the moment. The breeze blew the long, white window curtains gently and caressed his body. Krish felt very well-rested and energized. He sat on the floor, enjoying the silence of his surroundings, and more importantly, the silence of his mind. He turned on the tap and aerated water came out, making a gentle sound as the water drops sparkled in the sunlight from the window.

When you're present in the moment, Krish thought, *you can experience real joy in the smallest things. Otherwise, you cannot find joy in even the grandest of palaces.* Krish visualized that his research was complete and that the truth of life had been revealed. He was internally enjoying the success of his quest.

"Uhhhhhhhh, sons of bitches," Krish heard a beastly, shrieking voice outside his window. His blissful state was shattered. He ran down to see what was going on. What he saw was absolutely mind boggling… and heartbreaking.

His dreams had collided violently with his reality. In his doorway was Prisha! She wore blue jeans, a black top, and sneakers. She was standing there with her carry-on and check-in bags. Her strong shoulders, long legs, and athletic body maintained in an erect posture. The cab that dropped her off had already left. She looked bewildered, confused, and agitated. Her eyes had the emptiness of a crazy person that had lost a part of their soul.

Her knees were hurt due to a fall. She couldn't stand properly. Her hair was disheveled, lips dry. Her face looked devoid of vitality. It was clear from her expression that she was thoroughly confused, lost, hurt, and angry.

"Fuck off," she shouted, looking toward the street as if someone was standing there hurling invisible insults at her. There wasn't anyone there. Prisha was in the middle of a strong auditory hallucination and a complete nervous breakdown. Her smart, intelligent mind was clouded by out of control emotions and thoughts. Krish felt that she needed a hug to calm her down. As he touched her to initiate the hug, she screamed, "Don't touch me scumbag, or I'll call the police."

Although he was trying to comprehend that this was her disease talking, Krish was hurt and slightly angry to be talked to this way.

She still stood in the doorway, shouting loudly. Somehow, Krish got her inside the house and closed the door. He showed her the bedroom, she was completely consumed by her thoughts. She changed, took a shower, and went straight to sleep.

Krish couldn't believe that the tall, confident, pretty, successful girl in her stylish pant suit who came to drop him off at the airport just a few days ago seemed like a totally different person from another planet here and now. That girl was full of life and hope. The woman standing in front of him had been destroyed from the inside by her own relatives and colleagues.

Krish thought, *the human desire for inflicting violence has changed the means of expression over the years. Humans have replaced spears and swords with toxic words and sharp back-stabbings as instruments of battle in the jungle of life. The former wounded and maimed people's bodies. The latter strikes their hearts and minds. If humans were aware of their true power, they wouldn't do such things. And even if they did, the victims, if self-realized, wouldn't be affected. Oh! My work needs to succeed so that people will know their power and won't suffer!*

With Krish's support and guidance, Prisha was receiving treatment for her mental illness by a psychiatrist and a therapist.

One evening, Krish and Prisha went out for a walk. The twilight sky seemed like a magnificent backdrop to the human drama unfolding. The dark blue looking mountains were like spectators enjoying the action. Tall trees with their brown branches and green leaves decorated the scene. Kids were playing by a water fountain. The girls gracefully jumped over small stones and landed beautifully on their toes, like butterflies moving from flower to flower. The boys were splashing around, wrestling each other, catching a ball, and frolicking. It was a relaxing scene.

"Let's go out for dinner tonight. I don't feel like cooking," she said.

Krish and Prisha drove to the world-renowned chef Niki Nakayama's n/naka restaurant in Los Angeles. The simplicity, elegance, and rhythm of the food served, along with the leisurely pace, provided a great experience.

"The owner, Niki, broke into the male-dominated world of Japanese chefs with her new way of thinking and her talent. I need to get back to work to take my mind off this illness," Prisha said, more to herself than to Krish.

Krish clasped her fingers in his gently, indicating his support.

"I'll pitch my projects to venture capitalists in Silicon Valley," she promised. "IOT is an upcoming area in the US too. I'll start brushing up my business plan first thing in the morning."

"Sounds like a plan, sweetie," Krish said. "I'm proud of you, Prisha. Show them how it's done!"

Prisha travelled several times to the San Francisco Bay area, San Diego, and Boston, meeting several venture capitalists. She presented her business plan, leveraging her experience in the IOT business space.

Krish accompanied her on one such trip. He could see that the venture capitalists sensed something was off. One investor was very candid with her.

"Miss, you have impressive qualifications and experience, but you're a newcomer with no product. You don't have a team here in the US—the market here is totally different. I suggest you take a step back, work at a company, get familiar with the conditions here in the US, build your team, and then start your own business," the investor advised. Sensing that Prisha was heartbroken, the investor decided to demoralize her further. "We need some whack jobs in the arena to take risks, but not on my money, sorry! We have too many chiefs already. We need some Indians too!"

People, being people, won't miss an opportunity to attack someone who is down on luck.

On the drive home, Prisha raged, "Did you hear that? I'm a whack job!"

"These kinds of things happen, Prisha," Krish said, "Some investors think they're angels who descended from the heavens and that everyone else is beneath them. You've got to be able to handle such things and move on."

Ordinarily, Prisha would brush off blunt and offensive comments, but with her psychosis and paranoia, she was vulnerable to verbal volleys.

"Oh my God, these people in my head. They're everywhere now! They don't want me to work. They want me to be a failure and a loser. I can't take these insults," Prisha said pressing her palms tightly over her ears and screaming loudly.

Krish tried to calm her. He could hardly focus on driving. Somehow, he managed to make it back home safely.

Prisha continued seeing her psychiatrist regularly. Her symptoms would blow up from time to time, interspersed with periods of relative calm.

Krish was performing a balancing act between his research and the ups and downs of his wife's mental health.

One such evening, he came back home from work. *What's it going to be today? Calm or agitated?* Krish wondered, trying to guess Prisha's mood as he drove home. He opened the door. It was dark inside; none of the lights were turned on.

"Prisha," he called, "are you home?" There was no reply. He turned on the lights downstairs and poured a glass of water for himself. *Maybe she went out to get groceries,* he thought. He turned on the TV and watched a new documentary he had recorded. He opened the fridge and had a slice of leftover pizza, then went upstairs to change. He opened the bedroom door and turned on the light. What he saw left him dumbfounded. His lips went dry, he took a step back, and reached out to the wall for support. He felt light headed and dizzy. The rise of bile in the back of his throat threatened to breakthrough.

"Oh my God…" he said under his breath. Prisha lay on their Victorian bed dressed in her red nightgown. She had a gun lying near her right hand, and the beige colored bed sheet was soaked in blood. Krish stood there, staring, unable to move, unable to breathe. He was numb. The sight brought back harrowing memories of the shootings he had witnessed. But it was even more horrifying to see his own wife—the woman he loved—lying there, bloodied, wounded, and possibly dead.

A few moments had passed, and his mind began to understand what he was seeing. He mentally passed the point where he could either panic or think rationally. His mind chose clarity. The enormity of the problem in front of him brought sharp focus, and his priorities became clear. He tried to put some mental distance between himself and the situation at hand, so as to not to be overpowered by it.

He adjusted his glasses, stood erect, and took a sharp breath. *Number one: see if she's alive. Number two: don't get in trouble with the law. Number three: call for help. Number four: you are alone in a foreign land—take care of yourself so that you can take care of her.*

He observed her. Krish could feel warm, shallow breath on the finger he held near her nose. Prisha's eyes were closed. She actually looked peaceful. Her mind was finally silent. She felt alive. The blood came from near her shoulder. There was a good chance that the bullet had missed her heart. He called 911.

Krish sat in the emergency room waiting area. The ambulance had taken Prisha directly inside. He was soon called in and after the nurse ascertained that he was okay, he was allowed inside Prisha's room through a sliding door.

Prisha was intubated; her wounds dressed. The attending physician informed Krish that all of her vital signs were stable, and that she was out of danger, but heavily medicated. The doctor finished talking to Krish and turned to consult with her nurse. She was interrupted by an announcement over the PA system.

"Code yellow, CBRN, chief to triage," reported a calm voice. Krish didn't know what to make of it, but the attending physician and nurse knew exactly what the code meant. They looked at each other to confirm they had heard correctly. Shades of fear and worry appeared in the eyes of the young nurse. Her shoulders dropped a bit, as if due to something heavy in the pit of her stomach. Her body tensed, her fight or flight response ready, as she felt a surge of adrenaline.

The doctor's eyes reflected authority and determination. Years of training and practice were kicking in. "Let's go save lives," she said to the nurse in a calm, but stern, voice. They dropped everything and ran toward the entrance of the ER, hurriedly shoving their stethoscopes in their pockets.

Krish checked his cell phone for breaking news. CNN reported developing stories about a bomb explosion in New York, a pair of traumatized brothers in Syria and the Olympics.

"I wish it was just the Olympics in the news today," Krish sighed and clicked on the news coverage about explosions in NYC. Reports showed victims with intense flash burns, possibly due to radiation. He didn't see any news about Los Angeles, however.

The ER chief, Dr. Guss, briefed all the doctors, surgeons, nurses, and visitors. He was an African American man in his late fifties—bald, clean-shaven, and tall, with a fatherly, compassionate appearance. He seemed like the type of person whom people would naturally rally around, particularly in a crisis. The chief took off his glasses and spoke in a clear tone with a sense of urgency, but not panic.

"I am chief of the emergency department. We're getting reports of a chemical, biological, radiological, nuclear, or CBRN scenario. Tens to hundreds of patients are coming in. In addition to the regular SOP with mass casualty situations—such as cancelling non-urgent surgeries and emptying rooms—special precautions are needed for radiation situations."

He paused to see the reaction of those assembled. "It's not clear yet, but paramedics are reporting elevated readings on Geiger counters. Dr. Wilson will manage triage and label patients for treatment as green, yellow, or red. He will maintain a safe zone where patient's external clothing will be removed to reduce additional radiation exposure, and they will be decontaminated. This is a mass casualty situation, so no need to contain the run off. Put on your personnel protective equipment, or PPE. Don't take the risk of not wearing it.

It's the last line of defense. I'll get information on radiation levels—alpha, beta, gamma, neutrons—and identify radio isotopes-plutonium, U-235 or U-238, cesium-137, cobalt-60 or other, so that appropriate treatments can be deployed. We need to know what we are dealing with. Most victims are burn victims," Dr. Guss concluded.

As the patients started rolling in, it was difficult to look at them. Faces, backs, chests, hands, and legs were burned—flesh left hanging at some places. People were screaming in pain. Some were searching for their loved ones. Dr. Guss was trying to maintain a steady pace as he made his way around the ER. Soon, the hospital was at capacity and couldn't take any more incoming patients.

"The radiation levels are very low," Dr. Wilson said. Dr. Guss didn't know why the radiation readings were so low when the burns were so intense. They were not as prominent as a nuclear explosion would suggest.

Dr. Wilson said, "I have an update from my source in the federal government. It's much worse in New York. They had an actual nuclear explosion there. Here, it seems that we have just encountered a dirty bomb—no uncontrolled fission reaction that would cause a nuclear explosion. Another difference between the situations, is that New York is tightly packed. The terrorists exploded the nuclear bomb at ground level. But here, they used a drone and exploded it above ground to spread the shrapnel and radioactive material over a large area. There is no nuclear reaction to our explosion here, and the radioactive material was not purified before use. Hence, the low radiation measurements in patients."

"You're right. So basically, we're dealing with burn victims," Dr. Guss summarized.

"Correct," said Dr. Wilson.

In a few hours, more details started emerging. Thousands of people had perished in New York, and fifty-five had lost their lives in LA. It was a terrible day. Everybody was stunned by the naked display of violence unleashed on the nation's two largest cities. News anchors could barely contain their sorrow as they broke more ghastly details about the terrible incidents. The television images of vaporized bodies, charred remains, death, and destruction made the whole environment gloomy, angry, and depressing.

Krish saw the burned and charred bodies, severed body parts, disfigured corpses with parts cut off brought in the hospital; the ugliness of it all was a slap in the face. *Man is such an ugly son-of-a-bitch. Man—the so-called pinnacle of evolution—is also a pinnacle of sordidness. Nature kills with finesse—even when it destroys with overwhelming power.*

Krish remembered the rumblings in Pasadena as he experienced an earthquake. The awesome power of the earthquake hitting, shaking everything, and passing through him. The whole house shook like a toy.

When nature kills—be it with floods, earthquakes, or wild fires—there is power, awe, and destruction, but not ugliness. When man destroys, it's ugly, macabre. It's driven by hatred and animosity—be it destruction in the form of murders, wars, riots, or terrorism. Man is so messed up and violent. In his mind, and physically, he does not deserve to be saved. Man deserves to be damned, Krish thought with disgust. He needed a break from what was happening around him. He went to the cafeteria and got some coffee. He held the hot paper cup in both hands to absorb the warmth as he sat there, staring blankly.

The smell of death, fear, and destruction was all pervading. It turned out to be a long and sad day—for him personally and for the country as a whole. The terror attacks exacerbated his own feelings of loss and loneliness. Krish's breathing was shallow. His eyes reddened due to stress. He had a tingling feeling in his lower jaw, and his heart rate was faster than usual. He took a deep, conscious breath, as if the few extra seconds to fill his lungs would give his body a break from the stress and strain of the situation. He felt a strange sensation on his tongue that eliminated any desire for food or drink. He dumped his coffee down the drain, thinking, *I don't taste it anyway.* He felt his stomach churning as acid was rising up in his esophagus.

At that moment of vulnerability, he thought about drowning his nightmarish life in alcohol—anything to take the edge off. He pondered it for a moment, then decided not to act. He let the thought pass. Krish thought about the possibility of Prisha's death. It felt like death was all around him that day—untimely death imposed by man upon another man. The physicality and reality of death hit him hard. Death was not some abstract idea. It was real, and it was right in front of him and all around him. Everywhere.

Is there anything more to life or is this it? He wondered. *When it comes to death, nothing matters but the truth—if there is any—of who or what you really are beyond the physical body and the associated mind. The futility of it all—the money, fame, power, mind games, physical beauty, fashion, cars, jewelry-in pursuit of which, man spends entire lifetimes; it's all so completely meaningless and hollow. Even relationships don't help.*

After this realization, he felt as if the weight of the nonsensical had been lifted from his shoulders. He felt a strange sense of relief, power, and focus. *Only the truth remains. All other acquired layers of mind, body, relationships, and society don't matter at all. I finally feel like I'm cutting to the chase and coming to the point of it all. Witnessing death can be the best teacher. A brush with death is the force that acts as the parasite that enters an oyster and stimulates a secretion of material that eventually forms a priceless pearl! My research is not just some bull crap mental gymnastics about life and death. It's getting to the truth of it all. Mathematically. Unequivocally!*

"And I *will* get to it," Krish said aloud with renewed determination.

CHAPTER 13
THE WAR

~~~~~~~

Ancient India

~~~~~~~

A way of life is destroyed.

Brother Ram," Lakshman said, "please put on this woolen shawl. It is biting cold."

Ram was sitting on a massive rock within his cave. He opened his eyes from the meditative state he was enjoying. "Lakshman, I don't care about the cold. What must my Sita be doing? I am worried sick for her. It has been several months since she was abducted."

Lakshman looked down, running his hand over the stubble on his chin. "Two months have passed since Hanuman left to verify her location. No updates yet." He had barely finished his sentence when loud cheers and shouts were heard from outside. "What is all the noise?" he wondered. He instinctively took out his double-edged, straight-blade sword from its sheath, placing his left hand on the Asi tucked near his waist. He would be ready to pull it out in a flash if necessary.

Ram said calmly, "Lakshman, we are in our own camp. No need to draw weapons."

"But brother, our enemy, Ravan, has an impressive spy network. And, they are well trained in conjuring various forms. You can never be too careful."

Ram nodded his head lightly, stood up from his seat, and looked in the direction of the commotion. At that instant, a Vanara guard entered the cave with a beaming smile upon his face. He somersaulted in the air to express his happiness.

"Hanuman and his troops have returned after completing their mission! They appear to have good news."

Cries of 'Victory to Shree Ram! Har Har Mahadev!' could be heard approaching the cave and growing louder. Hanuman entered with folded hands. He looked absolutely joyful.

He put his mace down and reported, "Shree Ram, I was able to swim the ocean as I found resting places on ridges and small islands. I entered Lanka in the disguise of an ape roaming around, looking for food. I located Lady Sita and assured her that you are coming to free her."

Ram was delighted to hear the news and embraced Hanuman like a brother. He stroked Hanuman on the back several times, expressing his utmost gratitude. Hearing Sita's name stirred several emotions in Ram's heart.

"She is very strong. I found that she is under house arrest," Hanuman further informed. "Lady Sita is holding on to her will power and sternly resisting Ravan's advances. She is safe for now." His gaze suddenly went to the floor, and he added in a low voice, "The situation could turn at any moment... she could be in danger."

Ram frowned and his brother grabbed his sword, itching to attack Ravan right then and there.

Hanuman met Ram's eyes again. "I noted all military installations and defenses on Lanka. One of Ravan's brothers doesn't support the abduction of Lady Sita. He is ready to desert and join our army when we reach the sea shore."

Lakshman said, "It is a hedging strategy. This way, he will ensure the survival of their kind and avoid the complete destruction of Lanka in the war."

Ram said, "That could be the reason, or he may have a genuine disagreement with Ravan. Hanuman, tell me everything about Ravan. I want to be able to visualize him. I need every minute detail."

Hanuman nodded, "Here is a profile of Ravan. I challenged him to a fight to get a glimpse of his prowess. Ravan is a colossal man, seven feet tall, weighing close to 300 pounds. He is lighter in skin tone than the army of demons he commands. He uses his muscular chest, mighty arms, and long slender fingers to easily wield his massive mace—with the same finesse as he masterfully handles the musical instrument, Veena. He has a huge handlebar mustache, thick beard, and long, black hair. His eyes always look drunk with power and contempt, and it is apparent that his lust has overshadowed a knowledgeable soul deep inside. He wore a special helmet made from a single piece of steel that is impenetrable by design, and adorned by a huge, blue diamond. He wore a white silk dhoti with a red embroidered border and intricately carved, robust armor. Ravan is a brave warrior, lover of art and beauty, and very learned, but his lust and ego have completely dominated his very being."

Ram listened carefully to Hanuman, trying to construct a picture of Ravan in his mind's eye. "He sounds like a gifted warrior and a scholarly, capable person. But, because of his actions, Karma will lead to his annihilation. Hanuman, may Lord Mahadev bless you for completing this crucial task."

"Great work Hanuman," Sugriv praised. "We need to know as many details as possible to be successful. Only you could have accomplished this near impossible mission. We are grateful. Our own preparations are going well. We have transported rocks and small hills containing medicinal herbs to the shore of the southern ocean. We used mechanical means to cut the rock. After that, it was mostly muscle power. We employed pulleys, ropes, and huge carts driven by hundreds of Vanara, bears, and elephants for transportation. We also used chemical energy sources to help with transportation."

Sugriv was overjoyed with their progress. He looked toward Lakshman, who he knew used to look down upon the ape-men, and said, "Good thing the scientists bred us this way isn't it? To be of super human strength. Otherwise, Lakshman would have to fire his missiles to burn down the hills and somehow transport the charred rocks." Sugriv's sarcasm did not go unrecognized.

Lakshman smiled, shook his head, and acknowledged his mistake.

Sugriv said, "We have made ample arrangements for food and water for millions of Vanara, cut trees and rocks for the bridge, and transported missiles. All the ground work is done."

"My friend Sugriv," Ram said, "I am forever indebted to you and the Vanara. I assure you that the apes will always be treated with love and respect in this land. You have done a great job. I could not have done this without your help, bravery, and strength." Ram hugged Sugriv warmly. The two walked out of the cave perched on the mountaintop.

The Vanara army was waiting on the plane below. Ram decided to put on some fireworks to charge up the troops. He raised his bow and fired an arrow into the sky. It was coated with explosives. In rapid succession, he shot another arrow with a fiery head. It hit the first arrow and made a thunderous sound. The technicians, who were always at the ready, saw the signal. They launched a type of missile that resembled an arrow without a head. The missile had a cylindrical metal portion containing explosives within. It made a deafening boom as it flew in the sky. Ram shot a fiery arrow precisely at the tip of the cylinder, causing it to explode. Given the distance from the ground, the impressive display was harmless. The Vanara cheered wildly as they gazed upon the dazzling show in the sky.

"Lanka, here we come to destroy you!" the apes roared. Cries of 'Har Har Mahadev! Jai Shree Ram!' filled the land.

The million-strong Vanara crossed three mountain ranges on their way to the southern ocean. The number of troops swelled as more fighters stationed for food supply and other duties joined the marching army. Road clearance and forward-march parties ensured safe passage of troops.

Ram, Sugriv, and Hanuman marched at the head of the army. The force was sub-divided into several groups of approximately a hundred thousand fighters, each led by a general. Lakshman led a team of special forces tasked with transporting missiles. Most of the army was unaware of their movement, which occurred mostly at night. There were more than five hundred missiles of various kinds that needed to be transported. Secrecy and the element of surprise were as important as the missiles themselves.

It was an autumn night. Hanuman was strolling through his camp to get a first-hand account of any difficulties the soldiers were experiencing. He saw a pair of soldiers were busy moving a heavy rock in the dead of the night with only torches tied to trees for light.

The Vanara said to his buddy, "For the first time, I feel as if I am fighting a war I believe in."

His companion agreed, "I feel like I am part of something historic, something much bigger than myself. Hanuman has provided a glimpse of something beyond this body, and it feels amazing. Ram and Hanuman are great leaders and teachers. They are leading us on the righteous path. I feel energy constantly oozing inside me, tirelessly, and it feels invigorating."

Hanuman smiled as he overheard their conversation. *I am glad the morale of the troops is high*, he thought and continued with his walk. Recognizing the historic nature of the war, students were embedded within the army. They noted every detail of the geography, seasons, and landscape to maintain accurate records for the posterity.

"Kindly note the seasonal changes and planetary positions," Hanuman instructed a student from the ashram who was traveling with the army.

The student replied, "Commander Hanuman, as we march to Lanka, the sky looks clear. Venus shines brightly, Dhruva-pole star and the seven sages-Ursa Major are seen shinning. Star Trishanku, Acrux, and his companion star shine ahead of us as we march southward. The Vishakha constellation is not affected by the unfavorable influence of Saturn or Mars, however, the constellation Moola is affected by a comet with a bright tail."

"Excellent work," Hanuman said. "I express gratitude for your important role in this historic event!" The student looked at Hanuman with a steady gaze, joined his palms together in Namaste to acknowledge the gesture, and got on with his work.

Hanuman remembered what the Muni had told him before the army marched toward Lanka: "In this hot and humid climate, it is difficult to preserve history through building monuments. Our plan is to compile all the details regarding Ram and this war into a grand epic. We will include all the vital information with flowery language, and tell it like a story, so that it can be transmitted for thousands of years—from generation to generation." Hanuman clearly remembered. The Muni had gazed at the sky and added, "Only truth lasts for thousands of years. Lies do not."

The Vanara army reached the shores of the southern ocean. The chief engineer had already picked an area with a ridge and shoals to build the bridge. They waited a few days for the low tide.

The chief engineer addressed the troops, "We will use wood from Sala, Asvakarna, Bamboo, Kutaja, Tilaka, Bilva, Saptaparna, Karnika, Mango, Asoka, and other trees to build the bridge. We have prepared long ropes to keep the structure straight. We will maintain the curvature, length, and breadth of the bridge to keep it stable for millions of Vanara to pass over."

"What about enemy ships and their attacks?" asked a soldier.

"I will let Hanuman address that," said the engineer.

"Don't worry, you are safe. We have small bands of soldiers who swam to the exposed shoals and ridges. They are protecting those areas until our arrival. Our flying machine will protect the bridge from attack. We plan to finish construction within four to five days. Let us get to work!"

The Vanara shouted, "Victory will be ours! Victory to Shree Ram!"

Precisely following the plan, the bridge was built with great enthusiasm and urgency.

One of Ravan's brothers, who was more ethical and felt isolated and cornered, had joined Ram.

After reaching Lanka, Ram addressed the army from a hilltop. "Our messenger just returned from conducting diplomatic talks with Ravan. Talks have failed. Our last attempt at peace has been rejected by Ravan. War it is!" Ram raised his bow high up in the air and pulled the string, symbolizing the onset of the war.

The entire army joined him, "War it is! Victory to Mahadev!"

"The war begins at sunrise," Ram said. "The enemy thinks of us as silly apes, monkeys, and bears led by a forest-dweller. We need to destroy their confidence. We are on their island far away from home. We cannot support a prolonged war. We need to keep this fight brief and destroy the enemy in a short time." Ram gestured to Hanuman.

Hanuman lifted his heavy mace off the ground, rested it on his shoulder, and announced, "The first attack will be an overwhelming one that will shake Lanka to the core and instill fear in their dark hearts. This will entice them to bring out their best warriors, weapons, and technology immediately when we are at our best—not worn out after a prolonged war. We will attack all four gates of the city simultaneously!"

"Jai Mahadev!" the entire army roared in one voice. The moment they had been preparing for all these months had finally arrived. They were eager to see it through.

Hanuman continued, "Two divisions of a hundred thousand Vanara each will attack the four gates of Lanka. Two divisions will be on reserve in the hills for reinforcement as needed."

Sugriv stepped in. "Medical camps are on the other side of the hill, along the beach. Medicinal supplies and herbs brought in from the Himalayas have been transported from the peninsula to the island."

Ram gestured for everyone to sit down. He led them through a deep meditation exercise. After the meditation, the ape king Sugriv exclaimed, "The fear of death has been killed from our hearts and our minds. We fight and die without fear!"

All the Vanara raised their weapons and shouted, "No fear! Victory to Shree Ram!"

And so the war began. On this, the first day of battle, unending hordes of Rakshas with arrows, maces, javelins, three-pointed weapons, chariots, and elephants poured out of Lanka in various battle formations. The Rakshas rammed full force into thousands of Vanara. The apes were arranged in formations of their own to counter the enemy tactics.

War cries and sounds of metal colliding filled the battlefield. Both sides fought valiantly. The land was quickly becoming littered with broken bones, limbs, smashed heads, and dismembered torsos. Streams of blood flowed everywhere. Weapons and chariots had been thoroughly destroyed in the battle—the debris lying amongst the carcasses of elephants and horses, Vanara and Rakshas alike. Vultures and jackals gathered for a feast. Freshly cut heads, arms, feet, and torsos moved erratically with involuntary motion. Blood flowed from wounds and loud screams of pain were heard from those who still clung to life. It was a macabre scene.

Ram, Lakshman, and Hanuman suffered from wounds all over their bodies. Their armor and weapons were soaked in blood. The city of Lanka—once enriched by Ravan's conquests from lands far away—shuddered at the sight of death and destruction at its doorstep. Ram had taken the battle deep into enemy territory, directly at their center of power. He had kicked a powerful enemy in his gut. There was no turning back now! Only one side would survive, and the other would be completely destroyed. Forever.

The fighting stopped at the end of the first day—per the rules of warfare. Both armies returned to their camps exhausted and broken. Soldiers from both sides were busy carrying the dead to a distinguished cremation site or for burial at sea. The wounded were taken to the beach for treatment. Medics applied various herbs and painkillers to the wounds. The cool breeze provided much needed relief for everyone. The reserve ranks were now at the forefront and had circled the resting and injured soldiers in a maneuver of protection.

Suddenly, in the dead of the night, loud warning sounds from the dholak and bells were heard. Shouts and emergency signals from sentries manning watch towers spread like wild fire. The Rakshas had attacked the Vanara camp, violating the rules of warfare. They stomped upon bodies of dead soldiers, flesh and blood, to carry out the surprise raid. However, the sudden attack was successfully repelled by the vigilant Vanara guards.

Hanuman said calmly, "It shows that our strategy has worked. Lanka is shaken from day one, and in a moment of desperation, they attacked us after sunset and broke the code of battle."

Ram nodded in agreement. He held his mighty bow high and shouted, "We continue with our offense and kill the minor leaders as soon as possible. Our leaders should not waste time fighting the enemy troops. Attack and kill their captains and generals right away. That is an order by your commander!"

Over the next two days, Lanka generals and captains were targeted and killed without reluctance. Ravan was annoyed by his losses. He blamed the ministers for their misguided strategy. He was frustrated by their incompetence. He shouted, "You good-for-nothing ministers need to be sent out to be killed in this war."

Controlling his frustration, he nearly growled, "These monkeys and forest-dwellers want to create panic in my ranks. I have not use my best weapons and technology to protect my island from the destructive power of those weapons. I wanted to draw out this war! But this forest-dweller has forced my hand. The enemy will see the full extent of Lanka's power now! Send my giant brother to the battlefield tomorrow. He has struck fear in enemy hearts for years. He is powerful beyond measure. He will win this war in one mighty swipe."

The next day at dawn, powerful missiles rained from Lanka. Fully anticipating this tactic, the Vanara army fired its own missiles from high in the hills to get a precise angle and accurate shot.

An enormous man emerged from the gates of Lanka.

"What the hell is that?" yelled a Vanara soldier in panic.

The apes dropped their weapons in shock at the sight of such a monster. It was Ravan's ten-foot-tall brother. He was sitting inside a fifty-foot-tall mechanical device that he controlled by sheer muscle power and a series of levers and shafts. The huge skeleton was made of iron and reinforced with steel, or Ayas. The structure imitated the appearance of a man, and was coated with heat resistant materials. The metal-monster was guarded and fed with weapons by hundreds of demons that walked behind it.

There were soldiers inside the huge mechanical structure as well. It was launching a continuous torrent of javelins, axes, chakras—sharp metal discs—and arrows from various openings. Hundreds of Vanara were crushed under its heavy feet. It was an ingenuous killing machine designed by the Lanka army. It was impossible to get close enough to even attempt a counter-attack. The steel beast created havoc amongst the Vanara ranks. It seemed the only option was to flee for their lives.

Hanuman said to Lakshman, "You must deal with this surprise enemy tactic. I will make sure you don't get flanked."

Lakshman agreed. He attacked the monster, firing powerful arrows, but they did not make even the slightest difference in the enemy's advances. "I need to get closer to this thing," he yelled to his captain. As Lakshman crept closer, a javelin was shot from the monster from a great height. The blow broke his armor and pierced his shoulder, even as he tried to dodge it.

"You are bleeding," his captain shouted. "We need to get you out of here!" He raised a flag indicating that an important soldier had been hit. Hanuman saw the flag and rushed to his aide. He formed a protective perimeter around Lakshman and removed him from the battlefield. Thousands of Vanara were slaughtered that day.

Hanuman shook his head, looked down, and said dejectedly, "A bad day for us. What are we going to do about this monster?"

Emboldened by their upper hand, the Rakshas army continued their fight into the evening.

The next day, Lakshman watched from the hilltop as the two armies crashed into each other relentlessly.

"I wish I could fight," Lakshman said impatiently as he looked at his injured shoulder. "I should be down there." He felt deeply disappointed in himself.

Hanuman took a break from the battle and came to the hilltop to check on Lakshman and to rest. "Another awful day. We have lost thousands of soldiers. It's heartbreaking to watch. That monster is a killing machine. We just don't know what to do!" Hanuman wiped blood from his mace and hands. Despite the winter season, he was drenched in sweat; the high humidity did not help either. He drank some water obtained from a fresh-water lake.

Hanuman and Lakshman observed the battlefield from the hilltop. The monster towered high above the sea of two armies. It was surrounded by dead and maimed soldiers.

"It reminds me of those tall coconut trees on the beach…the ones that tower above the ocean," Hanuman said to take his mind off the war and think about more peaceful times. "We uprooted a lot of them for the bridge. They look intimidating, but fall easily because they are so top-heavy."

Lakshman listened carefully to Hanuman—lost in thought for some time. He then got up from his resting position and got ready to go back to the battlefield.

"What are you doing? Your shoulder is injured. You cannot lift your heavy bow—consider using a lighter one," Hanuman suggested. Lakshman took a step toward Hanuman and hugged him. Hanuman was puzzled by this display of emotion from a man who had always been very short-tempered.

Lakshman said excitedly, "You have given me a powerful idea. The monster is tall and heavy. It has very long legs. All the weight is concentrated at the top to protect the controls, the weapons, and the rider from enemy strikes. We cannot use big missiles due to the possibility of damage to our troops. It is difficult to fire such missiles with the high precision needed to bring down a single structure. Small missiles will not be effective as the structure is protected from heat. Its metal dissipates heat rapidly, and it has the ability to duck to avoid strikes."

Hanuman said, "Yes. We have to kill this machine fast. It is spreading panic amongst the troops."

Lakshman's eyes brightened, and he forgot all about the pain from his javelin injury; his excitement was growing by the moment. "Although the structure is protected from heat, we will use shock waves from the missile explosion to bring the giant down. We don't need to rely on precision. We will explode missiles simultaneously in front of the chest and near the lower knee region in the back. This double strike will push the monster in opposite directions and bring the creature down. You launch a ferocious attack on the troops accompanying the monster to create sufficient space for the missile to fly near the knee area. Once it comes crashing to the ground, we'll finish it off."

Hanuman listened patiently as Lakshman spoke with tremendous enthusiasm. He looked at this new, friendlier side of Lakshman with interest.

"Is it the effect of the pain killers or the javelin injury?" Hanuman chuckled. He got up from his seat and walked around, thinking about the proposal.

Lakshman was waiting eagerly for some feedback and support for his idea. To burn his nervous energy, he blew air gently over his wounded arm and applied herbal extract to the lesion.

After mulling over the plan for a while, Hanuman said cautiously, "Only you and Ram have the archery skills needed to pull this off, to hit the missile at the precise time when it is near the structure. Also, the wind direction has to be perfect for this to work. Wind seems calm today. Shall we execute tonight?"

"Tonight? That is against the rules. We have not initiated breaking rules from our side."

"Yes, but the element of surprise may prove to be our only option for true success. Besides, the rules have already been broken by the enemy—that makes them void for the remainder of this battle."

Lakshman was even more excited by Hanuman's line of reasoning in support of his plan.

"All right then, let us do it! Har Har Mahadev!" Hanuman declared. Lakshman was in his element.

"Call the missile technicians and Ram. Time to work out the mathematics—trajectories, draw weights, and arrows, grips, and all the other details to make sure everything goes per my plan. It all must be perfect!"

That evening the fight was winding down and the sun was about to set. Hanuman shouted orders to the troops fighting the monster, "Withdraw! Everyone, now! Turn around and withdraw!" As the troops followed their order, the monster made a huge turn to return to Lanka.

All of a sudden, Hanuman yelled at the top of his lungs, "Har Har Mahadev!" and ran towards the Rakshas soldiers who stood guarding the monster. Hanuman's soldiers followed him and hundreds of Rakshas soldiers were killed in no time.

Out of nowhere, Ram and Lakshman appeared on either side of the monster. Ram shot an arrow that signaled the heat missile. With precise calculations of trajectory and timing, he shot a fire arrow that exploded the missile the moment it was close enough to the giant metal creature.

The Vanara troops yelled, "Jai Shree Ram!"

Simultaneously, Lakshman accomplished the same task from the opposite side of the monster. The 'one-two punch' strategy was a success! The monster lost its balance and stumbled.

Hanuman charged in. "Attack the legs with boulders and maces!"

King Sugriv shouted, "I will maintain the outside perimeter around the monster and prevent any help from coming in."

As the monster tried to balance, it made a few erratic movements and crushed some of the soldiers under its incredible weight. Ram shot another arrow signaling one more missile to be fired. He made sure that this missile exploded near the chest area. With the massive shock wave that emanated from the detonated missile, the monster finally came crashing to the ground.

Hanuman took a giant leap, twenty feet in the air, and brought his heavy mace down with considerable strength on the steel head. The creature's head had softened due to the blunt force; it's shape now deformed. Ravan's giant brother had become stuck inside his metallic tomb and could not remove his head from the mechanical device. He was trapped.

Hanuman threw giant boulders at the deformed structure, until he had crushed it completely. Blood, broken skulls, and squashed brains splattered out of the monstrous structure.

"Victory to the Vanara!" shouted the ape-men.

"Destroy it! We must ensure that it cannot be reused," ordered Hanuman.

At his palace, Ravan was shaken to the core by the death of his brother.

"Oh! These blasted monkeys and those two loser brothers!" Ravan screamed. "They deserve no mercy. They need to be slaughtered like the animals they are!"

One of Ravan's ministers stepped forward. He clenched his throat and hesitated, but decided to speak anyway. He said sheepishly, "Clearly we made a mistake. The enemy is not a rag-tag team of forest-dwellers. These are seasoned warriors, led by astute commanders. We should negotiate peace."

Deep down, Ravan knew his minister was finally giving him sound guidance, but speaking of peace this late in the fight meant accepting defeat and humiliation.

"Behead this minister right now! I don't like cowardly and unsolicited opinions," Ravan shrieked. He got up from his throne and announced decisively, "Tomorrow, my son, who has never seen defeat in a battle, will avenge the death of my brother."

Even the gods could not defeat Ravan's powerful son, and he had assumed the title of Indrajit, the God Conqueror! Ravan's son had a reputation for being more cruel and deceptive than Ravan himself.

Indrajit launched a spectacular attack on the Vanara army. He killed thousands more with his astra weapons, which were capable of hitting multiple targets simultaneously.

Indrajit had a strong steel helmet and an impenetrable chest plate. He carried cloth rags drenched in various chemicals, different types of arrows, two bows, javelins, and swords in his huge chariot drawn by twelve horses. He carried pieces of equipment for conjuring images and fake forms as well. The instruments produced energy that could assemble matter particles into desired shapes, even multiple copies of the same shapes. He also carried several lifelike replicas of the severed heads of Ram, Lakshman, and Sita. The replicas were made from human skulls coated with animal tissue and skin to look very real.

He caressed his thick, horseshoe mustache and roared, "Come to your death, you filthy animals! The cruel demise that awaits you will make your mothers repent birthing you. Where are the two brothers? I cannot wait to burn them and serve their meat to Ram's wife before I kill her. Pour blood on these animals! Ram and Lakshman are beheaded!"

His soldiers aided in spreading the rumor by shouting, "Ram and Lakshman are beheaded. Victory to the Rakshas!" The soldiers then poured the blood and flesh of the Vanara killed in the war over the heads of the ape army that stood below their towers. They also threw the fake severed heads of Ram and Lakshman into the gathering of troops below.

Their gruesome tactics were creating a lot of confusion and fear within the Vanara ranks. Worry and doubt began to spread among the troops.

"Is Ram killed?" the apes cried out. Just the thought of such horrid acts broke their hearts.

"Drench these monkeys and set them on fire!" Indrajit ordered. "I don't care if my men burn too."

Indrajit's soldiers poured chemicals onto the Vanara army, creating an explosive gas that settled as a cloud over the troops. He set fire to one of his arrows and sent it flying into the gas, igniting all within and around the cloud. Indrajit had taken the war to a new, menacing low, and he was only getting started.

"Spread the gas that paralyses and slaughter them the moment it takes effect," he ordered. "You will spare no one—not even those that claim surrender. Eat them alive, feast on their beating hearts and livers, if you are hungry!"

At this point, some of the Vanara troops had lost their will to live. They had never even heard of such horrific tactics. There was nothing they could have done to prepare themselves for this kind of brutality. They began fleeing the battlefield, away from the carnage, and running for their lives.

"Huh! These cowards are running! Use the same tactics at all other gates in the city. Herd these animals in one direction. Once I have them right where I want them, I will launch my radiation device and fry them alive!" Indrajit ordered his captain. "Ask the royal family to take cover in underground caves to protect themselves from the radiation."

In the ape camp, Lakshman thundered, "The demons are getting desperate. They are using increasingly inhuman tactics and breaking all rules of warfare. Order me, brother Ram, to take the fight to the enemy!"

Ram said, "Do it brother, but be careful. Indrajit is sleazy. We have killed a lot of morally corrupt demons, but he can degrade to any extent." Ram added in a cautious tone, "Be mindful of his tactics. Deploy all weapons necessary to contain the threat."

Lakshman signaled the special forces to accompany him. Hanuman commanded the remaining troops. Fresh and well-rested soldiers had replaced the fleeing troops.

The fires set by Ravan's son were raging and burning everything in sight.

As soon as Lakshman reached the battlefield, he declared, "Deploy a missile to the northwest portion of the enemy army—that will create a low-pressure zone near the demon army, and the wind will blow, taking the flames with it."

The wind started blowing, just as predicted, toward the low-pressure zone, and the raging flames tormenting the apes changed direction; now burning the demons.

Indrajit's voice dripped with contempt, "Look who is here... one of the brothers who is desperate to die! You seem to be the younger one. Let me send you straight to hell." Indrajit welcomed Lakshman with a torrent of arrows, hundreds of them flying at high speed.

Lakshman showed great skill and quickly exploded a small missile precisely in the path of arrows, rendering them ineffective. Without giving his enemy a chance to launch another attack, Lakshman showered a slew of his own arrows at him.

Indrajit responded by splitting the incoming arrows with another onslaught of his own, skillfully moving his chariot and using a huge metal shield, along with a mace and other weapons to defend. The brawl between the two highly skilled warriors went on for a few hours—both fought tirelessly.

After some time, Lakshman said to his captain, "I sense that Indrajit is displaying some fatigue. Corner him!" The captain nodded his head, and the troops started to flank Indrajit's chariot from all sides. Lakshman took a deep breath. His helper quickly restocked his belt quiver.

Lakshman's captain announced, "Your path is clear."

Lakshman grabbed five arrows at a time in his shooting hand and launched a ferocious attack on Indrajit while speeding towards him on foot—simultaneously avoiding incoming arrows. All his arrows were precisely targeted at his enemy's chest.

Indrajit's chariot had been slowed by some dead horses, and the charioteer had been badly injured. However, Indrajit was still able to shoot arrows back at Lakshman with great speed.

Lakshman was hit in his bow-wielding arm, but did not let the pain from the impact affect his precision. He changed his angle of attack by shooting with both hands and constantly moving. In no time, Lakshman was only ten feet away from Indrajit.

Indrajit looked around and realized he was getting flanked from all sides. He shouted to his charioteer, "This mad ascetic is closing in!"

The charioteer smiled wryly and said, "He is walking right into the trap!" The next moment, Indrajit met Lakshman's eyes calmly, as if he was ready for anything that could happen next.

Lakshman was very close to the chariot now. He noticed that Indrajit's armor was showing chinks due to his sustained attack. Lakshman could feel the rapid breathing and neighing of horses as he touched them. Blood was dripping from their foreheads. He tried to steady his own breathing after the rapid approach.

Seeing the fearsome Lakshman up close, the smirk vanished from the charioteer's face. He was awe-struck by the huge bow and the speed and precision of Lakshman's shooting ability. He stared blankly, waiting to be killed.

Lakshman ignored him and shot three arrows at Indrajit, standing next to his chariot.

However, before the arrows could reach him, Indrajit turned into five conjured forms of himself—complete with chariots and horses.

Have I been shooting at an image all this time? Lakshman thought. He was shocked and perplexed.

Lakshman's captain was bewildered too. He pointed his sword at five images, encircling them. "What is happening here?"

Arrows were coming at them from all five chariots, but only one stream of arrows was real. They did not know which ones they truly needed to defend themselves against. They were taking hits one after another.

"Let us end this trickery." The quick-thinking Lakshman shot an arrow, signaling a missile from the sky. His crew immediately recognized the signal. Within a few moments, a missile exploded high above them. It seeded the clouds and started to rain.

"The conjured forms are beginning to disappear," the captain said with relief.

However, just before the fake forms disappeared completely, Indrajit threw a javelin, immediately following it up with an arrow that contained a small radiation device, and a second venomous arrow—all aimed directly at Lakshman.

"Time for you to die, son of a whore!" Indrajit yelled.

Lakshman roared back, "Not so fast! Let me first send you to your uncle. In hell!" Lakshman dodged the javelin, but the two arrows hit him in the arm and chest. He collapsed to the ground and instantly lost consciousness.

Lakshman's captain ordered, "Retreat!" With great skill, he immediately threw a protective barrier of soldiers around Lakshman and evacuated him from the battlefield. Lakshman was taken to the other side of the hill, toward the ocean.

Ram was gravely worried about his brother. He ran his fingers gently over the wounds and flinched when there was no reaction from Lakshman. He looked at the wounds his brother had sustained fighting for him; some were raw, some partially healed. Ram gently stroked Lakshman's hair.

"I have never seen Ram so disturbed," one ape said.

"Lakshman has been hit by a radiation device and toxic venom," the Vaidya, medic, said. "He needs antidotes immediately."

Ram asked worriedly, "How bad is it?"

The medic paused, weighing his words carefully. "He needs antidote within a few hours, or he cannot be saved. I am sorry."

Although Hanuman was anxious, he asked hopefully, "So, there is an antidote for this double strike of radiation and venom? What is it? Where can we get it?"

The medic replied, "There is an herb found in the Himalayas, thousands of miles away. Thankfully the Vanara army has brought these herbs from the Himalayas in anticipation of its need. The herb is ineffective in sunlight. Fortunately, Lakshman was hit in the evening. We have time. The herb is also very short-lived, so you need to transport the whole rock here. Then, I will pluck it fresh and use it for treatment."

King Sugriv said, "How do you suggest we transport a huge rock over this stony, bumpy bridge in such a short time?"

Hanuman instantly came up with a plan and said, "We will use the flying machine. I will remove the unnecessary parts of the machine to make room for the rock. As a backup, we will also make the bridge smooth with deposits of sand in between the stones and modify a chariot to fit the rock so that we can transport it that way if need be."

Sugriv responded cheerfully, "Hanuman your intellect is lighting fast, just as your movements in combat. You came up with not one, but two plans. Use all the troops you need and start working on your plans right away. I will assist in whatever way I can to make sure you are successful."

Hanuman acknowledged the kind words from his king and turned to Ram, who was lost in his thoughts. *The brave prince of Ayodhya has so many wounds on his body… perhaps more on his mind.* Hanuman thought, *His wife's, and now even his brother's, life is hanging by a thread. I have to make this work for Ram.*

"This rock is too big," one of the Vanara said. "There is no way it will fit in the flying machine. It will fall in the ocean during the flight. I am sure of it. This is a rare herb—if we lose it, we are finished."

"I will make it work," Hanuman said confidently. "I will hang from the side of the flying machine and support the portion of the rock that does not fit on my shoulders."

"Jai Hanuman!" the Vanara shouted with relief and joy at his bravery.

"Another flying ape will win this war today," said a veteran, reminiscing about King Vali's famous leap—the one that had ended Ravan's aggression in years gone by.

True to his word, Hanuman delivered the herbs in time and Lakshman was already showing signs of recovery.

Ram hugged Hanuman. "I have been blessed with three great brothers—one who was ready to give up his throne for me, a second who has followed me loyally no matter how far into the jungle I travel, and a third—you Hanuman—who has always stepped up whenever the need arose. You will live forever and your actions will guide humans for thousands of years to come."

"The Rishis created this body of mine for moments such as these, I am just doing my duty. I am fortunate to be blessed by you." The great warrior Ram could not stop his tears at the display of unparalleled devotion by Hanuman and Lakshman.

A Vanara observing the strong bond of brotherhood between the commanders said, "I feel so energized, even after long fights, due to the camaraderie of our leaders. I am ready to die for them."

This coherence at the head of the huge army led the troops to a higher morale than they had felt the entire length of this brutal war.

A Vanara spy disguised as a demon came running into the encampment. He looked terrified. He was dripping sweat and shaking uncontrollably. He had wounds all over his body, bleeding profusely.

"A huge radiation device is being packed into a flying machine," he said. "The enemy caught me watching, somehow I…Shree Ram, bless me…" He suddenly lost consciousness from the tremendous blood loss.

The medic shook his head and said, "I can't save him, apologies. There just isn't anything I can do. He's lost too much blood."

It was only a few moments before the poor soldier took his final breath. Ram approached the dead soldier and said, "With brave soldiers like you, my friend, our victory is assured. Rest in peace."

Ram placed a gentle hand on the body—noticing that it still felt warm—sat in a yogic posture, and closed his eyes.

"The enemy's plan is clear. They want to drop a radiation device from a great height and poison the entire island. They want to kill us so badly that they don't care if they also kill themselves in the process," Sugriv said in exasperation.

"Consult with Ravan's brother about the location of the enemy machine, and ready our flying machine. I need to destroy the enemy machine before it is launched," Ram ordered.

Ravan's brother was summoned. He was eager to share what he knew. "The machine is located in the north-west part of the hills, outside the city. The royal family, as well as all the people critical to the kingdom, will be safe in an underground location. They have set the Prachanda, the immense plan, in motion."

Hanuman chuckled sardonically. "Great leadership! Let others die while you are safe with your own family. You must repent being in the open with us, rather than safely in an underground location at this moment!" He teased Ravan's brother.

"After being with Ram, I have realized that I am beyond this physical form. That has changed my life forever. And that is priceless. I don't care if I die. It is better to die in a battle, than be beheaded by my own brother." He added in a lighter tone, "On the other hand, joining you has forced me to hang out with more apes than I ever wanted to."

All laughed with a sense of gallows humor.

Lakshman was fully conscious now. After sharing that light moment, Lakshman said, "All right we have very little time. I am feeling significantly better. Brother Ram, I need to finish what I started. I need to kill Ravan's son."

Ram blessed him, "May you be successful."

Lakshman said to the student pilot, "Bypass Lanka to avoid wasting time in confrontation with the main defense of the city. Head north-west, quickly."

Indrajit was ready to take off when Lakshman's machine appeared in the sky. "I thought I killed you," he said with disgust. "My traitor uncle must have given you our location. No matter… I have no problem killing you again!"

The student pilot said, "Lakshman, this location is a small cave like structure carved into steep hills. There is barely enough space for one flying machine. There is no room to land. What should I do?"

Lakshman's voice was steady. "Let me think. We need to get him before he takes off. His machine is faster than ours. We will not be able to catch him once he is in the air."

The pilot agreed. "Yes, sir. Our machine is not in good shape, especially since transporting the rock earlier tonight. We did not have time to refuel either. My estimate is, he will take off in less than one ghati, about twenty-four minutes."

"Okay, approach the cliff as slowly as you can. I will jump when you are close."

"What? Why don't you jump directly from here to your death? At least then I will not crash during your misadventure."

"Do you have a better idea in that bright mind of yours? Don't forget, I am ranked higher than you. Follow my orders."

"All right, let me make a practice run first. He is shooting powerful arrows at us!" the pilot exclaimed as the flying machine approached the cliffside.

"No time for this. I am jumping, slow down," Lakshman said. He left his bow behind, carried his sword in one hand, and jumped toward the cliff.

"How very stupid of you!" Indrajit yelled. He had used a very heavy bow to shoot at the flying machine. As a result, his reaction time was slightly slower. Before he could draw an arrow, Lakshman landed close enough to him to leap and stab him in the arm. Blood gushed from his arm—the brachial artery had been damaged. Indrajit dropped his bow, took out his dagger, and ran to take cover.

Lakshman chased him, took a mighty leap, leaned forward mid-air to cover more distance, and landed firmly on his feet. He kicked the dagger out of Indrajit's hand, and with a clean cut from his double-edged sword, separated his head from the trunk. Blood spurted from the torso while it made some erratic, involuntary movements before falling on Lakshman, bathing him in blood.

The Rakshas soldiers who had come to their superior's help, felt paralyzed by the ghastly sight of their headless leader. They stood, frozen in fear, and could not move their weapons.

Lakshman too trembled in shock after killing the great warrior and being drenched in his blood.

He gathered himself and declared sternly, "Take his body, put it in your machine, and get lost or I will kill you in much the same manner."

After the soldiers left with their master's body, Lakshman's machine landed and carried him back to Ram's camp.

At Ravan's huge palace, decked in gold and expensive garments, laid the body of his son. He could not take his gaze off Indrajit's severed head.

"Great King, what do we do next?" asked a minister meekly.

Ravan shook his head as those words brought him back to the present.

He screamed with fury, "I wish a coward like you were dead instead of my brave son! I want to burn the whole planet down!" He paused for a moment, eyes burning with anger. "But first, let me burn that woman, Sita, alive! She is the reason for all this!" He picked up his sword and prepared to leave the chamber.

Ravan's wife was standing nearby, wailing for her son. She wiped her tears and said coldly, "Our son was killed fairly in a battle that *you* started. He fought bravely, and so did the enemy. I suggest you do the same and fight, instead of attacking a defenseless woman. I thought you were a warrior!"

"Shut your mouth! I am Ravan, the Great King! I don't need your advice, woman." He silently wondered what to do next as fury and sorrow clouded his mind. His wife's words created further turmoil within him. At that moment of indecision, a soldier came running in. He was almost out of breath.

"Forgive me Great King, the Universe Missile! The Universe Missile! Enemy! Go Underground!"

Ravan slapped the soldier hard in his face to bring him to his senses. "Stop stammering, you useless creature. What are you trying to say? What about the Universe Missile?"

The soldier rubbed his cheek. He looked down to hide his watering eyes. He took a deep breath in an attempt to calm himself. "The enemy is ready to launch the Universe Missile. They have it ready over the hill!"

Ravan kicked, then pushed the messenger away and shouted, "I see. Now get lost before I chop off your head on this awful day." Ravan addressed his minister, "So, this missile is a warning to us, not to use our Universe Missile, or the two sides will be annihilated."

His minister cast his eyes to the floor and nodded in agreement. Ravan took a sharp breath and made up his mind in that moment.

"Get ready for a final assault," he ordered his general. "I will lead the charge today and send those monkeys and disgusting humans to the bottom of the ocean. By the time today's moonless night approaches, their lives will be submerged in darkness!"

Ravan's wife stood stone faced and watched her husband. She wondered, *Will I ever see him again? This war has taken everything from me. My entire family has been killed, our kingdom is ruined, and an entire generation of Rakshas has been slaughtered. Is this it? Is Ravan going to die today?* Her heart skipped a beat and sweat trickled down her brow as she considered the consequences of Ravan's terrible mistake.

She said to her maid, "This all feels like a drama enacted by the evil gods to destroy our way of life! This cannot really be happening! My world-conquering husband, god-defeating son, and colossal brother-in-law cannot fall like autumn leaves! I curse the gods for their evil tricks and for misleading my husband!" She suddenly felt sick to her stomach and began vomiting the anxiety from her body.

CHAPTER 14
THE FINAL ASSAULT

~~~~~~~~

Ancient India

~~~~~~~~

I am the force!

IN THE VANARA CAMP, HANUMAN SAID TO RAM, "OUR strategy of preempting any misadventure from Ravan by displaying our readiness to use the Universe Missile worked. I think this will help protect Lady Sita's life as well."

The mention of Sita made Ram reflective for a moment. He tried not to think about his beloved Sita, and focused instead on the battle.

Ram addressed his troops, "From the war cries emanating from Lanka and the high morale of enemy soldiers, I am sure the great Ravan himself will lead the attack today. There is no need to be afraid. Ravan will be determined to avenge his brother and son's death! My guess is that he will come straight for me. Be assured, we are ready for him!"

Sugriv stepped up and declared, "Yes, we are ready to unite Ravan with his brother and son... in hell!"

The apes roared back, "Jai Vanar-raj! Send Ravan to hell!"

As the new-moon day broke, a lone shining star could be seen in the sky as other stars and planets disappeared from view.

Hanuman said to his captain, "Wow! I can feel that this day is special. Something big will happen today that will change this planet forever." Hanuman looked around from his vantage point. He observed, "It seems as if the stage is set for the biggest battle of our lives to unfold. The two armies are lined up in battle formations. For some reason, it reminds me of stage shows. How the stage gets bathed in light and eventually the audience disappears from view. It seems the stars and planets have disappeared like the audience and are eager to see the drama. The lone shining star is the compère host. He will disappear soon, too. The whole world and indeed the universe is playing spectator to this battle!"

Hanuman looked at Ram and thought, *The Great Shree Ram! Steady gaze as ever as he gets ready to fight what could be his last battle! My heart fills with love and bliss every time I bear witness to this great man!*

Hanuman glanced at the enemy side, "And there is Ravan! He has lost his entire family, including his son, in this war! Yet, no sign of sorrow! Only eagerness to get on with his Dharma, his duty to fight! His eyes have a veneer of arrogance, hiding a deep and wise soul. One who wields the musical instrument Veena with the same skill as his mighty mace and bow! It is a great privilege to witness this epic battle between two great warriors."

Hanuman's captain agreed, "You are right, Hanuman. It is not just another battle, but a turning point in history! It is my honor to fight under your command." The Captain gently clinked his mace against Hanuman's.

Many of the Vanara were seeing Ravan for the first time.

One said, "Look at his big handle-bar mustache, thick beard, and blood shot red eyes. He looks crazed."

Another ape standing on the other side of the column of soldiers was not impressed. He had wounds all over his body from the hard battle he had fought thus far. "I see a demon who abducted a lady. That is all."

His buddy said, "This is the demon who mistreated our commander's wife, kill him! Kill him, like his brother and son, kill him!"

All the Vanara joined in, "Kill Ravan!"

Seeing the enemy face-to-face added to their determination to achieve further success in this war. The two armies prepared themselves for their final encounter.

Ram wore his armor, a helmet, simple cotton dhoti, and wielded a huge bow and quivers full of various kinds of arrows. He also carried a shiny sword and dagger.

Ram observed, *Ravan is a great leader and a supreme warrior. Despite all the losses he has suffered, look at the confidence his men have in him! Their morale is so high today! But, I am confident we will win!*

A nameless messenger approached. He wore a white dhoti and had a tuft of Shikha hair on top of his shaven head. A Yagyopaveet consecrated thread could be seen running across his left shoulder. It seemed he had his attention centered on something within as he went about his activities.

Hanuman stopped him.

The messenger recited a hymn. "Message from the ashram for Shree Ram."

Hanuman allowed him to pass through.

The messenger dutifully approached Ram. "Identify yourself," he ordered.

Ram recited the Aditya Hridaya stotra-hymn. After verification, the messenger handed over an arrow covered with a protective sheath. He informed Ram, "This is from Agastya Muni. This is not the first time you are using this arrow. You are the seventh avatar! You have used it six times before!"

Ram glanced at him knowingly. "I am aware of that. Gratitude."

The student nodded his head. "Good. This arrow has been activated. It is a small radiation device made from impure fissile material. It generates a lot of heat, but very little radiation. As per the rules of warfare, such a device can be used directly on an individual enemy. May victory be yours! Jai Shree Ram! Oh, and one last thing," the student said as he got ready to leave. "Don't forget to use the chariot today."

Ram nodded in agreement.

The final battle began with a clearly noticeable sense of vengeance. Ravan attacked the Vanara army with all his might in this final push. He was flanked by his generals. They killed thousands of Vanara and rained arrows, javelins, and missiles down upon the rival army.

Sugriv sent an order to Hanuman, "You get the generals on the right. I will take the left flank. Ram and Lakshman will be at the center and attack Ravan directly."

"As you command, my king. Har Har Mahadev!"

As soon as Ravan saw Lakshman, his primal fatherly instinct at the thought of his beheaded son pushed him over the edge. Ravan let out a blood-cuddling scream, "You filthy son of a whore! I will smash you to pieces!"

Lakshman responded, "You are nothing but a cowardly demon! You dared touch my brother's wife. I only dreamed of spilling your brains on this cursed land since that depraved day. I promise, you will not return home today. You are going to die in this filth."

Both warriors were overwhelmed with fury. Their weapons created a deafening roar as they collided with one another. The Vanara and

Rakshas were being slaughtered mercilessly. Because of the immense hatred between the two leaders, the soldiers were even more savage with one another. One Rakshas danced on the body of a Vanara he had recently killed. His partner encouraged the overkill by exclaiming, "Gouge out his eyes!" He promptly tore out the eyes to further disfigure the body.

On the other side, a Vanara had pinned a Rakshas under a huge boulder and tore out his arms as he screamed in pain. The hatred between the troops was naked on display.

Ravan and Lakshman attacked one another, raining arrows in rapid succession.

Ravan's charioteer advised, "Remember, Lakshman was hit on the right shoulder with a javelin. He is slower on that side. He is also on foot, so you have the advantage of height."

Ravan took out a javelin drenched in deadly toxin. His driver maneuvered the chariot to Lakshman's right, and when Ravan was close enough to strike, he threw the javelin with full force from atop his chariot. It stuck Lakshman exactly in the location of his previous wound. He screamed as the pain coursed through his body.

Sugriv noticed Ravan's maneuver and rushed to cover Lakshman and bring him to safety.

"Attack Ravan!" Ram shouted as he saw his injured brother being taken away. Ram's chariot immediately moved toward Ravan.

Ram addressed Ravan in a steady, but dominating voice, "Attacking somebody on foot from a chariot is cowardly! Have you not an ounce of bravery left in your entire body? I guess we can't really expect much more from you, now can we?"

"You know all about bravery, don't you Ram? Especially when you killed King Vali from hiding!"

Ram answered, "Yes, and don't forget, I killed King Vali. The same king who pinned you down in his armpit, Great King!" Ram readied his weapon. "It is your turn today! Consider this punishment for abducting an innocent woman and spreading your wrongful ways."

The two warriors attacked each other with all their might.

Ram sent a barrage of arrows, but every single one was precisely blocked by Ravan. Ravan's attacks were skillfully dealt with by Ram's charioteer and his lightning fast reflexes. The fight went on until midday. The sun was now moving to the western horizon.

"I have bad news and worse news for you!" Ram taunted Ravan. "Your generals are killed, and your flanks are unguarded. That's the bad news. And the worse news is, Lakshman is out of danger! He will survive and assist me in your death!"

"My spies informed me a long time ago. As such, I am more than enough for both of you!" Ravan shouted to his captains, "Go now! Take over the flanks and hold your position. Go!" Ravan threw his huge mace and javelin with great force, damaging Ram's chariot and killing some of his horses.

The charioteer assured Ram, "Don't worry, this chariot allows me to release the dead horses quickly." He skillfully created an opportunity for Ram to strike swiftly.

Ram shot an arrow straight at Ravan's head. The helmet sustained a mighty crack, but before Ram could shoot at Ravan's bare head, he had replaced the helmet with another he kept ready in this chariot. Ram was amazed by how quickly Ravan had been able to retrieve this new helmet.

Ravan launched a counter attack, sending multiple arrows that injured Ram in several places all over his upper body. "Here comes your death and my wedding gift to your wife!" Ravan's arrow whizzed passed Ram's head, injuring his neck.

Ram's charioteer created another opportunity for him. Ram hit Ravan's head, only to see him replace his helmet almost instantly.

Ram clenched his bow. *His head is well protected. His chest plate has multiple layers of steel, and is impossible to break. How do I get him?* he wondered. Then, he had an idea. Ram ordered his charioteer, "Get me closer to him, so I can penetrate his helmet and get his skull."

Ram shot another arrow at Ravan's head from close range.

Ravan attacked in retaliation with his javelin. "Even if you stand next to me, you will not be able to penetrate this helmet!"

Ravan's attack had injured Ram's thigh this time, and he was bleeding profusely. Given his other wounds, be was beginning to lose blood, and strength, quickly. Ram saw a horseman approaching fast from his left flank. The horseman had broken through the Vanara ranks.

"He appears to be friendly," the charioteer noticed. "He is from the ashram!" The horseman got Ram's attention, then disappeared into the fighting hoards.

Ram said with relief, "Oh! He has come to remind me of the arrow he gave me this morning. The small radiation device should melt Ravan's chest plate!"

The charioteer said, "But, the sheer size of his chariot makes his chest area difficult to target."

"Let me get him out of his chariot then." Ram applied pressure to the wound on this thigh in an attempt to slow the bleeding. He felt better, drank a sip of water from the leather bag in the chariot, and tested putting a little weight on the leg. Once steady, Ram was able to fire several enflamed arrows at the wheels of Ravan's chariot.

"Finish him!" Ravan yelled to his charioteer, knowing that Ram was growing weaker due to his numerous injuries. As Ravan maneuvered his chariot to the right, he exposed two wheels completely.

Ram's charioteer shouted with excitement, "There! Get the wheels! He is coming to your right!"

Ram promptly dispatched a slew of fiery arrows upon both wheels. The wooden spokes caught fire and buckled, nearly throwing Ravan from his chariot.

Ram's charioteer cheered, "Get him!"

Ram loaded the radiation arrow and aimed it directly at Ravan's chest. Ram let out a sharp breath. He said to his charioteer, "Now that Ravan is in my strike zone, I realize I cannot break the rules myself and taint my victory with deceit forever! In the heat of battle, I did not think of it before. I am in a chariot, and he is on the ground. I will not shoot. I will not break the rules of warfare!"

Ram's charioteer shook his head in disagreement. In the moment of Ram's hesitation, one of Ravan's captains took the opportunity to insert his own chariot in between the two leaders.

Ravan immediately pushed his captain off and took over the chariot. This was a much smaller chariot than his own. Ravan took a deep breath, and declared, "I can't wait any longer. It is time to launch the Universe Missile and destroy everything!"

Ravan reached for his quiver to retrieve the arrow that would signal the launch of the Universe Missile. Traditionally, the arrow was kept way in the back of the quiver to make sure that it was not used by mistake. His right hand was raised to reach deep into the quiver. His left hand, holding the bow, was naturally bent down to provide extra depth for the right hand. This exposed his chest completely. The small chariot did not offer any protection.

Ram was prepared for this opportunity. Ram's special radiation arrow crashed into Ravan's chest plate. It generated intense heat upon impact, softening the armor.

Ram was ready with a broad-head arrow for greater penetrating force. He balanced his body properly on both legs, enduring the pain in his thigh. He stretched the string until the bow almost buckled, and locked his mind onto his target. His breath was steady and balanced. He shot the venomous arrow. It entered precisely where the armor was softened, penetrated the chest plate, broke Ravan's rib cage, and lodged itself in his heart, poisoning his blood stream instantly. Ravan fell to the ground in a heap of melted metal and blood.

Ram stepped down from his chariot and approached Ravan with a steady, although painful, gait and a calm gaze.

All the soldiers stepped aside to allow his passage. The will for the Rakshas to fight lay dying with their king.

Ravan was bleeding profusely. Due to a lack of oxygenated blood, his lips were becoming blue, his face pale. His pulse grew weaker with each passing moment.

Some Rakshas soldiers gathered around their king, wanting to take him away. Ravan gestured, 'no' and pointed to Ram.

Ram advanced and stood close to Ravan.

Ravan tried to smile, then mumbled, "The mistake of abducting your wife was made due to bad habits, and karma, accumulated over the years. After that, I was overtaken by events and could not turn back. It was better to die fighting than to live defeated!"

Ram shook his head as he understood Ravan's viewpoint.

Ravan continued in a very feeble voice and pointed to Ram. Ravan's eyes started rolling back into his skull. All the victories, carnal pleasures, fine food, power, and wealth he had earned seemed to hold him down rather than making him feel satisfied, free, and ready to die. His heart was trying its hardest to keep beating and keep him alive. His face displayed the anguish of his mind—a mind that wanted to live and enjoy more pleasure, while his body could not, would not, sustain any longer. The mighty Ravan had only a few beats left before his heart would stop anyway, no matter what his mind desired.

The memories of all the lives he had taken to satisfy his ego rattled him. He could feel the spirits of his brother, son, and parents waiting for him. He could feel his own spirit preparing to leave his dying body. Ravan was perplexed as he wondered, *Am I the body or the spirit?*

At that moment, Ram got down on his knees and gently touched Ravan between the eyebrows with his fingers. The anguish suddenly evaporated from Ravan's face. Ram pressed on the top of Ravan's head.

Ravan was immediately reminded of his vast nature—the one not limited by his dying body. Ram had activated the yogi within him—the intelligent soul who lay buried under the filth of his own mind. Ravan died a truth-realized yogi.

Hanuman watched all this intently. He touched Ram's feet and said, "For the Great Ravan, this immense war was all worth it, as he received a privileged death in your presence. You help even your sworn enemies realize their true nature. Your compassion is unparalleled."

The Vanara, in unison, let out a loud cry, "Jai Shree Ram!"

The war was finally over, and the sun was preparing to set. The scene along the western horizon looked beautiful; the splendid evening was filled with clouds of various colors—orange, light pink, white, gray, and shades of purple.

Hanuman dropped his weapon and absorbed the serenity of the landscape. He thought, *Plain, colorless water vapors in the form of clouds, when powered by the mighty sun behind them, appear so vivid and beautiful. But, once the sun is gone, the clouds lose their beauty, their color, and turn back into their true, simple form. Similarly, the body shines in all its splendor until the life force that powers it is gone. Then, the body is simply earth and water. The trick is to realize and experience that I am not the body. I am the force that powers the body!* Hanuman concluded in his peaceful reflection.

CHAPTER 15
THE RULER WHO LISTENS

~~~~~~~

Ancient India

~~~~~~~

People rule over the king.

THE DAY FOLLOWING RAVAN'S DEATH, BACK IN THE VANARA camp, Lakshman came running to his brother with excitement and relief. "Brother Ram, Devi Sita is here! Thanks to Lord Mahadev, she is all right. She is accompanied by some ladies from the Lankan royal family, favorable to us."

Ram glanced at Lakshman. Ram was seated on a huge stone at the beach, accompanied by the generals, King Sugriv, and Hanuman. Ram looked as steady as ever. Without showing any emotion, he said dispassionately, "Good. I am glad Yogi Sita is safe."

"Did he say Yogi?" Sugriv whispered to his general. The general nodded.

Ram got up from his seat, and said in an un-characteristically commanding voice, "Lakshman, please request Lady Sita to walk through fire to prove her chastity of thought and action."

Ram's command shocked everyone. Sugriv looked away nervously, shaking his head. Hanuman, who had met Sita and knew how much Ram loved her, could not believe what he was saying. Hanuman watched Ram with raised eyebrows.

The volatile brother Lakshman felt a surge of anger and warm blood gush through his entire body. He then realized that his anger was directed at his dearest brother. He was dumbfounded. He could not control his emotions and started sobbing.

"I understand your intentions," Lakshman said in a hoarse voice. "This action must be to settle doubts about Lady Sita's character in the minds of the population. I get it. But, how is this fair to her? The lady was abducted and forced to live in someone else's home. She didn't go there by choice. I feel ashamed even talking about such things. I thought you were a just king."

Ram looked at his brother with a steady gaze.

Lakshman added angrily, "Lady Sita is the one who deserves the title of Vishnu, the Savior, not you!" Lakshman spoke what everyone in the assembly was thinking. After venting, Lakshman was able to calm himself and accept the inevitable. He realized that his brother must have come to this decision with great difficulty and pain. He must be heavy with a lonely heart. Despite his feelings, he went and hugged Ram.

Lady Sita was informed of Ram's order. After the initial surprise, she brought herself back to calm and smiled gently. "My husband has showed great love and respect for me by waging this great war and destroying Ravan, who dishonored me. I am the one and only woman in Ram's life, and he is, and always will be, the only man in my life. He knows this well. But, nobody is above the law, especially not the ruler! And the population follows the actions, not the words, of their ruler! Lakshman, please make necessary arrangements."

Lakshman and his soldiers arranged several rocks to create a five-foot-long square structure with openings on two opposite sides for entry and exit. They cut many trees and arranged them around the stones. They covered the floor of the square box with tree branches. Teary eyed, Lakshman set the cut trees on fire. Dark smoke and huge flames rose high into the sky. All the Vanara warriors were sickened by this merciless test.

Lady Sita appeared tiny standing in front of the huge flames.

"She will be eaten alive by these flames in no time," whispered a Vanara.

"I would never subject my wife to such a humiliating death," argued another.

"Shree Ram is truly the greatest leader ever to undertake such a severe task for his own dear wife," a third commented.

"Victory to Lady Sita! Victory to Shree Ram!" the onlookers shouted out of genuine love and respect for their leader.

Sita was calm. She sat near the fire. She closed her eyes and performed several yogic postures and breathing practices. She reached a state where she felt one with the fire. In a trance-like state, she slowly stepped into the fire.

The Vanara cringed at the thought of the flames burning the delicate skin of the princess who was brought up in royal comfort.

Sita, however, walked through the fire effortlessly. The smell of her slightly burned clothes brought her out of her trance, but she was otherwise unharmed.

The entire Lankan and Vanara army witnessed the Test by Fire in awe.

"If Lady Sita was not of pure thought or action, she would not be able to experience this union with fire and would have been burned alive!" Everyone present was shaken by the seemingly gentle, but powerful, energy of the lady.

"Victory to Lady Sita! Long live Lady Sita." They shouted. The entire army got down on one knee and bowed their heads in respect to the awesome power of Lady Sita.

≈

Ram, Sita, Lakshman, Hanuman, and other important members of the army travelled back to Ram's kingdom of Ayodhya. Ram was a popular prince when he was exiled more than a decade ago, but now, after his heroics and defeating the demons, he was a living legend.

In the capital of Ayodhya, at the harvest festival to celebrate recent good yields from crops, a wealthy trader said to the revenue minister, "King Ram brings new possibilities with him. The entire southern part of the country, which was hostile to us, is now friendly. And beyond that, now we have a friendly port in Lanka. Our ships can trade across the southern ocean to a new world! There is no limit to how much we can expand our business!"

An army general standing nearby said, "The threat of the Rakshas, who made southward expansion impossible, has been permanently eliminated! And with Ram's valor, nobody will dare threaten Ayodhya from east or west, so our borders are safe too!"

The Prime Minister said, "Another important factor is the king himself. Ram's brother was taking care and keeping the kingdom safe, but his heart was not in ruling. He felt guilty that he was the reason Ram was exiled. The grand vision, quick decision making, vigor, and energy were absent due to conflicted leadership. Now everything will be smooth and fast!"

A local farmer served freshly made alcoholic drinks to everyone. "The common man has not seen any increase in income for fifteen years now! There is plenty of water and fertile lands in the south. Our kids will have new frontiers to explore! Ram has instilled great vigor, optimism, and energy throughout the population!"

The farmer's wife joined in the exuberant toast. "We are all planning a grand welcome for King Ram and Queen Sita. The entire city will be decked with flowers, all the houses have been freshly painted, and decorative wooden sticks have been installed. Plenty of food, meat, and drinks will flow limitlessly. Music, dance, and festivities will go on for weeks!"

Her young daughter could not stop giggling. "I have heard Ram is so handsome and strong! I can't wait to see him! He went all the way to Lanka and fought a war to save his wife. I wish I could find a husband like him!" Everybody had a hearty laugh!

Ram was coronated as the king and ushered his kingdom into prosperity like it had never seen before. His kingdom served as an economic engine driving the development of the rest of the country. So many economic and business opportunities were created that it would take several generations to fully realize their potential.

A few years had passed, and the economic boom was in full swing. Everyone was making money as if there was no tomorrow. There were no poor, hungry, homeless, or untreated sick persons left in Ayodhya. Signs of opulence such as huge houses, elephants, chariots, expensive jewelry, and proliferation of the arts were seen everywhere.

Ram enjoyed his time with his loving wife and soon she was pregnant with their first child. Ram ruled his kingdom exactly as prescribed by the scriptures and surpassed the lofty standards of governance set by other kings of his famous clan. One important part of governance was maintaining a feel for the pulse of the nation. This was accomplished through spy networks. Spies would constantly feed information about what the general public was thinking directly to the king, bypassing the ministers and bureaucrats. Recently, King Ram had received feedback that was troubling. Winds of change were blowing through his kingdom.

At one such meeting, the chief spy said, "Great King Ram, people are prosperous and can't stop singing your praises, but they have become very indulgent. Here are some reports for you directly from the spies who saw it. 'Consumption of meat, alcohol, hallucinogens, and the business of prostitution are at an all-time high. Most people are drunk and spend all day enjoying song and dance. Making money is so easy that people are becoming lazy. Nobody wants to study the scripture for wisdom. Nobody performs meditation, self-introspection, or pursues higher goals in life.' And this is not the worst part!"

Ram was surprised to hear about this turn of events. "What do you mean this is not the worst part? The news you are providing me is very bad. It is as if my kingdom is strong from the outside, but hollow and weak from the inside!"

The spy chief said, "Forgive me, my king, but you have not heard the worst yet."

Ram was losing patience. "Out with it then!"

"Forgive me, my king. I am just the messenger. People think you are responsible for this."

Ram could not contain his bafflement. "Elaborate," he ordered sternly.

"I dare not speak another word. I fear for my life at the hands of the mighty King Ram," the spy chief said, trembling with fear and appalled by what he had heard.

"You should remember, your king did not shoot at the powerful King Ravan even when he himself was about to die from bleeding. You are only performing your duty. Don't be afraid."

The spy hung his head in shame and looked downcast, teary-eyed. He said, "These ungrateful people say that the king was so enamored by his wife, he accepted her even when she had lived in another man's house for months! And because of the loose morals of the king, the entire population has a right to be lustful and indulgent!"

Ram responded calmly, "I had anticipated this. Queen Sita went through the Test by Fire."

"They say that only silly apes and bears witnessed it! Who knows what really happened?"

"I see. My gratitude to you. You may leave now." Ram was deeply hurt and disappointed.

He thought for a while, then said aloud, "Economic prosperity is useless, even harmful, without moral and spiritual development. A king is like a father, and a queen like a mother. When parents see their child headed down the wrong path, they must take action. Our society is headed in the wrong direction and needs an urgent course correction. And as the rulers, Sita and I have to bring them back, and if necessary, pay the price for such an action."

Ram gathered his brothers in the palace and shared the sensitive news with them.

Ram's voice was laced with sadness. "I have made my decision. The Queen has to leave the kingdom. This will give me moral authority. I will lead from the front and steer the population back in the right direction."

Lakshman could not even begin to contain his anger. "Ram, why don't you leave? Why does Devi Sita have to pay the price for your greatness and popularity all the time?"

Ram had been expecting such an outburst. "Lakshman, you are the voice of truth, always! You say things that I want to say, but cannot, and I am thankful to you for keeping my conscience clear, dear brother. You took deadly arrows for me. You put your life on the line for me. I am thankful to you for that and for presenting facts as they are. I am ready to leave with my pregnant wife, right now! For me, this is the easiest thing to do as I don't care about the title or the palace."

Lakshman was disgusted by the unfair treatment handed out to Lady Sita time and again. "I don't care about all that," he lashed out again. "Whenever I think of Lady Sita, I feel a motherly energy and grace filling my heart. She is an ideal human in all respects, even more so than you, because she does not get all the glory for her greatness.

And I know you realize this. I don't understand why you want to save these miserable people. These barbarians in civilized clothes are worse than the Rakshas we killed. Let me chop off a few wagging tongues and everyone will fall in line."

Ram's other brother intervened. "This is Ram-Rajya, the rulership of the ideal King Ram. This is a yardstick by which other rulers will be judged in the future. Make no mistake, we are creating history here. Punishing people for expressing their views, however false they may be, shall not be practiced. Lady Sita is being treated unfairly. There is no question about that. But, we need the king here. Who will oversee the economic development? And who will guide the public along the right path? If the king leaves now, the economic engine will come to a halt, rebellion will spread everywhere, and there will be chaos. All the good work will be brought to nothing. The king must stay."

Lakshman knew his brother's assessment was correct, but he did not want to admit it. He bowed before the king and walked out of the assembly room with heavy footsteps. The painful decision had been finalized. Just as a mother goes through unbearable pain during childbirth, true leaders suffer the pain for giving birth to a new social structure.

The very next day, pregnant Queen Sita was dropped at an ashram by the river Ganga. She gracefully accepted the separation from her husband. King Ram was completely heart broken, but he knew he had a job to do. Ram summoned the ever-dependable Hanuman.

"We need to bring people back to the spiritual path," Ram said. "Their moral compass has gone completely wrong because they have forgotten what it means to be human! They have become too indulgent and lazy. They need to be made aware of their true nature and the greatness of being human. I cannot think of a better person for this job than you!"

Hanuman agreed gladly, "Oh wonderful! I get to talk about my beloved guru Ram all the time, and spread his true teachings? It is my good fortune to do so! Once they taste this potion of your spiritual grace, they will completely forget about the silly indulgences. I guarantee you, my lord. Please do not worry, my king. I will accomplish this mission for you!"

Hanuman was a natural leader. He spread yogic practices, created training centers, trained several disciples, and made spiritual pursuits part of everyone's daily life.

Hanuman advised his followers, "The scriptures describe how to eat, drink, exercise, procreate, and enjoy life while not getting too attached to it, and maintaining a constant reminder of your true nature beyond the body. Create temples, festivals, and customs such that reminders of your true nature are intertwined with your daily life, and it becomes a way of living. This is the only way a balanced life and a balanced society will be created."

A few years later, people slowly awakened to their mistakes and were gradually turning toward a more balanced life. A just king, such as Ram, positively influenced the general population with his actions and energy.

The chief spy met with King Ram to inform him of the latest news. "My great king, your sacrifice, leadership, and Hanuman's efforts are paying off. The people are being nudged toward a more balanced lifestyle."

"As per the scriptures, humans should spend the first quarter of their lives in childhood and education. The next part, they should spend as a householder, accumulating and enjoying wealth and pleasures of the senses. The third part they should devote to spiritual pursuits and development. Then guide others on the right path in the last part of their lives. I am glad to inform you, mighty king, that this population is moving in that direction. And this is not the best news, oh great king," the spy declared, beaming from ear to ear.

"The people want their queen back! They have realized their mistake and are thankful to have a merciful king, like you. They acknowledge and accept an ideal lady like Queen Sita as their ruler! They also want the twin brothers that Lady Sita gave birth to as their princes!"

Although inwardly ecstatic, Ram spoke calmly. "I will send Lakshman right away to retrieve Lady Sita and invite her back. My people's wishes are my command."

The very next day, Lakshman left for the ashram where Lady Sita stayed. He brought the two princes back, but could not bring Lady Sita with him. He delivered a letter from Sita for Ram. It read:

My Dear King Ram,

I am always fortunate to be your wife. Here at the ashram, I have practiced more meditation and evolved spiritually. I also befriended a princess of the people who live in underground caves. As you know, my birth was non-uterine. I was a queen, but hardly lived in palaces. I was a wife, but separated from my husband for long and painful periods of time. And now, I am sending my sons to their father. I am glad to hear that the people have realized their mistake and want me to come back, but I have decided for myself. The last few days of my unusual life shall be spent with the underground cave people. I will then leave my body voluntarily as per the yogic process.

Your loving wife,
Sita

Ram was completely devastated to realize that he would never see his wife again. He contemplated for a few days, made all the arrangements, and decided to address his ministers and common people of the court.

Ram said in a steady voice, "My fellow citizens, I have decided to give up this body as per the yogic practices, having realized my true nature a long time ago. My work is done here. The entire nation is safe, prosperous, and on a path toward a balanced life. My brothers and sons will take care of the kingdom. You are in capable hands."

Everybody in the court was shaken; some could not control their sobbing. However, they knew Ram's word was always final.

Ram addressed Hanuman next. "You are designed to be immortal by the Rishis. As you have seen, it is very easy for society to stray from the right path. You need to stay on this planet and make sure history is not forgotten. Guide the people when they need help." Ram got up from his seat, walked toward Hanuman, and gave him an exceptional arrow. "This arrow is powerful like a thunderbolt. It is decorated with gold, its wood is from the reed forest of Kartikeya, and it has eagle feathers for fins toward the end. Its nodes are very smooth, the tip is extremely sharp, and its egress is flawlessly straight. It will always show you the right path forward!"

Hanuman bent one knee, accepting the arrow with both hands. He respectfully touched it to his forehead. "My dear guru Ram, I accept your command. I assure you that, as long as humans live in this country, Devi Sita's name will always be remembered ahead of you. As long as both of your names and history are not forgotten, I will stay here and guide the people on the righteous path."

Heartfelt cries reverberated throughout the city, "Victory to Sita-Ram! Victory to Hanuman!"

Ten thousand years later, even today, due to the power of their actions and energies, Sita-Ram and Hanuman continue to be the beacons that guide humanity on the path to righteousness! They were humans who became Gods due to their actions. So can every human!

CHAPTER 16
THE TENTH AVATAR

~~~~~~~

Modern Day California

~~~~~~~

This is who I really am.

KRISH DECIDED TO TAKE PRISHA HOME FROM THE HOSPITAL after she was sufficiently stable and had recovered from the self-inflicted gunshot wound. Her psychiatrist was an older lady in her early sixties, with wrinkled skin, slightly disheveled grey hair, and tired looking eyes. It seemed that her body had withered from the ravages of time and her soul had as well, from dealing with people whose minds had started working against them—in the process of ruining them from the inside.

She delivered an ominous warning to Krish. "People who hurt themselves once are very likely to do it again."

On the way home from the hospital, Krish connected his phone to the Tesla Model S bluetooth system and listened to the news. "I miss newscaster Gwen Ifill's cultured and soothing voice on the radio," he said to Prisha, attempting to warm the silence. "She was only sixty-one when she died."

Prisha appeared lost in her thoughts. Krish breathed a sigh and thought, *I'm glad she didn't hear about someone else dying. It might have reminded her of her own near-death experience. Oh man, it's going to be like walking on eggshells now.*

As the news went to commercial break, Krish reflected on the last few weeks. Although he had faced tremendous difficulties in his personal life, his professional life was going well. He was getting paid handsomely for the intellectual property and patents he had generated. He had also published scientific breakthroughs in highly rated peer reviewed journals from his work at CERN and his collaboration with world-renowned physicist Professor Anton Kimble from Cambridge.

The press was fascinated by his work. He had done interviews with Hollywood celebrities and entrepreneurs on TV channels and some talk shows regarding his groundbreaking research. It was rare for a young scientist to receive such a high profile in the media.

Krish's advisor's, Dave's, ego was hurt due to his student's fame. Dave secretly hoped that all this hype about Krish's controversial theories would be over one day when it was just proven to be hot air. Then, Krish's career would come to a grinding halt. Additionally, Dave was not fond of the eccentric Anton, and what he thought of as his conceited British accent. Dave had wondered loudly if Anton would be so famous were he not handicapped.

Krish shook his head and said softly, "Ugh, office politics." He breathed sharply and diverted his attention back to the radio as the news was back on. From the reports, it was clear that the persons and governments responsible for the horrendous, simultaneous, and highly coordinated twin nuclear attacks over the United States were brought to swift justice by the most powerful war machines created in modern times.

Krish shook his head, trying to not remember the horrible day of the attack. Just then, the news stopped playing through the car speakers and an incoming call was seen on the screen.

Prisha turned sharply to notice the call; neither one recognized the number.

Krish answered.

A professional sounding voice responded on the other end. "Sir, this is the FBI. We need your help with an investigation. Please visit our field office in LA tomorrow."

"Sure, I'll be there."

"The address and further instruction will be sent to your email via a secure server."

"You have my email address? That's not creepy at all," Krish said sarcastically.

"Yes sir, always watching, always listening. Glad to hear that your mom and dad are well." The agent played along. "We will expect your presence at tomorrow's briefing. Good day."

The line disconnected without further discussion.

The next day, at the FBI field office on Wilshire Blvd in Los Angeles, a special agent briefed Krish. "The attackers used very sophisticated detonator with the drone to trigger the dirty bomb. We have their top scientific talent in custody. We need help deciphering some of the notes and mathematical formulae we recovered."

"All right, let's get to it," Krish said sitting down at a table. After studying the notes for some time, Krish was alarmed. "I need to talk to this guy. This is not some rudimentary work here. They seem to have even grander plans than what has already been carried out."

The special agent asked with anticipation, "What do we know so far?"

"They plan to modify a long-range missile to make it nuclear capable. They came up with approximately 850 different changes to the existing missile to make it nuclear capable. They needed to run a simulation to find the most optimized path with the material constraints they had. That requires a sophisticated model of the system and a lot of computing power. I want to find out how he got from close to 850 design change paths, down to a 100 or so—and he was on his way to narrowing it further. That means they're that much closer to achieving a nuclear missile attack!"

The special agent was trying to process everything he heard. He got up from his chair and paced the length of the room. "Well first, it's a woman, not a man, that we captured. And second, I need to talk to the New York office about what you just told me. The risk is real. I'm sure there are others working on different angles of this."

After pulling some bureaucratic strings, Krish could question the captured scientist through an intermediary. At one point during the interrogation, the captured woman was pressed hard for information. The interrogator got in her face, mere centimeters away, screaming, "How did you get access to super computers and sophisticated models? Which governments are supporting you?"

The captured woman looked very upset, she spat in the interrogators face, looked straight into the camera, and started banging her head violently on the table. Blood dripped from her forehead. The interrogation had to be stopped; she wasn't going to talk.

Krish looked at the special agent, ran a hand over his face, and said, "I told you what we could decipher from the notes you showed me. Let me know if you find out more and if I can be of further help."

"Yes, sir."

On his drive home, Krish thought, *when people are frozen in their beliefs, they refuse to look outside the constraints of their worldview. Throughout human history, religious and ideological zealots, dictators, and warmongers have frozen their thoughts and views to an extreme level.*

But, in our day-to-day life, even some scientists have frozen views about some things and refuse to consider other possibilities. In any case, I need to keep an open mind and figure things out. I have seen enough death and destruction in the last few days. Plus, things could escalate further based on what I just saw—with an even more devastating nuclear attack. I've had close calls with death myself. My wife almost took her own life! I need to get to the bottom of this and figure out the true nature of life before death catches up to me.

Krish developed a keen sense of being on a mission; a mission to understand the reality of life before it was too late for him, his loved ones, and perhaps the planet! As soon as he reached Pasadena, Krish got together with Kathy and Professor Kimble.

"We have published a lot of high-impact papers, generated ground-breaking patents based on the data from CERN, and mathematical formulae from Ramanujan's lost pages. But, that was not the goal. I really wanted to understand the true nature of life and the universe."

Kathy nodded in agreement. She habitually spun her pen in a circle, balancing it skillfully on her thumb and forefinger. "Yep, that was your mission, and we became part of it." She paused and added half-jokingly, "What were we thinking! Anyways, let's summarize what we have and what the missing pieces of the puzzle are."

Professor Kimble moved his wheel chair toward the desk, clicked on his custom software, and pointed to the diagram depicting galaxy clusters separated by empty space. "Each one of these yellow spots represents a galaxy. The known mass of matter is not sufficient to keep these galaxies, which are moving at great speed, from escaping from the center. So, there must be something holding it together. We call this unknown material dark matter. We cannot detect dark matter, but we see its effect. For example, the extent of gravitational lensing— light bending around galaxies that distorts their apparent shapes and even causes two galaxies to appear in place of one!"

"To me, dark energy is the wild card. From the study of type 1A supernovae or explosive dying stars, we know that some seven billion years ago, this dark energy appeared and accelerated the expansion of the universe," Kathy added. "This acceleration can be seen by a shift in wavelength toward the longer end of the light spectrum by a factor lesser than 0.49. A factor of 0.49, for a plot between distance and red-shift, would indicate an expansion at the same rate as in the past. A redshift less than 0.49 indicates an accelerating expansion."

Professor Kimble said, "We don't know why dark energy appeared suddenly, its nature, or how it will behave in the future."

"Or perhaps, more significantly, it could indicate a fundamental gap in our current model based on the understanding of physics," Krish concluded.

Kathy leaned back in her chair. Her diamond shaped eyes showed a little surprise. She adjusted her brunette hair over one shoulder. "Well, dark energy and dark matter are some of the missing pieces in the current physics model, which has served us quite well, by the way. Let's not abandon it so quickly. Dark matter is illusive to detect. It could just be an effect of dark energy. We have not seen any evidence of the alternative hypothesis—massive particles interacting weakly."

"I see your point," Krish said, "but here are the big unknowns of the current model. In addition to not knowing much about dark matter and dark energy—which together constitute 96% of the universe—we don't know how matter was produced from energy after the Big Bang, or how mass was produced from the forces that created protons and neutrons."

Kathy agreed. "Yes, there are still a lot of unanswered questions."

Krish got up from his seat, crossing his hands behind his back. "What bothers me most is the Incomplete Theorem."

Anton sounded amused, "I don't get it... how is that related?"

"As you know, Kurt Godel, an East European mathematician, came up with the Incomplete Theorem. Any logical system cannot be self-contained and cannot explain every logical assertion within that system. We need a bigger system than the one we're studying to explain everything."

"So, to understand this universe, we need something bigger than the universe? What does that even mean?" Kathy said, challenging Krish's claim.

Krish shook his head, defeated. "I don't know."

"I guess we summarized all the problems facing physicists today," Anton said. "And still, we're not any closer to solving one of them. Good day's work, I reckon."

"We're completely useless," Kathy added, resting her chin in the palm of her hand.

Anton couldn't miss an opportunity to showcase his humor. "I'm sure the rest of our colleagues—whom I refer to as cubical rascals—are even more clueless. I'm sure they're devising twisted mathematics as we speak to claim the fame for solving these fundamental problems!"

Kathy winked at Anton and adjusted her hair back over to the other shoulder. "Cubical rascals, you mean rascals from all sides," she giggled flirtatiously. "That's a good one. Where did you get that?"

"Love Brit jokes!" Kathy said. Everyone had a laugh and decided to call it a day.

When Krish got home from the lab, he checked Prisha's room. She was sleeping and had an erratic breathing pattern. *She must be dreaming*, Krish thought. He tiptoed over and checked the medicine cabinet to make sure she had taken her medications. He then went to his room and thought about the problems he had discussed with Kathy and Anton that day. He took out the mysterious arrow and Hanuman statue from his bag. Krish put the statue and arrow down and sat cross-legged on the floor, closing his eyes to think deeply about the obstacles he faced.

Spontaneously, he felt a strange energy inside him. His awareness was withdrawn from everything around him, and only focused on his breath. With each inhalation, he could feel a tide of energy coarse through him—increasing, rising steadily. And finally, it erupted within him and a crackling of energy rose through his back, toward his forehead, and into the center of his brain. He began shaking uncontrollably. The energy caused a sweet, joyous effect throughout his entire body. He felt completely elated. Krish could feel a warm, comforting glow near his heart. He experienced the entire length of his spinal cord suddenly lighting up like a live wire.

Completely lost in his experience, Krish felt pleasant sensations spread to every cell in his body. He felt every cell bathed in some sort of nurturing energy field. He was smiling, overwhelmed with sweetness, as tears rolled down his cheeks. He felt free from everything—all the painful, as well as the pleasant, memories lying dormant in his mind. He felt like a ball of unbounded energy. The energy kept rising inside him in waves, and he felt as though he was floating.

In this state, he could hear sound waves emanating from a cave somewhere. Somebody was uttering some words at a particular frequency, rapidly, and with very high energy. He could feel the vibrations of the word 'Ram' from that sound. His awareness locked onto that word. The energy waves inside him started vibrating at the same frequency as that of the sound 'Ram' emanating from the cave. Now, the two waves were synchronized and reached a resonant frequency. Slowly, the vision of the person reciting those words came into view of his mind's eye. Krish focused on the being sitting in a cave, chanting Ram's name. It was the Vanara, Hanuman! Krish couldn't believe what he was seeing.

Taken over by the unfamiliarity of the whole experience, Krish was glad to see a being with a physical form that he could turn to for some understanding of his current state. Krish mentally urged Hanuman for help, for clarity and direction. Krish then saw the mighty Hanuman, in energy form, appear next to him. He could feel Hanuman's presence near his own body. Slowly, the energy form pulled matter particles together. Then, Krish saw Hanuman in physical form standing right in front of him! Krish could physically touch and feel Hanuman. Hanuman's body was strong, like armor. His simian face was compassionate, and his eyes were energetic and gleaming. Hanuman maintained a kind gaze. He looked at Krish lovingly. Hanuman then reached out for something lying near Krish. He put the arrow in Krish's hand.

"This arrow is powerful, like a thunderbolt. It is decorated with gold, its wood is from the reed forest of Kartikeya, it has eagle feathers for fins toward the end, the nodes are very smooth, the tip is extremely sharp, and its egress is straight. Lord Ram gave me this arrow for this very moment, with these exact words! This is the same arrow you saw at the presidential debate hall when you heard these sacred words! That was a clue to nudge you in this direction of exploration. This arrow has been used nine times in the past. This is the tenth time it will be used. You are the Tenth Avatar. Please realize you true nature. The right time is upon us! I have lived all these years awaiting this moment…waiting for you! I'm here to help you. Once you realize your true self, you will guide the world! This is the purpose of your life!"

Krish was shaken by these words. The illusion of the world created by his mind had been completely shattered! As soon as Hanuman touched him, Krish became completely disconnected, not only from his body, but also from the world created by the current model of physics his mind was conditioned to believe in. His own body had conspired to make him believe in this model. His senses of sight, smell, touch, taste, and hearing—that had evolved to protect him from outside threats—had built their own model of reality that presented information in a form that would keep him alive and safe from predators. In addition, his mind was always buzzing and creating all kinds of stories to keep him occupied with one thing or another. To experience life in its native form, he had to abandon this model.

He stepped out of the model and saw things as they were, without the constraints of physics, mathematics, and biology. He had broken through and stepped outside the model-based reality. He could see life and the universe exactly as they were—in their true form! Not in the form presented by his brain for protecting and sustaining his body.

In his energetic form, Krish could not distinguish himself from the rest of the universe. The bubble of his physical limitations had burst, the fake boundary had been eliminated, and his true self was released from the trap of his body to be one with all that surrounded him! He saw himself as a small bundle of energy whizzing around, looking for an appropriate physical body to land upon. He looked down and saw his own body sitting cross-legged and motionless. He drifted downward gently, landing back in his body.

Krish stayed in his meditative state for what he thought was just a few utterly pleasant moments, but it was late morning by the time he emerged from his ecstatic state. He had all the answers he needed. With Hanuman by his side, he was a transformed and self-realized being.

In his elevated state, Krish was like a thunderbolt of energy, greatly affecting everything around him. He immediately got up and called Kathy and Anton to his home.

As soon as they saw him, they felt dizzy under the influence of his power. Spontaneously overcome by energy radiating from Krish's body, Kathy couldn't contain what she was feeling; they were the purest emotions she had ever experienced. She started crying like a baby and shaking involuntarily. Her stomach churned as a strange energy pervaded her whole body. From the depths of her stomach rose deep feelings of joyous energy.

Brimming with ecstasy, she sobbed, "You're a changed man." She pulled Krish into a bear hug. Her tears soaked his shirt. "I just want to be in this rapturous state forever. I don't care about physics and mathematics. Don't ever ask me to go away from you! Take everything from me, but let me just be in this state! What have you done to me? Why haven't you ever shown me this state before?"

Anton was also profoundly impacted by Krish. He cried loudly, throwing his hands up in the air and beating his chest. Everything he had been holding back was finally allowed to come to the surface and was bursting out. He was overpowered by an intense experience of unfathomable energy he couldn't even begin to express.

"I feel like I have new powers inside me. Krish, what is this? I feel this intense love toward you. I'm drawn to your energy, man. Help me, help me, Krish. Help me. Please." Overpowered by an intense pull, Anton tried to get out of his wheel chair to reach Krish.

Krish stepped forward and hugged him. He sat down, closed his eyes, and tried to reduce the intensity of the situation. He tried to lower his energy to reduce its impact. Gradually, everyone calmed down.

Krish told them about his experience from the night before and about his encounter with Hanuman.

After hearing that, Kathy said, "If I hadn't experienced the impact first hand, I would've accused you of popping some of Prisha's pills!"

Krish laughed. "I would've thought the same! I guess I need to learn to control this energy so that it doesn't send everyone around me into a tail spin."

Kathy said, "Wow! Just wow! I don't even know what I'm going to do next!"

Krish said, "Guys, let's get ahold of ourselves. We have a responsibility to explain all of this mathematically and to spread this experience and knowledge to everyone! Imagine what a fantastic world could manifest from all this!"

The three of them shared a group hug. Anton said, "Krish, this is so much bigger than academic papers, patents, money, and prizes. This is real-fucking-life man! A revolution, a transformation! This is REAL life, in every sense! Historic, my friend! I assure you, both of us will always be there with you, every step of the way!"

Krish smiled gently. "I'm counting on it! Let's get to work."

After the transformational experience, Hanuman directed Krish toward a master yogi who was visiting the US at that time. Krish decided to attend a yoga program that the master was conducting.

As soon as Krish walked into the hall, the master was hit by a bolt of energy. He couldn't see Krish, but he clearly felt his presence long before Krish even entered the room. A very composed, compassionate, and serious person, he got up from his seat and ran like a long-lost child running to his mother. He made his way through the assembled people and headed straight toward Krish.

Krish tried to bow in respect, but the master hugged him tightly and whispered, "I have been waiting for you! What took you so long, my dear? Remember, I helped you before in the jungles of Kishkindha!"

Krish had goose bumps all over his body. He couldn't stop weeping. "Why was I lost for so long? Why didn't you come sooner?"

"You tell me!" the master said. "Everything happens at the right time. You, the Tenth Avatar, the incarnation of the very energy that constitutes everything—which some people refer to as God— were still completely lost in this world. The purpose was for you to experience first-hand how ordinary people feel and experience the world! But, now the time has come for you to realize your true self and guide all who are willing to be guided!"

Krish and the master shared a soulful connection. The yogi taught him how to control his experience and the intensity of his energy. He taught Krish how to always be in a meditative state while going through his daily activities.

Within a few days of practice, Krish could experience the meditative state at will. His experience of life had changed immensely, in a way he could never have imagined.

Krish met with Kathy and Anton. Now, they always looked at him with a loving gaze, as if he was the source of their happiness.

"Guys, we need to focus on our work. We need to spread this wealth to as many people as possible! Everyone should have this experience. And it starts with you two. So that you aren't dependent on me for your spirit-centeredness I'll start training you. As for the physics, here is what I have:

"One, we know space-time is not flat, but curved and distorted by mass and energy. Conscious life and energy are interlinked. That means energy, and in turn a conscious life, can shape space-time and affect mass. Thus, a conscious human who has realized his true form can rearrange space-time in a favorable manner.

"Two, a conscious life, such as a yogi, can step out of the physical and biological model-based reality any time to witness the world as it is and understand the mechanism of how the world functions, using it to solve the mysteries of the universe."

Kathy interjected, "That's good, but how do you explain the strange effect you had on us when we saw you for the first time after your self-discovery?"

Krish nodded his head. "That's a good question. The real question is, how can the energy of one human affect another? The reason electromagnetic forces are not significant in large bodies, such as in human beings, is because they cancel each other out. At the atomic level, all reactions take place due to electromagnetic forces. So, if we start changing a big body from the atomic level, that person can have a net energy that is not zero and this energy has the ability to affect other humans. And with practice, I can generate this energy on demand. That's how my energy was influencing you. This is also the energy one can use to step out of and refine the scientific model. It can also be used to accomplish several super human tasks such as lifting objects, flying, etc. Now, we need to prove this mathematically and unequivocally so that all the disinformation from religious, political, and other sources will be discarded, and spirituality at last won't be tented by national, religious, geographical, or any other discriminatory factor. It will be the same for everyone and will be backed by science! The time for such a transformation of human society is upon us!"

Anton said, "Wow! Krish, that sounds like a wonderful idea. The world has no idea what's going to hit it!"

Kathy listened to everything excitedly. She habitually flipped her pen and said, "Hate to be the devil's advocate here, but what if this awesome power is misused by individuals? Second, how do we convince fellow scientists that one can actually step outside the model-based reality and that the model will rearrange itself to accomplish the change desired by the individual?"

Anton jumped in, "I have an idea. A quick history lesson is in order. The scientist, Fred Hoyle, took an intuitive leap and predicted the existence of an excited state of carbon to stabilize the fusion of three helium nuclei to form the carbon. He proved it experimentally at Cal Tech using one of the few particle accelerators at that time in 1950. Of course, he was a Brit, and he was right. He didn't get the Nobel Prize. The Americans got it. That aside, he essentially determined the excited state of carbon solely based on intuition, then provided experimental proof later on!"

Krish said, "Great idea! We'll do the same thing. We'll provide the theoretical basis using the mathematics found in Ramanujan's lost pages. And experimental proof will be the people and their transformed lives! The ultimate experimental data. The data that really matters! As for the misuse scenario, I don't think anybody could think about petty, selfish desires once they have an experience this extraordinary. In any case, it won't be a majority. As with any new power, be it guns, cars, the internet, or anything else, ultimately it will work out for the betterment of the majority."

Krish and his team, in a burst of creativity, published three major papers in the premier scientific publication Nature, boasting the highest impact factor among peer-reviewed journals. The titles of the research articles took the academic world by storm. Headlines flashed: 'Effect of conscious energy on space-time and mass,' 'Redefining the current physics model by stepping outside the model,' and 'Electromagnetically charged macro objects.'

In the academic world, some researchers supported the ideas and some opposed them, but nobody could deny that they were provocative and the supporting mathematics was solid.

The outside world took notice as well. First local, and then national and international, news channels picked up the story. Krish was busy explaining his work for days. Soon everyone was talking about these mind-boggling, but exquisitely explained and mathematically backed, ideas.

Spiritual masters from various religions and countries, ascetics, saints, and truth seekers who had always had these insights were brimming with joy that their life long quest had finally been proven mathematically. Now, the whole world could potentially benefit from it.

Krish had been invited to an interview on a national television, primetime show. On top of being watched by millions of viewers, the anchor was taking questions from live audience members. Most of the questions were about the science and mathematics that went into the research.

One older woman stood to ask a question. The wrinkles in her face and slightly disheveled white hair hinted at the many years behind her. She wore off-the-rack grey pants, a grey top, and a checkered red scarf around her neck. As the cameras turned toward her, Krish noticed she wore minimal jewelry.

The woman held the microphone that had been handed to her too close to her mouth at first. The rest of the audience could hear her wheezing breath as she took a few seconds to calm herself. When she did speak, her voice carried a slightly irritated tone.

"Hello, my name is Shirley. Sir, you sound like a smart person. I don't understand most of the things you're talking about, but before I walk out of here, do any of the things actually mean anything to me? My husband was a veteran. He shot himself after a long fight with depression. My son is addicted to pain medication and lost his job after he injured his back and neck trying to save the victims of recent terror attacks. Does your science help me solve my problems in a way that's real, tangible? Thank you very much."

There was silence in the studio. The anchor looked at Krish to judge his reaction. Krish was quiet. He could have dodged the question by saying something about how his research added to human knowledge and such. But, instead, he saw an opportunity. He cleared his throat, took a sip of water, and spoke with genuine compassion.

"Ma'am, I'm very glad you asked this question. First of all, thank you for your husband's service and your son's willingness to help others. Please see me after the show. I would like to introduce you and your son to meditation—to help you realize your vast, true nature. Let's see what impact it has on your life. I'm confident that you will see improvement."

The rest of the audience broke into spontaneous applause. The moment went viral on YouTube and received more than a million views. Suddenly, the art of meditation was all anyone could talk about.

Shirley and her son spent some time studying with Krish and his master.

A reporter from a TV channel in New York, where Shirley lived, decided to do a follow-up on her question. The reporter interviewed Shirley in her home several weeks later.

"Did you follow-up with Krish? What did you experience?"

Shirley looked strikingly different. Her eyes were full of energy, there was a spring in her step, and she was beaming with positivity and joy. She displayed a huge smile as she answered. "I did. I'm so peaceful now, so happy. My circumstances don't affect me anymore. Secretly, I was taking pills for chronic panic attacks. I haven't needed them at all since my work with Krish began. And the best part is, my son's pain medicines are much more effective at a much lower dosage. He's getting better. My life turned around that day! Things have absolutely changed for the better."

Shirley was showered with affection and support by total strangers. Her success only fueled the incredible interest in Krish's research and accomplishments.

When Krish saw the video, he was with Kathy and Anton. Both of them had undergone training with Krish and had also seen spectacular improvements in their energy and satisfaction with life.

Anton said, "My chronic pain is easing. I feel much better now. Using more advanced prosthetics, I'll be able to take a few tentative steps with my own feet next month! Can we do some meditation together Krish? It's much more effective when you guide us."

They sat down and were about to start the session, when Prisha entered the room.

"What are you guys up to?" she asked sounding annoyed.

"We're doing some mediation. Would you like to join?" Krish asked. He had tried several times, but Prisha didn't trust this 'meditation voodoo,' as she called it.

"I don't believe in this non-sense," Prisha said dismissively before walking away.

Kathy looked at Krish sadly. "I can't stand to see her suffer like this while you help so many others! Think about it… meditation is better than what she has now—nervous breakdowns and numerous side effects from her medications. You need to convince her. It's like she's dying of thirst, yet standing right next to a river! It's right here for God's sake! What's wrong with you?"

Krish replied calmly, "She was very unstable during the summer and due to changes in her medication. I can't force her."

Anton interjected, "I think she likes Brits better. Let me try." Anton convinced Prisha to just sit there and observe as they practiced their meditation.

Prisha witnessed the whole process from a unique vantage point and saw the joy radiate from their faces. She felt the vibrant energy shift all around her and slowly started to pay attention to her own breathing. Although she didn't fully trust these methods, she had to admit that she felt better from the experience.

Within just a few days of practice, she saw an amazing improvement in herself. Her moods were more stable. The bitter experiences and scars from her job loss, the struggles she'd faced in the US, and even the conflict with her parents didn't seem to affect her as much. She realized the tremendous energy she had inside of herself and that enabled her to break out of old thinking patterns and work toward a new beginning. Her medications were effective at much lower doses, and more importantly, the frustration and hopelessness she felt were replaced by a new zeal to live life to its fullest.

After his initial success with Shirley, Prisha, Kathy, and Anton, Krish contemplated ways to spread the sweet nectar of his realizations to a wider population.

"Traditionally, to sell any product you need capital, right?" Prisha asked one day with great enthusiasm. "But, in today's world, dominated by social media, decimation of information about your product can be achieved by directly going to the masses! I think we should start a social media campaign."

Krish smiled. "Wow! Thank goodness we have a business person among this gang of scientists. Only your mind could think of this valuable wealth we have as a commercial product!"

Prisha shrugged her shoulders, feeling quite proud of herself. "I know what I'm talking about. It's marketing. You've got to think along these lines if you want to spread your ideas. Period. The most common mistake entrepreneurs make is being too attached to their products. You can be passionate about your product, but you also need to be savvy when it comes to marketing."

Kathy smiled as she witnessed Krish and Prisha interacting like a normal couple for the very first time. She sensed the warmth and enjoyed the healthy, witty back-and-forth between the couple she now considered close friends. She sat down next to Prisha, held her hand, and looked at her lovingly. Kathy hugged her genuinely.

"What's wrong?" Prisha asked, unsure of what had triggered this act of affection.

"It's just so good to see your brilliance shine once again! God bless you both."

Just then, Krish received a call.

"Is this Krish?"

"Yes."

"This is Elton Hardy. I saw your interviews and YouTube videos. I would like to talk to you about your work. Is this a good time?"

"Hold on one minute. Let me step outside." Krish placed his phone on mute, and whispered to the group, "It's Elton Hardy!"

"Elton Hardy, the billionaire, serial entrepreneur, philanthropist, environmentalist, founder of Europa Inc., who wants to be the first private company to land on Jupiter's moon?" Anton exclaimed.

Everyone looked at Anton, amused.

"Are you a member of his fan club or something?" Kathy teased.

"The president actually," Anton announced proudly. "I get daily updates on my LinkedIn feed. He's an icon!"

"All right then. I guess I better take this call." Krish walked out of the room.

"Thanks for taking my call," Elton said. "Let me get straight to the point. I'll be blunt. I'm piqued by your research. I think it's bullshit. How many attempts at this spirituality thing have there been before? It didn't work. How is what you're propagating any different?"

Krish responded calmly, "Well, let's see. The scientific work is published in top-tier, peer reviewed journals. If you have any questions about it, I'm happy to discuss it with you, or if you don't know enough mathematics, someone who does." Krish paused to feel the effect of his statement on the other side before he continued. "As for the practical aspect of meditation, so far it has helped five people, and they're very happy with the results. Try it out for yourself. If it doesn't work for you, discard it and move on until you find something that does work and that you consider fundamentally sound."

Elton smiled on the other end. "Okay, I'm going to take you up on it. Come visit me in the San Francisco Bay Area. I'll have trusted people from the Powell Foundation and other like-minded, top-tier billionaire philanthropists there. And we'll throw in some mathematicians and physicists from UC Berkeley and Stanford too. Are you up for it?"

Krish remained steady. "Are you? Are you open to a life-altering possibility?"

"Great… I'll see you next week then."

Krish presented the mathematics and physics related aspects of his work to a group of twenty individuals from the world of academics, entrepreneurship, and billion-dollar philanthropists who genuinely wanted to improve life on this planet. His presentation was impeccable. In fact, as he concluded, he received a standing ovation from his audience. Krish warmly acknowledged the adulation.

"Enough theory, let's get to the practical side of things. A picture is worth a thousand words, and an experience is worth a thousand pictures, so let's start with that." Krish closed his eyes for a moment and took a deep breath. "Please sit up as straight as you can in your chairs. Close your eyes, breathe deeply, and repeat the sound I make."

Everyone repeated it three times and slowly opened their eyes.

"The gist of the matter is that, if you felt something in the last few moments, you need to follow that experience and see where it takes you."

"I didn't feel nothing!" one physicist said in a thick Russian accent.

Everyone chuckled at his comment.

Someone else joked, "Maybe you shouldn't have had that shot of Vodka this morning."

The group shared a big laugh.

The Russian physicist played along with a big smile, "I did actually!"

Krish steered the discussion back to the topic, "Yep, Vodka would do it. But, jokes aside, even if you didn't feel anything now, let me share some experiences to help with the discussion." Krish took a few steps away from the podium to allow the energy to flow between him and the audience. He mentally scanned through the compartments of his memory banks. "There are experiences in life that make you question whether there is more to life than what you can see and touch. It's the same in science also. You reach a point where you feel there is more than you can measure and observe."

Krish had the audience's attention—some nodded in agreement while others stared at him sternly. "For example, a few years back, I clearly remember, I was in Pasadena, at my work desk that Sunday morning. I felt some sort of signal in my mind, someone was saying something to me. It was like a ping. Slowly I realized, it was my grandfather saying goodbye. Thus, I clearly knew my maternal grandfather had passed away in India before I heard the news from my mother, an hour later. He was old, but in good health when he suddenly passed away.

"Besides experiences like these, there is always a yearning inside every human to find out the true nature of life. Some bury this feeling in work or whatever else they like doing—good or bad. Many of us don't have a choice but to carry on with work due to responsibilities and bills to pay and can't afford to explore, so we ignore! But, what about those of us assembled here? You're billionaires. If you choose, you could decide to just sit in one place or play golf all day. But look at you. You cannot stop working. It's not just empathy and compassion for fellow humans or about having a purpose in life. Even if everyone in this world was happy, you couldn't stop your activity."

Krish was interrupted by an old man with greying hair. The man wore an old sweater, khakis, and worn tennis shoes. He had thick glasses that covered the wrinkled skin under his eyes. His hair looked as though it had been combed in a hurry. He tried to sneak in without causing a disturbance, but everyone in the room noticed him and stood up to welcome him. It was James Powell, the second richest man in the world!

He grabbed a seat in the back of the room and said apologetically, "Sorry, didn't mean to interrupt. My secretary, Ana, texted me just now saying that I needed to check this out. 'This is the real deal', she said. Please continue."

Krish seemed to be focused on something within, and said without fuss, "Welcome Mr. Powell. We are glad you joined us. As you have seen, the mathematics and physics behind this research is solid. Meditation has improved the experience of my life exponentially, and I finally know what my yearning was for. All I must say is, if it helps you in any such way, keep it. Otherwise, keep looking for something that works for you. If what I have is the truth, you will come back to it eventually. If this isn't the truth, it will wither away. It's like the scientific approach—you always challenge the working model, make sure it predicts experimental data and observations, and if it doesn't, you modify it or replace it with something that does. It's really that simple."

James Powell raised his hand. "What's your vision for this work, and what's the execution strategy to expand it to the rest of population?"

Krish thought for a moment before answering. "I have a slide for that. First things first, I would like to train people in this room so you have the opportunity for a first-hand experience."

Krish browsed through his slide deck until he found the one that contained the action plan. "My master and I will train and certify as many teachers as needed. We can do this in small groups of forty to fifty interested practitioners. It will take each group two months to be ready to train others. As many people as possible need to be trained in these simple practices. It's crucial to reiterate that people should only keep these practices if they work for them, if it answers their yearnings, if it improves their life in any way. Otherwise, they must keep looking until they find something everlasting and fundamental.

"Slowly, these practices will need to become part of the public and private school curriculum. One final aspect is this—the person at the top needs to have impeccable integrity. If he falls short or passes away, the entire structure will falter. The best way to ensure this doesn't happen is with diffused leadership. We must go back to the traditional teacher-disciple relationship—individualized approaches where these practices are part of everyday life. I would like to remove myself from the picture and make the whole system as self-sustaining as possible. Slowly, it will become part of everyone's daily practice, like brushing your hair or eating breakfast. Components would need to be added to the training so that people don't become disconnected from life. A certain percentage can, if they wish, but others need to keep working on sustainment and diffusion of experiences and leadership. Again, analogous to the scientific world where some do pure research and others do applied research and engineering."

Everyone in the room listened carefully.

One person finally spoke. "I would like to opt out. I'm not interested. Sorry." He briskly got up and left the room.

Krish was unaffected.

Elton Hardy said, "I'll decide what to do after going through the training you provide."

"Wonderful. I'll get my colleagues here, and you will be the first receiver of the Quantum Democracy Program. I hope it works for you."

After the training, there was no response from Elton Hardy and the group. While the elitists and wealthy were undecided about their own experiences, treating it like a philanthropic investment decision, the common people were utilizing these tools readily to solve their problems and change their lives for the better.

Krish, Prisha, Kathy, and Anton began putting their own money into the program. The participants were making voluntary contributions as well.

More and more people were trained as teachers.

One afternoon, Prisha was reading a selection of numerous 'thank you' e-mails, and comments on videos and websites, to Krish. The feedback was mainly from the Southern California region, near their home in Pasadena.

"'I feel more alive and energetic every day!' this person writes. Oh, and here's another, 'Keep up the good work, God bless you.' 'I can sleep better. Thanks.' This one says, 'My dosage for pain meds has gone down. I don't feel drugged-out all the time.' 'I take very few psychiatric drugs now! Lot less anxious :)' 'You are so cute.' I'm going to have to agree with that last one," Prisha said planting a light kiss on his mouth.

Of course, there were also a few that said: 'You are Satan. Get lost, dumbass!' But such things left Krish unaffected.

As the program grew in popularity, the big money finally decided that it was a viable destination for their investment dollars. Funds started pouring in. With more resources, the program spread throughout California.

Back home in India, Krish also received an abundance of support—helped partly by the international recognition. People were improving their lives by implementing the meditation practices he was teaching. Slowly, local and state governments noticed the positive changes occurring in the population: dramatically reduced crime rates, increased productivity, a sharp decrease in health care costs, childhood and maternal survival rate close to 100%, and a burst of creativity with new business ideas resulting in 99% employment rates among those seeking work. A new outlook toward life was taking hold.

Two years had passed since Krish first launched the program. The meditation practices had spread to almost all countries. Some countries and individuals rejected it for ideological and other reasons, but they were in minority. Signs of progress were seen everywhere. The happiness index in most countries increased considerably. People were living stress-free and satisfied lives. There was a fundamental change in people's mindset. Fear for survival and distrust were slowly being replaced by the realization that true human nature is too vast to be shackled by such primitive concerns! Happy people were slowly making the whole planet happier, safer, and more stress-free.

Krish was enjoying time with his newborn daughter. Fatherhood was a tremendous new experience for him—even when he thought he couldn't feel any more peaceful.

One such day, Krish received a call from Sweden, "Congratulations! You're the winner of not one, but two Nobel Prizes! This is the first time in our history that a person has won two Nobel Prizes in the same year. You will be receiving one each for physics and peace! Congratulations, sir!"

Krish smiled gently and reacted calmly, "Thank you very much for your generosity. It's an honor that I will cherish deeply."

At the ceremony awarding the Nobel Prizes, the presenter announced, "Ladies and gentlemen, before I announce the next awards for physics and world peace, let me tell you a short story. In the history of India, it is believed that a person rises to the challenge when human society needs guidance. A few years ago, we were in a situation where the planet was on the brink of permanent damage due to human activity, war, terrorism, and population explosion. Most of us were lost and hopeless. At that time, this man rose to the challenge and guided us. He used his skills in physics and math, combined with a yearning for truth, to realize the true nature of life.

"As I mentioned, as per Indian history, there have been nine individuals who have risen to the challenges humanity has faced at various times during our evolution on this planet. These nine individuals have been conferred the title of 'Avatar of Vishnu'—meaning 'Incarnate form of the Savior'. Today, I present to you, a man deserving of being called the 'Tenth Avatar', the only recipient of two noble prizes in one year. Ladies and gentlemen, I proudly present, our beloved master and visionary scientist, Krish…nanujan Bhat!"

The whole auditorium was on its feet with thunderous applause.

Krish calmly walked onto the stage. He wore a simple, but well-fitted, grey suit. He bowed to acknowledge the applause and the honor. He signaled everyone to take their seats.

After the excitement had died down, he addressed the gathering in a steady voice, "Thank you very much for the privilege. I would like to take this opportunity to remind everyone that the best days for this planet are ahead of you! If you continue this path of seeking and realization, well-being will follow naturally as a byproduct of your endeavors!"

Another thunderous round of applause followed.

Krish then gestured to the organizers. They cleared a few tables and chairs and created some empty space. Krish took off his tie, shoes, socks, and coat. He sat down in the middle of the stage on a cotton sheet. In a booming voice, he announced, "I have an important decision to share with everyone."

The excitement in the crowd was palpable.

One man whispered to the person next to him, "Is he going to reveal another layer of truth about life?"

His colleague said, "Perhaps some new scientific breakthrough? Or a program for the betterment of society?"

Krish raised his arm and requested, "Please do not try to guess my announcement." He paused, then said calmly. "The time has come for me to leave this body as per the ancient yogic practices!"

232

The audience was shocked and hushed in utter disbelief.

"What? What does that mean?" What had been a joyous and cheerful atmosphere was instantly transformed into a somber, funeral-like state. There were sobs and loud cries of protest.

"Are you leaving us? Don't leave us! We love you!" someone shouted.

Krish spoke with power behind every word. "With Hanuman's help, I have shown you the correct path. Due to our interconnected world, these meditation practices have spread to every corner of the planet. There are many capable leaders here who will continue the work. The system was designed for diffused leadership. I don't want you to be dependent on me. If I stay around for too long, another risk is that these practices will come to be considered a cult or religion. Before you know it, temples and churches will be formed. Today it's the Noble Prize, tomorrow it'll be political posts bestowed upon me. Seeking will be completely forgotten, and it will be replaced with blind practices and followers. Groups will be formed and they will start fighting with each other. Some will want to follow their own path to truth, but will be prosecuted by the majority. I need to go so that you will continue to seek and not be stagnated by my idolization. The timing is perfect."

"What if we get lost along our path?" Kathy pleaded. She had come to the stage and sat down next to him.

"Only my body will perish. I will always be available when you need me," Krish assured.

Prisha couldn't control her tears. "Our daughter is just six months old! What about her?" she begged.

Krish smiled and said, "You're quite capable, my love! For the work to continue, and humans to evolve, individuals need to take responsibility for their own well-being. There is no God up in the sky. The God is within you! Seek that and your life will be fulfilled. You will have all the help you need! You will all be successful in your pursuit, cared for, and looked after! I promise you. Do not fear, do not worry! Love you all!"

Krish then performed some yogic practices and breathing exercises. His eyes looked glassy, attention laser focused between his eyebrows. He slowly drew his awareness inward.

There was complete silence in the hall. The whole world watched this incredible event with bated breath via TV, webcasts, and social media.

It seemed that Krish had completely disconnected from everything around him, but also still occupied every single particle in the room simultaneously. He sat straight, his eyes rolling back into his head, and his breath becoming more and more feeble until it was barely noticeable. Krish gently lay himself down on the cotton mat, flat on his back. His head was held upright, arms gently resting by his side. With his eyes, focused inward and partially closed, his chest stopped moving completely. His head was still held in position as if being supported. The life force had left his physical body, but it still looked so full of life!

The imprint of his last moment was left on his lifeless body. Krish's body appeared in a deep meditative state with attention centered consciously in his forehead.

Slowly, the ultimate realization dawned upon everyone assembled. Krish was very much still present, although his body lay discarded. There was a sense of pleasantness about his passing. An uplifting emotion rose in the crowd! The theoretician had given the ultimate experimental proof of true human nature beyond any physical limitations of matter and time. Sadness no longer spread throughout the room. Krish had demonstrated how to conquer death—the ultimate fear! The Tenth Avatar had taught the entire world how to live fearlessly and return to their true selves when desired!

CHAPTER 17
BEYOND THIS WORLD

~~~~~

California, 20 Years Later

~~~~~

The next evolutionary step.

K RISH'S DAUGHTER, BROOKE, WAS A GROWN WOMAN NOW. She was named after the federal agent who laid down her life to protect Krish and other innocent travelers during a bomb threat. Typical of her generation, Brooke was trained in mediation practices at a young age, and she was already an accomplished Yogi.

"Today is the twentieth anniversary of your dad's transformative experience," Prisha said to her daughter one afternoon. "He became a self-realized person that day. A lot of people, including me, didn't recognize it then. But, today, you can see the transformative impact of his work and energy all around you."

Brooke smiled gently. She had inherited Krish's lively eyes and sharp mind, combined with Prisha's light brown, wheat-ish complexion, long, dark hair, tall body frame, and outgoing nature. She was a beautiful and brilliant young lady. She didn't have memories of her father physically, but his presence had always guided and protected her and her mother. Brooke was teary-eyed thinking of him. She missed her father. She wrapped her arms around her mother, hugging her tightly.

Prisha now ran a highly successful firm that optimized scarce power resources in the lucrative interplanetary space flights business. A few grey hairs had appeared in her curls, however, due to regular meditation practice—under Kathy's guidance—she was at her peak physical, mental, and emotional health. That day, her morning was spent receiving calls of support from presidents and prime ministers from across the globe. Krish's day of truth realization was celebrated the world over as 'Quantum Democracy Day'.

Brooke attended a prestigious conference that would analyze the progress the world had made in the last two decades. She wore a flowing, golden, silk gown, with a matching rose-gold backdrop, and a diamond pearl necklace for the event.

The occasion had generated a lot of media attention. Many people attended the program without being physically there or without the aid of any technological devices. They could hear and see everything clearly by tapping into their highly evolved faculties. There were representatives from various fields of research, arts, and governance at the conference who presented their studies on the impact of Krish's work on the world.

Brooke heard everything calmly. She then got up from her seat, gracefully walked up to the stage and said, "I now request the honorable president of the Earth Body to address this august gathering of top representatives from diverse backgrounds, including Nobel laureates, industry leaders, humanitarians, top bureaucrats, celebrities, and artists. Please join me in welcoming the president. Thank you."

The Earth Body was an organization that represented the entire planet—along the lines of the United Nations. The president of the

Earth Body was directly elected by a simple majority by the entire world population. Individual countries were free to enact laws and policies as per the desires of the local population. A very compassionate and smart man, in his forties, walked briskly to the stage. Everyone welcomed the president with a warm round of applause.

The president addressed the gathering in a rousing speech, "I am honored to be here. As is the case with most of the people in the world today, I was also enlightened by our beloved leader, Krish's, mediation practices. I thank him, and many other teachers, sons, and messengers who came before him, from various parts of the world, from the bottom of my heart."

Everyone in the audience clapped and cheered.

The president continued, "The mediation practices, pioneered by Krish, spread throughout the world because of an organic growth led by people themselves, rather than being prescribed by governments and powerful leaders at the top. As a result, the societal structure is stable and sustainable. This is true quantum democracy!"

The audience showed their strong approval with thunderous applause.

Once the roar had dinned, he continued. "The principle that scientists can witness natural phenomena as they are, without any preconceived scientific notions, meant that answers to long standing questions in the field of physical and other sciences were known with great precision. New states of matter have been discovered, riddles of dark matter, dark energy, and other outstanding physics problems have been resolved. The details will be covered at another event.

"As humans realized the vast nature of their truth, the need for biological propagation has reduced. People do not work to keep up with their neighbors, but they work for the betterment of society or to express their creativity. Computers and highly advanced robots are available to do all menial work, such as driving, cleaning, manufacturing goods, etc. The world population is on a rapid decrease and approaching the six billion mark. All activities are carried out in harmony with the environment. The planet is finally healing and recovering from the damage done by humans. It can almost be likened to the image of an obese person losing weight. They can finally breathe properly, feel light and fit once again!

"Corporations have stopped making environmentally harmful products, as there was no longer demand for such products. They also got away from the need to generate profit every quarter and could invest for the long term. Markets are efficient because the humans handling them are highly evolved and self-realized. There's no need for a constant prodding by the financial markets, competition, or Wall Street to realize profits and efficiencies."

The business leaders in the audience were seen smiling. A CEO in his sixties whispered to his colleague, "It's almost silly to think how we used to operate, just driven by profits and incremental growth. But now, it's different. I just commissioned a fully automated plant that manufactures hand-held positron emission tomography (PET) scanners. These were expensive machines, traditionally used to trace metabolic molecules to study the spread of cancer and potential treatments. Now, they're also being used to study the interaction of plants, animals, and humans. PET scans are being used to study how everything physically responds to everything else by producing different molecules! It's a truly disruptive application and will take a long time to be profitable. But my board of directors fully supported me, and knew I could do it!"

His colleague pressed his hand and mouthed, "Amazing. Congrats."

The president continued, "Most of the human population is self-realized now. These beings have experienced being part of the same energy that resides in all the plants, animals, and the entire universe. The very basis for all the divisions among our species—nationality, religion, skin color, race, gender—have been eliminated from the root! There is no motivation for war or conflict. But, that does not mean we are docile. We are ready to protect the planet from any extraterrestrial threats or any sudden development of rogue humans. Highly advanced weapons, such as solar blockers that can turn entire countries temporarily or permanently dark by blocking the sun's rays, have been created. Our space probes can get past our sun's plasma bubble and reach interstellar space within a year, compared to the almost thirty-five years needed by Voyager 1. Interstellar space is being continuously monitored, and we get regular updates about low magnetic fields picking up ions and anomalous cosmic rays.

"In effect, all the unnecessary expenses, activities, and resources dedicated to artificially created conflicts, wants, and divisions have been removed. The efficiency of deployment of capital, resources, and the increase in productivity is many orders of magnitude higher compared to just twenty years ago. The world economy has grown to more than four hundred trillion dollars! Humans have achieved the real pinnacle of evolution and live in harmony with themselves, others, and the planet. Happy people make for a happy planet. Let us keep up the good work!"

Everyone applauded enthusiastically as the president elegantly summarized the amazing changes brought about in the last two decades.

Once the planet was in complete balance and on a sustainable path, human creativity needed further expansion. The solar system had already been explored. For safety, and for continuity of life in case of a disaster, all the necessary knowledge and means for repopulating society were stored, including energy forms, in various parts of the solar system. Places with liquid water were preferred. Space vehicles that could reach various planets in a few minutes were realized.

Humans could choose to stay in energy form at different levels of existence, or just be free and dissolve into the all-occupying energy after the death of their physical bodies.

Some humans had already travelled to other galaxies. Interstellar transport across different solar systems and galaxies was in energetic form. With mastery over space-time and energy, humans reached distant worlds instantly. Humans could move there in energy form, and create a body and an environment friendly for themselves from the matter around them on that planet. They could also adopt a form suitable to the environment of the place, instead of modifying the existing conditions.

During one such trip to another galaxy, a young woman communicated with her father.

"Pitashri—honorable father, I like this planet and solar system. Shall we start a new cycle of life here?"

Her father considered the question carefully. He said...

To Be Continued...

REFERENCES AND INSPIRATION:

1. Valmiki Ramayan, valmikiramayan.net

2. Through the Wormhole with Morgan Freeman, Science Channel

3. Advancement of Ancient India's Vedic Culture, Stephen Knapp

4. The Historic Ram, Nilesh Nilkanth Oak

5. The Grand Design, Stephen Hawking and Leonard Mlodinow

6. The Beginning and End of the Universe, Jim Al-Khalili, BBC

7. Inexplicable Universe, Neil deGrasse Tyson, The Great Courses Signature Collection

8. The Shiva Trilogy, Amish Tripathi

9. Nirvana: The Journey Unfolds, MJ

10. The Krishna Key, Ashwin Sanghi

11. BBC documentary on Ramanujan -Legendry Indian Mathematician

12. The Meaning of Ramanujan and His Lost Notebook, University of Illinois at Urbana Champaign, George E. Andrews

13. https://www.youtube.com/watch?v=y_0NuOBNobk

14. http://www.ancientmilitary.com/ancient-india-military.htm

15. Dhanurveda. http://www.atarn.org/india/dhanurveda_eng.htm

CUTTING-EDGE NAVAL THRILLERS
BY
JEFF EDWARDS

www.braveshipbooks.com

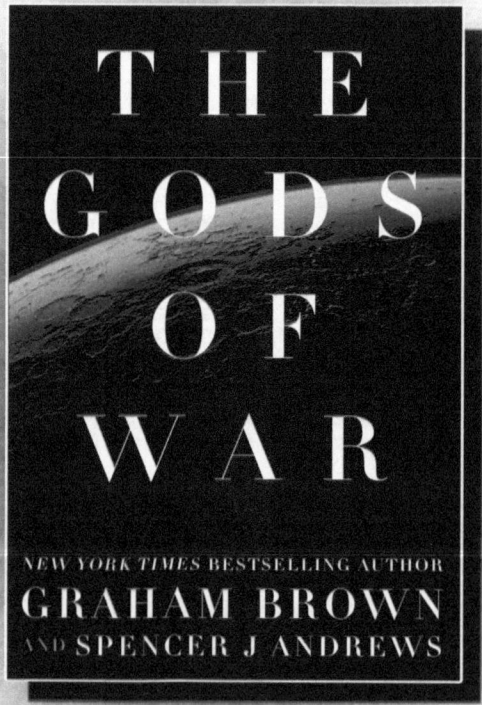

HIGH COMBAT IN HIGH SPACE

THOMAS A. MAYS

"Solid adventure, intrigue and speculative space-tech, from a rising star in military science fiction."
— DAVID BRIN, Hugo and Nebula Award-winning author of 'EXISTENCE,' 'THE POSTMAN,' and 'STARTIDE RISING'

A SWORD INTO DARKNESS

THOMAS A. MAYS

The Human Race is about
to make its stand...

www.braveshipbooks.com